Copper Kiss

Tom Neale is a freelance writer whose work has appeared widely in the national press. He lives in London.

Also by Tom Neale and available from Headline

Steel Rain

COPPER KISS

TOM NEALE

headline

First published in 2006 by
HEADLINE PUBLISHING GROUP

First published in paperback in 2007 by
HEADLINE PUBLISHING GROUP

1

Cataloguing in Publication Data is available from the British Library

ISBN 978 0 7553 2242 8

Typeset in Palatino by
Palimpsest Book Production Limited,
Grangemouth, Stirlingshire

Printed and bound in Great Britain by
Clays Ltd, St Ives plc

Headline's policy is to use papers that are natural,
renewable and recyclable products and made from wood
grown in sustainable forests. The logging and manufacturing
processes are expected to conform to the environmental regulations
of the country of origin.

HEADLINE PUBLISHING GROUP
A division of Hachette Livre UK Ltd
338 Euston Road
London NW1 3BH

www.headline.co.uk
www.hodderheadline.com

For Guy and Davina

Prologue

They killed the old man as he slept. When they pulled back his coat, they could smell the liquor rise from him and he was too stupefied to fully realise what was going on. This was a mercy. Three blows to the head with a tyre iron, and it was all over for him. Then they stole his boots.

He had not been easy to find. He'd dropped off the grid, as many long-term alcohol- and substance-abusers do. He had no lodgings, phone number, cell phone, bank account or credit cards. Any necessities, such as cheap vodka and cigarettes, were paid for with crumpled dollar bills or the coins he got back on collecting soda and beer cans.

His last known address had been in Boston, when he'd spent some time at the Pine Street Inn homeless shelter, the city's largest. However, the staff there hadn't seen him in a while. Then they had a sighting in Florida. Bums like Florida: it has kinder winters than Boston. But by the time they got there, he'd gone. What they did get was the identity change. Their man had become Hank Porter, although that wasn't the surname he was born with. That was something altogether more famous.

When they caught up with him, he'd made it across the country to San Diego. Hank Porter had eaten at the Market Street soup kitchen and drawn clean clothes from the Treat Street shelter. As was the norm, the latter logged him on the San Diego Social Register computer database: *Henry 'Hank' Porter, W/M, 5' 10", 62 years of age, balding, gray beard, scar on left cheek, 160lbs.* It was enough to put him back on the grid. They flew out to find him.

When they got to the charity centres, they discovered that Hank Porter didn't actually stay at the shelter. He preferred to sleep rough, mostly on the ornate benches in Balboa Park, where he could hit on tourists outside the zoo or the Museum of Art. He'd told the people at the hostel that he didn't think shelters were safe.

A week later, someone beat him to death in the park, just so they could steal the used Timberlands he had recently drawn from the clothes exchange. Or so it seemed.

The park ranger who discovered the body reported

it to the SDPD, who went through the motions of trying to discover if Hank had any next of kin. A man who was not, in fact, his son came forward and claimed to be just that. He paid for a quick, simple cremation.

Hank Porter had, on the face of it, been a threat to nobody, but that wasn't the case. He had a history, including a conviction for second-degree murder, that could be embarrassing to important men, one very important man in particular, if anyone – say, some crusading journalist – had tracked him down. It was better if he was out of the way.

The group who ordered the killing were pleased with the outcome, but they knew that it had been a simple elimination of someone already on the margins. The homeless and the destitute are rarely missed, and Hank was no exception. The next one would be more difficult, require a better team. After all, murdering a hobo in a San Diego park is one thing. A hit in the centre of London, that is something else altogether.

One

United States: Early November

Outside, the temperature has dropped into single figures Celsius but, thanks to over-efficient underfloor heating, the classroom is hot and stuffy. Vincent Piper hesitates before opening the window. With it ajar, his students can hear the shots from Hogan Street South, one of the FBI's famous training mock-ups. As he swings it wide, the trainees stir in their seats and several look wistfully in the direction of the flat crack of blanks being discharged. They'd rather be doing practice than theory. And who can blame them?

Piper strides back to the whiteboard at the front of the classroom and most of the dozen trainees dutifully turn their gaze back towards him. There are nine males and three females, all in their twenties, all given the rare chance to become a Federal Agent. Piper tries to prevent himself from identifying those who will wash out early. Perhaps Mike, the lanky kid at the back, who still has an ear cocked for the sound of bullets.

'So, as I was saying, Mike.' The boy spins in his seat, a shy grin on his face. 'Whidbey Island was one year before Waco, but there are certain similarities. However, the senior figure in this particular cult, the self-styled "Father" William, had had military training. His defensive positions,' Piper points to the diagram on the whiteboard, which shows a series of slit trenches that had been prepared around the organisation's headquarters, a converted and fortified farmhouse, 'were exceptional. If you look at page sixteen of your dossier you will see a full description of how they were constructed and their firing lines. Ranged against them were a SWAT team from Seattle, local ATF and FBI officers and State Troopers. Inside the compound and the trenches were thirty-seven male members of the American Free God Association and twenty-two women, each one armed with assault rifles, recoil-less rifles, grenade launchers and so on. The law-enforcement officers had a hogjaw to help shield their approach.' He points at the picture of an armoured bulldozer pinned on the wall behind the board. 'But as far as hardware was concerned, that was it.'

5

There were TV crew helicopters, he wants to add, but nobody had thought to do a full aerial survey of the hold-out. If they had, they might have seen just what they were up against.

Piper looks at his watch, just as the minute hand hits the hour. 'Right, your assignment for next week's class is to analyse the police and Federal actions that left seventeen dead and twenty-seven wounded, and to identify six key errors in the tactics. Then, to devise an alternative strategy, which you believe would have avoided that bloodshed. See you then.'

The trainee agents gather up their papers and leave, murmuring their thanks, while he moves to the window and loosens his tie. He has been teaching this unit on classic FBI cases for close to a year now. Making the move into training from fieldwork had been a godsend, there was no doubt about that. Following the death of first his daughter, then his father, he had needed time to get grounded again.

There is a knock at the door and Senior Special Agent Roscoe Mitchell steps into the room, pressing past the last of the trainees. Mitchell, an urbane black man in his early fifties, is Deputy Director of this satellite unit of Quantico, set up after the surge in recruitment, following the terror alerts of early 2005, had stretched the original facility to bursting point. 'Vince. Got a minute?'

'Sure.'

Mitchell looks at the board. 'Whidbey?'

'Yup.'

'Thank God we haven't had too many of them since.'

'Doesn't mean we won't,' says Piper. 'It's just at the moment we got bigger fish to fry than the odd nutty cult where some guy decides he's Jesus, so he can get laid.'

'Yeah.' Mitchell parks himself on one of the desks. 'I hear you wanna get back in the fish-frying game.'

Piper feels himself colour slightly. 'I might have mentioned it. To—'

'Leo Masterman. An old friend of your dad's.'

'Yeah.' He doesn't ask how Mitchell knows. These things got around. He should have foreseen that.

'But not to me.'

'No. I was just dipping a toe in the water.'

Mitchell smiles. 'It's OK, I'm not going to give you a hard time. You're still young, you have plenty of experience – I don't blame you.' He wags an admonishing finger. 'You should've followed procedure, though.' As the FBI has expanded over the past four years, so its despotic faith in procedure has increased exponentially. Procedure said there were to be no requests for transfers until the matter was cleared with your immediate superior.

'I haven't heard zip, though, Roscoe. I still might not. You know there's the odd glitch on my file.' Piper had screwed up on a case in London eighteen months previously, the one involving the death of his daughter, Martha. However, he had been treated leniently by the subsequent enquiry because he was deemed to be operating under the psychological impact of her death – and because, in the end, the plot to kill him, his ex-wife and the Ambassador of the United States to the Court of St James had failed. Only barely, though.

'Well, someone loves you,' says Roscoe, reaching out the piece of paper he has been holding. 'You know about SOCA, over in the UK?'

Piper flips through the vast bank of acronyms in his brain before he gets it. 'Serious Organised Crime Agency? Heard of it, that's all. It kicked in after my time over there.'

'Well, they heard of you, too. I got this. Through official channels.'

Piper takes the letter, notes the heading and address, and scans the contents. 'I don't quite—'

'They are doing their own version of this, is what I hear. Case analysis. They had half a dozen big foul-ups, just like us,' he points at the diagram of the Whidbey scenario, 'and some successes. They want an overview of what went wrong and what went right. They asked for you.'

'Why?'

Mitchell spreads out his hands, like it was the dumbest-ass question he had heard in his entire career. 'I don't know. Maybe because you know both countries, you are now an expert on FBI history and, even if you don't always follow it, procedure. Now, it's up to you whether you go. It would be a six-month secondment – by which time, maybe Leo would have found you something. You been back over since . . . ?' Mitchell lets it trail away.

Piper shakes his head quickly. The tightness is in his chest, the one that squeezes his ribs every time he thinks of Martha. He waves the letter at Roscoe. 'Well, it's nice to be wanted by someone.'

'I want you here, Vince. But I understand if you got to go.'

Piper looks Mitchell in the eye. 'I haven't got a problem here, Roscoe. I just feel I'm not quite played out yet.'

Mitchell laughs. 'Me neither, Vince.'

'I didn't mean . . .'

'I know.' His superior walks over to the whiteboard and shakes his head as he examines the play sketched out before him. When he turns, his eyes are hard and flint-like. 'I was there, you know. At Whidbey. Junior Agent, of course.'

'You never said.'

'No, and apparently there weren't any Federal Agents at Waco, either. Or at least, none who'll admit to it.' Piper opens his mouth, but Mitchell guesses what is coming. 'And don't ask me to address the class on what we did wrong.'

Piper snaps his jaws shut.

'So, I got no problem with you going, Vince, if London is what you want. But can I just say, I ain't never been back to Whidbey.'

Piper nods, understanding what the other man is saying about opening an old wound. He folds the letter into a small square and pockets it. 'Can I think about it?'

'Sure. I would. Hard.'

Piper isn't certain why he has asked for time. He knows straight away that the answer is yes: he is going to return to London.

With the sound of its brakes muffled by the howl of the first blizzard of the season, the unmarked bus glides to a silent halt near the subway entrance at 231 Street in the Bronx. It comes at the same time every Monday and Friday: five-thirty in the morning, give or take ten minutes. Normally, like every other neighbourhood in the city, these ill-lit streets would be all but empty, especially given the bleak weather. This morning, though, there are three coffee stalls fired up and steaming, an assortment of well-wrapped characters huddled in doorways, and several knots of underdressed working girls clustered beneath the streetlamps, eyes red-rimmed and bleary, exposed flesh pricked into goosebumps.

Along the streets, parked cars, engines still running, spew out coils of water vapour into the night air. A pawnshop has rolled up its shutters, a couple of moneychangers are open for business, and the Italian bakery has begun making the focaccia a half-hour early. An NYPD black and white sits at the end of the street, the two cops within sipping coffee, their hooded eyes taking in the scene, scanning for any signs of trouble.

The bus stops rocking on its worn shocks, the doors hiss open, and a ripple of expectation runs through the watchers. The twice-weekly deposit of released, pardoned or paroled federal prisoners has begun.

There are thirty-three men on board, eighteen Afro-Caribbean, seven Hispanics, the rest Anglos. Some of them last saw this world in a time before universal cell phones, terrorist attacks, and smoking bans in bars. They will be as confused and disoriented as any recent immigrant. More so: because they think they know this country.

The first of the ex-inmates hits the ground running. Claude Podoma, automobile thief turned bank robber (failed), ignores the shrill entreaties from the hookers, who figure they can do good business from guys who haven't banged a woman in an age. Not with Claude, though. He is head down, collar up and into the subway. The second guy off the bus is a tall black man by the name of Macrae, a murderer, who always maintains that, if he had his time over, he would kill the son-of-a-bitch a second time, only slower. This one heads straight for a dog and a coffee, and a satellite group of girls detach and follow him. One of them will strike lucky, if not exactly paydirt.

The third man to put his free foot down is the extortioner, blackmailer, horse nobbler, cardsharp, all-round grifter, Jeffrey Reid aka Brandon Lewis aka a dozen other names. He alights and stops, blocking the entrance for others trying to step down. Despite the protests from behind, he takes his time working the street and smiles when he sees headlights flash at him twice in welcome. He heads towards them. The hustler expects it to be his long-suffering, and bigamously married, second wife. It will be too late when he gets in and realises that the car might belong to Marie, but it contains representatives of some of the people he grifted out of thousands of dollars. His body will be found in three days' time, a single shot through the skull, but minus many extremities, which the Medical Examiner will determine were removed before the merciful bullet.

So it goes on, rapists, robbers, blackmailers, muggers, even the occasional innocent man, each anxious to feed one appetite or another, often being welcomed by friends, loved ones or sometimes enemies. For one man, there is a reunion with his dog, the frisky Alsatian now lame and almost blind, but still yapping as his fur is ruffled and the ex-con's hot tears fall onto his head.

A significant proportion, however, have nobody to greet them, and they disappear into the early morning.

Of the thirty-two who have so far stepped out into the lazy swirls of snow this night, nineteen will eventually find themselves taking a return trip into the bosom of the corrections service, either state, city or federal, within the next twenty-four months.

The last man to step down does so casually yet assuredly, as if he has taken the cross-town bus rather than the Con-Metro. Neither furtiveness nor desperation on show, he stands for a second and sniffs the air, turns on his heel, buries his hands in the pockets of his leather jacket and heads for the subway. He quickly becomes aware of a slow-ticking engine directly behind him, and turns to see who is shadowing him. The window cracks free of its rubber seal and glides down to reveal a familiar face, which breaks into a smile.

'Hello, Lawrence.'

Lawrence Hooper doesn't react. He hasn't seen the man in the Acura for six or seven years, and he isn't certain he is pleased to see him now.

'Are you going to get in? I'll give you a ride to wherever you want to go.'

'Albany?'

'Well, Penn station. Buy you a drink first. Been a while, Larry.'

Hooper hesitates. 'There's a diner three blocks down on the right.'

'Hop in.'

Hooper shakes his head; he needs to think. 'I'll see you in there, Colonel.'

There are a few cabbies and a couple of cops in the diner, but Hooper ignores their stares and slides into a booth with the Colonel, who has already bought him a coffee. Hooper stumbles for a second, as if his legs have failed, and steadies himself on his old employer, before flopping back into his place opposite. He examines the Colonel, who looks much the same as he remembers, face a little gaunter, hair going over to mostly grey.

'Black, right?'

Hooper nods, picks up the glass sugar container and lets a stream of crystals fall into the coffee. He stirs them in slowly, the metal spoon scraping on the rim of the mug.

'You look good.'

Hooper weighs exactly what he did when he was twenty-five, and his waist measurement is only an inch more. He's kept himself in shape. 'You were the last person I expected to see here.'

'Who were you hoping for?'

'Jennifer Lopez would've been nice.'

The Colonel laughs politely. 'What about Renee?'

'I told her not to come. We got to do this real slow.'

His wife is living with her mother in Boston; Hooper knows that the various and differing expectations of his release could implode the already fragile shell of a marriage. He wants to get some heavy scaffolding in place before they try to rebuild it.

'Out for Thanksgiving, though.'

'Yeah.'

'That's something.'

'Only if you like turkey.'

'You'll see Renee, though. Thanksgiving.'

'We'll see. Like I said . . .'

'Slow.'

'Yeah. Colonel, forgive me, but they haven't moved you across to Social Welfare, have they?'

'No.'

'So . . .'

'So,' repeats the Colonel. 'You want anything to eat?'

Hooper yawns and shakes his head. 'In five minutes I'll take that ride to Penn. You got something to say, I'd rather you got to the point.'

'They took your money.'

'They said it was all proceeds of crime.'

'You didn't mention us. That was good.'

'You think they'd believe me? I'd've sounded like . . . what's that guy? Chuck Barry.'

'Barris. What do you want to do now?'

'Finish my house.'

Hooper had been building a house on a lake in upstate New York – modern, Scandinavian-style, hugely energy efficient, designed to blend in with the background – and when his employment with the Colonel had terminated, he had foolishly tried to top up the construction fund with an armed robbery. He still asks himself why.

'How much do you need?'

'How much have prices gone up?'

'A lot.'

'Then I need a lot.'

'I have a paint job I can offer you.'

Hooper narrows his eyes and squints, trying to read the face before him, but the Colonel never gives anything away. 'How big a team?'

'Two man.'

'Who else?'

'Kolski.'

He could live with that. Not everyone could, but the guy knew what he was doing, even if he could be an irritating prick. 'I wasn't going to go back to painting.'

'You lost the moxie for it, Larry? Or are the reflexes shot?'

'You know, Beretta started out making stilettos.'

The Colonel looks puzzled at the change of tack.

'The finest personal protection known in Northern Italy in the fifteenth century,' says Hooper. 'Then they discovered matchlocks. Never looked back since.'

Hooper places the Beretta 9000S model on the table and watches the Colonel's hands twitch before he checks himself. No point in reaching for his belt: he knows the holster will be empty. The Colonel quickly puts his fingers over the weapon and slides it out of sight. 'Very good. When?' Hooper doesn't answer; his face remains impassive but for a slight lift at the corner of his mouth. 'As you slid into the seat, right?'

'Tell me who, what, where,' Hooper says brusquely. 'And how much.'

So the Colonel tells him, although not in that order.

Two

London: Mid-November

'It's a great idea.'

'It's a daft idea.'

'That girl got a film deal out of it. A million dollars.'

'Zip me up and shut up.'

Roddy Young yanks the zipper on his sister's dress and watches as she examines herself in the mirror. They are in her Chelsea townhouse, and she is about to leave for a lunch-date. He knows he has less than a minute to convince her of his scheme's merits. He smoothes down the back, closing up the material over the zipper, running his hand over the silken taupe fabric. 'Nice dress.'

'Paul Smith.'

'Bit low rent for you. Strapped for cash?'

She glares at him from the mirror, but doesn't dignify the jibe with an answer. There is only one of them in the room in need of cash, and it isn't her. 'It's always a million dollars, isn't it?' she sighs. 'And we both know nobody sees any worthwhile cash until the cameras roll. Before that, it's all hot air and prayers and PR.'

'Look, I know a film producer—'

'Half the scum washing around London claim to be film producers.'

'A real one. He says once the site is up and running for a couple of months, has created a bit of a buzz—'

'No.'

'Can't you at least ask the others?'

'No, Roddy.' Celeste turns and stares him in the eye, trying to convey finality. 'They will not be interested.'

Roddy lets exasperation creep into his voice. 'But you lot will do anything for money.'

'Is that right?' she replies frostily.

'Oh come on, Cel. You know what I mean. You don't mind taking money for sucking some old man's cock.'

'Roddy!'

He realises he has overstepped the mark. 'Sorry. But where's the harm?'

'In sucking an old man's cock?'

'No, in this. Look, if you just let me sell The Stables . . .'

That old one. She works hard to prevent herself exploding at him. Instead, she snaps: 'No.'

'Why not? We'd get a good price.'

'No, we wouldn't. It's only half completed.' The Stables is a series of stone dwellings in the Cotswolds that their father has left them. The place is slowly being restored, with the intention to let it out as an upmarket B&B. However, Celeste is sick of being the only one able to fund the project, and is waiting for Roddy to stump up his half, plus arrears. 'What would Mummy say?'

'How would Mummy know?'

Their mother is in a nursing home, her grip on reality increasingly tenuous. This probably isn't the time to remind him that the reason she lives in relative comfort is down to her. Instead Celeste says: 'Besides, it will give us an income one day.'

'You have an income,' Roddy retorts irritably.

'It's not my fault you don't.'

'It is if you don't let me at least pitch my idea.'

She blows out her cheeks in frustration and exhales in a long sigh. Where is the harm? With Roddy there was always a downside, although it has taken her many years – and much cash – to comprehend that.

Schemes that seemed surefire winners quickly turned into quagmires of lost funds and legal writs. Only Roddy, it seems, could have failed to make any cash from internet gambling, but he managed it. Still, all he is asking for on this occasion is some of her, and her friends', time. Despite a drawerful of reservations, she merely says: 'I don't like it one bit.'

He senses the slight weakening and gives his best puppy-dog grin. 'It will all be anonymous, that's part of the whole allure.'

Celeste picks up her Goyard handbag and checks the contents. 'You'll have a ten-minute window over apéritifs,' she says coolly. 'Then you leave, and we'll talk about it. I'll let you know this evening.'

'Great. You won't regr—'

'Please,' says Celeste, holding up her palm. 'Don't ever, ever say that.' Because she knows, one way or another, she always regrets it.

The bar is called the North Pole, for reasons nobody recalls, not even the current owner. It is on Baltic, four blocks from Atlantic City's boardwalk, some distance away from the well-lit areas usually patronised by the city's customers. This section of town is all dilapidated storefronts, broken chainlink fences, burned out tenements and cars with cinder blocks for wheels.

Hooper steps into the bar and waits for his eyes to

adjust to the gloom. The place is smoky, sweaty, the atmosphere thick with the rancid odour of the over-worked deep fryer out back.

He crosses the floor to the bar, the sticky carpet sucking at his soles, and finds a place on the u-shaped counter. The clientèle is mostly black, an equal mix of men and women, vacant-eyed, staring up at the TV, all ignoring him. Something strikes him as odd. He has been in some dives in his time, a few in the last couple of hours, but he is aware of a missing element. Then it hits him: no slots. Every Atlantic City bar he has been in has table-top slot machines as well as their ubiquitous big brothers. Not here.

Hooper orders a beer from the barkeep, a woman either a young forty or an old thirty, who sports a spectacular black eye. He tries not to stare as she pours him a beer.

'Need anything else?'

Hooper, unsure of just how loaded that question is, shakes his head. 'I'm good.' He joins the others in watching the football on TV.

He slips so much into Baltimore Ravens at the New York Jets that the hand on his shoulder five minutes later makes him start. He spins on the stool, expecting trouble of some kind, but then relaxes. It is Kolski, dressed in combat jacket, thick leather gloves and a woollen hat, which he yanks off. He is sporting a full beard, black flecked with coarse grey, and those piercing green eyes are as unsettling as ever. 'Hi, Buddy.'

'Hey,' he says, equally careful not to use Kolski's real name. You never knew.

'Over here.'

He takes his drink and follows Kolski to a booth in an even darker corner of the place, the cheap plastic of the banquette squeaking as he slides in. The black-eyed barkeep brings Kolski a beer and chaser without being asked.

'You should cap him, Phoebs,' says Kolski, looking up at her and indicating the yellowing corona around her eye.

She nods. 'Give you a hundred bucks to do it for me.'

Kolski shakes his head. 'Wouldn't pay for my bullets.'

'How come?' she asks.

'Gonna need silver ones to make sure that bastard is dead.'

She smiles mirthlessly. 'Got that right. You want another?' She points at Hooper's glass and he nods.

'Nice place,' he says when she is gone.

Kolski smirks. 'Yeah – not like you're used to, I hear.'

Hooper smiles, drains his glass and accepts the replacement with a nod.

'It's a casino workers' hangout. Dealers, pit bosses, waitresses. It's always dark like this. The casinos run twenty-four hours, see, on three eight-hour shifts, so there really is no day and night. You live a different rhythm from normal folk, so when you clock off, you need somewhere like this, somewhere that won't throw your new body-time out. And you don't want to be around the jerks you been dealin' to all day, which is why you come to this part of town. Plus, no slots. Last thing these folks need is to see more flashing lights, rolling tumblers and jackpot promises or cracker-jack crap like that. Know what I'm sayin'?'

'Ah reckon.'

'Ah reckon, too,' Kolski mimics.

Sometimes, Hooper still has the panhandle in his voice when he speaks. His father was a Primitive Baptist preacher in a fly- and mosquito-blown town at the top of Florida. Father and son never did see eye to eye about the Creation, sin, retribution and redemption, right up to the day he beat the old man to a pulp with a fence-post and went off to enlist. One thing he had from that church upbringing, though, was a great singing voice. Even Kolski, who has only heard him sing in the shower, reckons his partner could have been a white soul star in a different life, like Michael MacDonald.

'The beard is new.'

24

Kolski tugs at it. 'Yeah. It'll go if we take the job. You get anything while you were away?'

Hooper shakes his head. No tattoos, no distinguishing marks at all, apart from a new scar on his back where he was shanked.

'Where you stayin'?'

Hooper tells him and Kolski gets out his cell. 'What you doin'?' Hooper asks, suspicious.

'Boostin' you up a floor or two. Hey, Frank? You got a . . .' He looks across at Hooper.

'Steve Drizer.'

'A Steve Drizer stayin'. Can you comp him up to five-oh-nine for me? Great. Owe you one.' Kolski closes the phone. 'Wanna get laid?' he asks Hooper.

'No. I appreciate the room—'

'You been laid yet?'

Hooper figures this is none of Kolski's business. His look conveys this.

'OK. Just that, you been away, there's some girls, not professionals, I could, like . . .' He lets it die a lonely death in the space between them. 'Please yourself.'

'What you doin' here?'

'In Atlantic City? Just some casino security work. Tracking down the off-site poker schools that get set up, helping bust 'em.'

'All of them?'

Kolski laughs. 'No. They let a few ride. You big

25

enough or mean enough, you can do what you like in this town.'

It was always the same. It is Hooper's third visit to the city and he hates the raw venality of it, feels the need to take a shower every couple of hours to try to scrub himself clean. 'You work for Wallace much?'

'These last few years? Nah.' Kolski downs the chaser. 'I mostly did some time in LA. Working for a fix-it lawyer. But, Jeez, I tell ya. Those guys – they got mansions, they got million-dollar salaries, but do they pay their bills? Do they fuck. Can pay, won't pay. What do you do when a lawyer owes you? Threaten to sue? Right.'

'But you got paid.'

'Eventually. You can't sue, best thing to do is tie his trophy wife up, douse her in gasoline and tell him the only thing'll be left that he'd recognise when you finish will be her silicone implants.'

He can't tell whether Kolski is riffing on a threat he made or an actual event. He has learned not to ask or guess. He usually gets it wrong. The fact is, the threats were never idle, so it was academic anyway. 'What you reckon on this paint job?' he says.

'Wallace always pays,' Kolski shrugs. 'Can't beat a government job.'

'No, I mean, you good to go on it?'

Kolski swirls the last inch of his beer round in the glass. 'I just got to get my dog looked after.'

'You got a dog?' Hooper can't keep the surprise from his voice. The idea that Kolski can care about any living thing enough to feed it, let alone get someone else to feed it, is something of a revelation.

The Black-Eyed Barmaid slams a plate of chips down on their table and moves off. Kolski helps himself to a handful. 'Only safe thing to eat in this place. Yeah, I got a dog – a setter. Nice. Good company. I think I like dogs better than people.'

'I think you like most things better than people.'

A cadaverous figure looms at them, a laminated menu in his hand. The odour of old frying oil is suddenly so strong, Hooper thinks he is going to gag. The man's chef's whites are that only in theory. They look as if they've been implicated in the derailment of a gravy train. 'You want to eat tonight?' the man croaks.

'No thanks, Maurice,' Kolski says quietly, 'I got some chips here. Maybe later, eh?' Maurice shuffles off. 'I know what you're thinking. Why do I waste my time here? I'll tell you. This is the kind of place that is the opposite of the bar in *Cheers*. You ever see that show?'

'I wasn't inside that long. I even know *Frasier*.'

'Sure. You know it ended, right?'

'*Cheers*?'

'*Frasier*.'

'I heard. So, this is unlike the bar in *Cheers*,' Hooper says, trying to get Kolski out of back issues of *TV Guide* and on track once more.

'Well, this is the place where nobody knows your name. Two days from now someone comes in lookin' for me, flashin' my mugshot, all he'll get is blank stares and shakes of the head. You walk out that door, you're history to these people. It's like collective Alzheimer's.' He finishes the last of the chips and brushes his hands together to flick off the crumbs. 'So, I get my dog looked after. We gonna do this thing?'

Hooper waits a while before he confirms. 'Yeah. We're gonna do this thing.'

'Good.' Kolski raises his glass, preparing to sink the last of his beer. 'Here's to London.'

'You all know Roddy, don't you?' says Celeste and the three women nod and smile in unison as they sit, flashing him a dazzling show of the best Harley Street cosmetic dentistry. They are in the corner of the Wolseley restaurant, a former car showroom on Piccadilly, built when such emporia were temples to the might of British automotive engineering. Jason has seated them well; the group is able to see the room without being jostled by waiters and customers, as can happen at some of the less desirable tables.

The Wolseley is still a place to see and be seen three years after its opening, so Roddy knows he is going to have a struggle to keep the women's attention focused on him in the ten minutes he has been given. He orders a bottle of champagne as a sign of his good intentions and examines each of his prospective clients in turn.

Opposite him is the immaculately preserved Natalie, who comes with a lovely complexion, only slightly tightened by the knife, and a delicious French accent. Celeste reckons she is forty-one. In certain lights, maybe, he thinks.

Timmy is a Croatian with blonde hair, once long, now cut dramatically short, who sports a spectacularly pneumatic figure: she has a tiny waist and enormous breasts which, she never fails to boast, are 'all natural'. She also has the dirtiest laugh he has ever heard. There was a time when he used to memorise jokes, just to make her laugh. Timmy is an uncomplicated girl: she likes sex, so why not make a career of it?

Sasha is the one that Celeste claims is Mayfair out of Macclesfield, a top-drawer construct, but that hardly matters to Roddy. A perky brunette, with sexy grey eyes that have a soft, smoky quality, she is by some margin his favourite of the quartet. His sister excepted, of course. She is his most-favoured high-class prostitute in the world.

29

'So,' he begins. 'The idea came to me when I read about the sexblog.'

'Sexblog?' asks Natalie, making the word seem at once alien and filthy.

There is a cheer from the table next door and Roddy glances over. A party of Russians. There is one of those Anglo-Soviet Economic Forums going on, which is an excuse for wealthy oligarchs to come over to eat and shop well. The windows of both Liberty and Selfridges are full of Cyrillic script and gilded domes. Roddy raises his voice slightly to drown them out. 'You all know what a blog is? A kind of web diary, a web-log. Blog for short. Well, this, um . . .' Not for the first time he finds himself stumbling for a euphemism for what these girls do.

'Sex worker,' says Celeste, taking a sip of champagne.

'Yes. This sex worker kept an on-line diary of her adventures, which became a complete cult. People logged on and paid to read what she had been up to.'

'Read?' asks Sasha. 'No photographs?'

'No, not on hers, but I was thinking of including some tasteful shots, just to put a body to the name—'

'Don't get ahead of yourself,' warns Celeste. 'Four minutes and then we order.'

Roddy pushes back his hair with his hand in what

he hopes is a cute-but-harassed gesture. 'Right. That web-log has been picked up as a movie. Now, I thought, what if you did that times four? A virtual chat room where the four of you discussed every aspect of your, um, business. Who you did it with, where, how much . . .'

Natalie makes a disapproving noise. 'But our clients want confidentiality. That's what they pay top money for – right?' She looks at Celeste, who vigorously nods her agreement.

'Of course there would be anonymity. All the names would be changed. You can use false ones or nicknames. Dick Thrust, that sort of thing.' Only Timmy laughs, bless her. 'I mean, think about it. You must have had Premier League footballers.' He looks around the table. 'Pop stars. Politicians.'

'So how does it work?' asks Natalie. 'This blag?'

'Blog. Well, every day there will be a tease page, but if you want to read the whole thing, then you need to be a member. A paying member. It'd be like *Sex and the City* but with real sex. Not so many shoes.' He senses he isn't pitching this as well as he might. 'Although there could be shoes if you want.'

'Are you ready to order?' asks the waiter.

'No,' says Roddy curtly, irritated at the interruption. 'A few more minutes.' He glances at Celeste who concurs with a small nod.

31

'And the members have to pay, you say?' asks Timmy.

'Yes. A monthly fee. Plus we have the chance to option the whole idea as a movie or TV series.' He pauses for breath. 'It can't go wrong.'

'You don't think,' says Celeste slowly, 'that when the press realise there are four anonymous women having sex with barely disguised celebrities – which I am afraid we don't, but I am sure a little creative writing will go into this – they won't move hell and high water to find out who we are?'

'It'll be a dead end,' he assures her. 'There's no way they can find out. We'll cover our tracks.'

'So if someone does want to do a movie, how do they get in touch then?' asks Sasha. Good question, thinks Celeste.

'Through the webmaster. Me.' Roddy drains his glass of champagne and pulls four sheaves of paper from his inside pocket. 'Look, I scribbled out some figures. You can read these over lunch, see what you think. Cel will call me later, tell me what you decide. Won't you?'

'Of course.'

'But let me say, you won't regr—'

'Roddy,' Celeste snaps.

'It's copper-bottomed. Trust me. Anyway, great to see you all. Natalie. Sasha. Timmy. Thanks.'

Roddy backs away from the table, spins and walks through the main room, stopping at a number of tables for a quick word and a handshake.

'Shall we order?' asks Celeste.

'Oysters for me,' says Sasha. 'He's nice, your brother, isn't he?'

'Yes. Which is his big failing.'

'How do you mean?'

'People say yes to him because he is nice, not because whatever he is up to is a good thing.'

'But this web-log, it's not a bad idea, is it?'

'Yes, it is,' says Celeste. 'It's a very bad idea indeed.' Even worse, she realises, Roddy hasn't paid for the champagne he ordered. She turns to try and catch him, but he is gone. She is unaware that, as she presents her face to the restaurant, a man sitting across the aisle surreptitiously captures her image digitally.

Roddy gets the call just after five, at his new office in Museum Street. Soho is now too expensive for him; in fact, he owes rent on the Greek Street premises he had taken when his internet future looked bright. Here, he has managed to pick up a short lease on the first floor above a Japanese restaurant.

The women at the Wolseley would hardly recognise this figure, sitting on a packing crate, chewing his lip, drinking from a carton of milk to try to calm the acid eating his stomach. Across the room, considerably more relaxed, sits Lennie, his partner and, of late, sole investor, who is speaking very cautiously on a landline. He puts down the phone and looks over at Roddy.

'What did Geoff say?' Roddy asks.

'We have two hours to make up our mind whether we are in or not.'

'Christ, Lennie, I'm not cut out for that sort of thing.'

Lennie shrugs. 'It's a good little number.'

'I know.' He looks across at his friend. Lennie, despite being dressed in a Spencer Hart of Savile Row suit and Tod driving shoes, is a Bethnal Green boy through and through. For most of his life he'd zig-zagged over the blurred line between legal and illegal activity – mostly involving supplying desirable cars to the Middle and Far East. The reason that BMW X5s and Aston Martin DB9s all needed trackers these days was down to Lennie, who had passed the operation on when the dollar, the favoured currency for payment, had slumped in 2003.

He'd linked up with Roddy at a dog track, where Roddy was promoting his internet gambling idea. Lennie had heard the sales pitch about the future of new technology, how it would transform their lives. It had certainly transformed Lennie's. He was dangerously close to poor now. It was, in his opinion, time to dabble in some old-school technologies.

'You don't need me at all really, do you?' says Roddy.

Lennie shrugs. 'I provide the spit, you bring the polish.' He laughs, pleased with the analogy.

Roddy's mobile chirps, and he takes the call. He listens, grunts and flips it shut.

'She said no,' says Lennie flatly.

'She said no. It was two-two. Stupid bitch.' He glares down at the phone in his hand.

Lennie tries to stop himself smiling. He always thought it was a rubbish idea, and he thinks Roddy's smart little sister did the right thing.

Between them, he and Roddy have raised a few grand in loans, mostly from friends, but that well is just about dry. So they have one last shot left. The cash is enough either to pay off their immediate debts and start up and market the whole blog idea – with no guarantee it will work – or they could invest in something Lennie has a line into. 'What now?' asks Lennie. 'Shall I tell Geoff we are in?'

Roddy chews his lip once more, until he tastes the iron tang of blood. Geoff is Lennie's brother, a man who normally would swat him like a fly, Roddy suspects. Lennie confers on him a decent amount of immunity from thugs. At last he says: 'I bet that Sasha is one of the pros. No pun intended. Rather than a con, I mean. We could use her, fake the rest . . .'

'Roddy—'

'No, it'll be great. Run it for a few weeks, then we can get Matt to push it to Working Title. They buy anything connected with London.'

'Roddy, the chances—'

'No, I'm sorry, Lennie. Look at me. This blogging I can handle.' Roddy is thinking back to his stint as a big-time drug dealer, which lasted all of two days and ended in ignominy. He spreads his palms out before him. 'Do I look like an armed robber?'

No, Lennie had to admit, Roddy didn't. But he did.

Three

The grave of Vincent Piper's daughter is in a cemetery on the fringes of a Manchester suburb. Even before he has checked in with the London Legat, as he should do if he were to follow strict procedure, he travels north by plane and takes a cab from Ringway airport to Didsbury.

The cab waits at the North Gate for him while he turns up his collar against the wind, walks down the cinder path, past the boarded-up and graffiti-ed Victorian chapel, to plot 50887. He takes the bunch of freesias from under his coat and lays it on the green marble chips, next to an urn containing fresh irises. 'I'm sorry, Martha,' he says softly as he kneels. 'I've been away so long. And I am sorry they disturbed you for nothing.'

The British police had exhumed the body to check

for traces of explosives on Martha's fingers. That way, they hoped to prove she had handled the very bomb that had helped kill her. In fact, they found no residues. Even so, Piper suspects they still think his daughter was trying to take both of them out that day.

Sunshine breaks through the sullen November clouds and warms him. He takes a deep breath and smiles down at Martha. He is glad he has come; it is easier to face this patch of ground than he had expected. He is remembering his daughter from before the revenge undertaken by two crazed women, who are now serving life sentences in federal prisons, not the dying girl he carried in his arms. As it should be. It is a small victory over the depression that sometimes clouds his mind.

He looks at his watch. Fifteen minutes before midday, the hour that Judy, his ex-wife, has told him she always sets aside for visiting their daughter. He had made certain he was here for her, but now he can feel his resolve ebbing away. He had thought he was strong enough to see both of them, Martha and Judy, but now he isn't sure he can face the icy undercurrents that flow between those left living.

As he stands, wiping his eyes, he sees a figure approaching from the South Gate. It's Judy, and she is early. She is still 300 yards away when she stops, unsure of what she is seeing. He returns Judy's gaze.

She stays immobile, but for the familiar gesture of pushing her hair behind one ear. He raises his hand in greeting, but there is no acknowledgement. He turns and walks quickly away, back towards his waiting cab. He will have to be stronger to face her. One small victory a day is his current limit.

'Sit down, Vince. It's good to see you.' Stanley Roth, his old friend and mentor, is now the Senior Legat at the London FBI office, with an impressive suite of panelled rooms at the Embassy in Grosvenor Square and his very own picture of the President on the wall. Hanging next to it is a selection of Roth's awards and citations, from his Quantico weapons training merit award – with a photograph underneath of him holding up his perfect score on the rifle range – to the last mentioned-in-dispatches for his part in breaking an illegal immigration scheme. The certificates stop around three years ago, when he became a full-time bureaucrat.

Still, the promotion obviously agrees with him. Since Piper was last in London, Roth has lost weight, as well as his beard and the lugubrious air that used to hang around him.

Piper lowers himself into a complex mesh-backed chair, which causes him to start as it rocks him back.

'Comfortable, eh? Got the whole place furnished

with them. Helps the back. You ever had back trouble? No? Once you get out of the field completely, that's when it goes. Too long sitting at this thing.' He thumps the desk. 'How are you, Vince? Lookin' good.'

'Fine. How are the kids?'

'Growing up Cockney. Might have to ship 'em back to the States for a while, re-Americanise them.'

'Must be big now.'

'Twelve and fourteen.' He points at the green assignment folder on his desk. The niceties are over. 'So. Bet you didn't expect to be back here. Not officially.'

'No. Did you—?'

'Me?' He shakes his head. 'I'll be honest with you, Vince. I said it was a bad idea to bring you over. That it might trigger . . . you know. An event.'

'Stan, spare me the psychology. I took the operational profile test at Quantico before I left. I'm good, all the marbles I should have, roughly in the right place.'

'Glad to hear it. No, you have your old chum DCI Fletcher to thank.'

'Fletch?' Piper had worked with her on APPLE, the Anglo-American initiative whereby the FBI helps Scotland Yard with crimes committed by or against US citizens.

'Yup. She is now part of the Home Office's task force on reviewing the performance of,' he slips on his glasses and reads from the assignment folder, 'SOCA.'

SOCA, a recently formed elite super-force, sometimes dubbed the British FBI, or by others 'the Untouchables', had been intended to streamline crime investigation in the UK by combining elements of the National Crime Squad (NCS), the National Criminal Intelligence Service (NCIS) and the investigative arms of Customs and Excise and the immigration service. Piper knew that, as in the US back when the Feds were formed by Hoover, there was much resentment among other agencies that had lost manpower and, more importantly, money and influence to the new boys. SOCA had trodden on similar toes, and its results hadn't quite lived up to the hype when Prime Minister Tony Blair had announced its creation almost two years previously. Hence the proposal by the Home Office Review.

Roth slides the folder towards him and Piper knows he is going to hear a resumé of his new role, even though he has sat through it a dozen times already. 'The assignment outline is in here. The first thing you have to do is get up to speed on how the system works now. They have allowed three weeks for that, not counting the holidays, which seem to go on for ever over here. You remember how the whole place shuts down for, like, two weeks around Christmas? Unbelievable. So, probably in the New Year, you will report to the National Hi-Tech Crime Unit in Docklands, where they have a suite reserved for you, to start shooting the breeze with a bunch of other so-called experts – no offence – examining individual cases to see where and why things went wrong.'

Roth adopts a smug expression which demonstrates that he has been doing his homework. 'And try to explain to the Brits why they have spent more than a hundred million dollars on SOCA and yet the equivalent of six billion dollars' worth of cocaine and heroin still came in last year. Then you report in six months on whether, in your working party's opinion, SOCA needs beefing up, or splitting back into its component parts.'

That is a slam dunk, thinks Piper. The new system might need tweaking, but the old one, with over-lapping responsibilities and conflicting aims, was a mess. SOCA has to be given a chance to work.

'Then you can go home,' Roth concludes, slapping the desk.

'Sounds easy enough.'

'Personnel fixed you up somewhere to stay?'

'Apartment near Dolphin Square for now.'

'Good. You might wanna move to East London in the New Year. Getting across town is worse than ever. Well, that's the formalities here taken care of. Fletcher's direct line is on page one. I suggest you tell her you're on board and set up a meet before Christmas comes along.'

Piper manages to swing out of the multi-pivoting chair and offers his hand. Stanley takes it. 'One more thing, Vince. You may be working for the Brits, but you are still FBI.'

'Of course.'

'Which means you draw a concealed handgun from the armoury.'

'What?' When he had served in London previously, access to handguns was strictly controlled.

Roth lets go of Piper's hand and flips back his jacket to show his holstered gun. 'Things have changed. We play by FBI rules now – armed at all times. So you don't have to go mugging Secret Service men for their weapons any more.'

Piper keeps his face impassive. 'Meaning?'

Roth cracks a grin. 'Just fishing, Vince. Just fishing. Look, when you do draw the weapon, do me a favour?'

Piper asks: 'What's that, Stanley?'

'Keep your nose clean. Just do your job and go home. And stay away from You-know-who. You two go together like acid and oil.'

After the meeting, Piper takes the chit down to the basement. He walks by the softly lit rooms where, behind smoked glass, the men and women from the Communications Division sort through myriad e-mails, faxes, cell-phone and landline intercepts. Some of these will be passed along to THRESS, the Threat Assessment unit next door, responsible for the daily report on who wants them all dead, and why. If not usually, unfortunately, exactly where and when they want to do it.

Piper takes a concrete flight of stairs and shoulders open the heavy steel, sound-proofed door to the lower level, where John Ditko, the Embassy armourer who now serves the various US security forces, has his little fiefdom known as the Gun Cage.

The ceiling is low, the walls bare cinder block, the lighting dim, and the place smells of oil and gunshots. Ditko is hidden behind a tough wire mesh, surrounded by a wall of grey gunsafes. This is where weapons are stored, issued and repaired. Quite why there needs to be such security is a mystery – the Embassy is one of the most impenetrable buildings in the world, and any interloper intent on weapon-theft would need a map and a flashlight to find this place.

Piper leans down to the opening in the wire barrier. 'Two Big Macs, fries and a Coke. Can you supersize that?'

Ditko shakes his head good-naturedly. 'Ain't heard that before, Vince. How are you? Long time no see.'

Piper indicates the size of the installation by spreading his arms. 'You got big.'

'Yeah. They finally saw sense. Now you can draw a weapon officially.' He winks. 'Without all that sneaking around the Fairmont.'

Again, Piper doesn't rise to the bait. The rumour is he once took out a Secret Service colleague because he needed a gun. The rumour is true, but he will never confirm it. 'What have you got?'

The armourer selects three models, each from a different safe, and lays them on the counter: a Sig P229, the Smith & Wesson auto chambered for 10mm and a Glock 32. He slides them through the narrow opening to Piper. 'This is our choice.'

'What do you think?' Piper asks Ditko.

'What do you use back home?'

'A Sig 226.'

He taps the 229. 'This is better. But they are all good guns. The ten-mil round on the Smith and Wesson is a beauty.'

'I had problems with it back in—'

Ditko holds up his hand. He knows all about the initial glitches with the ammunition. 'Yes. All addressed. But it is a thicker, heavier cartridge. It stops real good, but ups the weight a couple of ounces. Why don't you put some shots through each, see how you feel?'

Piper collects a pair of ear-defenders from the rack

on the wall, moves across to the two narrow firing ranges they have somehow managed to shoehorn into the space, and fills it with noise and smoke for fifteen minutes. He opts for the Sig, chambered for 9mm, the more common cartridge in Europe. Ditko compliments him on his choice then makes him sign a stack of forms as fat as a telephone directory, before he measures him for a holster. He tells him he can pick up the whole rig in twenty-four hours.

After the shooting, the detonations still ringing in his ears despite the defenders, Piper walks from the Embassy north to Oxford Street. He keeps going north, heading up Baker Street through the thunder of one-way traffic, wandering aimlessly past Selfridges ground-floor food department, and up towards the Sherlock Holmes Hotel. The weather is turning spiteful, and icy squalls of rain keep dashing into his face.

Piper feels the depression he fought off at the grave-yard curling around him. It weighs on his shoulders and heart. He knows he will open a bottle of wine tonight and then a second. Yes, he'll regret it in the morning when he has the shakes and the flashes of nausea strike, but for the moment, he just wants to stop thinking too much.

At the big junction, opposite the Mosque, he stops, aware of the direction in which he is unconsciously heading: Regent's Park and Winfield House, the US Ambassador's Residence. This is where the final, gruesome and insane act of Martha's death was played out, and where he was saved by the woman Roth calls 'You-know-who', as if her very name, Celeste Young, is contaminated. Like that Shakespeare play British actors don't like to mention, in case it curses them. *Hamlet* or *Macbeth*, he can't recall which.

Celeste Young is the woman who helped Piper when Martha had been fooled into planting a bomb in a Charing Cross Road bookshop; it had gone off and seriously injured her. In the aftermath of the carnage, Celeste had driven his daughter with maniacal skill to the nearest hospital. It wasn't her fault that his daughter died anyway.

Piper had then stupidly got involved with Martha's tutor, Sarah Nielsen, when in fact he really wanted Celeste. The tutor turned out to be the real bomber, intent on a public act of execution, a Big Dance, as she called it. She had tried once more in the grounds of the US Ambassador's house in Regent's Park, by detonating a device hidden in a statue to commemorate Martha. The explosion would have devastated the crowd, taking out Piper, Judy, Jack Sandler – the US Ambassador – and dozens of others. Again, Celeste had saved the day, taking a bullet for her trouble.

After he'd made sure Celeste was OK, and that the FBI knew she was a hero, Piper had returned to the US to see his dying father. His feelings for Celeste remained unresolved. He knew what she did for a living, but it didn't matter. Well, it did – of course it did. He just wanted her anyway.

Celeste is just one thread in a complicated mess of emotions, like a ball of wool after a kitten has finished with it. Snarled in there is Judy, his ex-wife, his ex-lover Rachel – the infidelity that wrecked his marriage – the death of Martha, that near-disaster at the US Ambassador's Residence and the slow death of his father, 'The Wolf', once a star FBI agent. Celeste and pain seem to be intractably intertwined in his mind.

Piper turns away from the park, hails a black cab and heads back into Town. No point in raking it all up, it hurts too much. As Roth says, 'Do your job and go home.'

Four

Even as Larry Hooper crawls across its underbelly, his face centimetres from the earth, he thinks: This is beautiful countryside. Kissed by a late-year yellowish light, the trees bursting with reds, golds and ochres, it is all rolling hills, white picket-fences and small-holdings, the last outpost of rural Americana, before the bland giant farms of the corporations begin a few miles further south. Winter hasn't quite bitten at this latitude, the storms that blasted Washington have stayed north, and there are still more leaves on the trees than on the ground.

From his final position on the edge of the woods, a prostrate Hooper assembles his weapon and surveys the Target through the Hensoldt scope attached to his SIG 3000 sniper rifle. His objective is walking across one of those fields, padding through the yellowing grass and its smattering of crisp leaves, unaware that Hooper has spent two days on what snipers call an RSTA manoeuvre – Reconnaissance, Surveillance and Target Acquisition – and has him framed in his eyepiece.

Sniper skills deteriorate over time. Hooper's stay in prison means that his eye is terrible, so while they wait for the Colonel to give them the green light on the paint job, Hooper trains. *Train like you fight, fight like you train.* That is the maxim that has been drilled into him. None of it is an exercise.

So, while Kolski does a little practice of his own around the city, Hooper has rented a car on a phoney licence and ID in Virginia and driven to North Carolina, scouting out something that would help his rusty reflexes.

He had found the perfect location after two hours of driving. It involved moving past two houses, both with dogs, across an open field, into this copse, and crawling, very slowly, with minimum noise, through the undergrowth until he reached the perfect spot for the kill.

At this stage, with the Target in his sights, a lesser man might have pretended to squeeze the trigger and called it a day. Not Hooper. Because after the RSTA phase of a hit, you have two more stages: Elimination, followed by E&E: Escape and Evasion. That is, getting away from the place of the hit without being detected. And killing anyone who does detect you.

For this particular training sequence, he has forgone the usual laser sight which 'paints' the target with a red dot. To rely on that at this stage would do him no good at all. He has gone back to basics with an optical sight and a five-round magazine. Could he get more than one shot in? The lock time – the period between squeezing the trigger and the bullet leaving the muzzle – is very short on the Sig, and in his prime he would reckon on getting three away before a body hit the ground. Regular Lee Harvey Oswald. That was then, this is now, he thinks. He'll be happy with two.

The Target turns and begins to walk the line, hugging the fence of the field, walking with big strides. Hooper inserts his auditory suppression plugs. He doesn't want to get cordite ear, the loss of hearing that careless riflemen suffer.

Some people think sniping is a cowardly way to wage a war. Hooper likes to tell them it has noble antecedents, and its own band of heroes. Like Simo Häyhä, a Finnish farmer who had nothing but an iron-sighted Mosin-Nagant Model 28 – not even a scope – yet when Finland was invaded by the Soviet Union in 1939, he was credited with killing more than five hundred Russians in a nine-month period. And he could do a decent E&E – as proved by the fact that he only died in 2002, aged ninety-six. He was The Man as far as Hooper was concerned.

A pheasant breaks cover to his left, and as the Target turns his head towards it, the scope's cross hairs meet directly between the eyes. Hooper hesitates. At this range – perhaps 700 metres – the PH, Probability of a Hit, is pretty good, but he wants a first-time kill, then the chance to put a second, maybe a third slug into the body. The Target turns his head away again. The Target: not flesh and blood, father or mother, brother or sister, not a living thing at all, he reminds himself, just something to be eliminated.

Hooper empties his mind of worries – about Colonel Wallace, about his wife Renee, about the wisdom of what he is doing. He shifts position slightly, the chestnut leaves crinkling beneath him, and begins to calculate the AAP, the Adjusted Aiming Point, allowing for variables such as gravity, wind and Target movement.

The Target halts, inspecting something snagged on the wire before him. Hooper quickly determines his new aiming point, makes sure his eye is a good three inches from the scope – he isn't so rusty he has forgotten how painful a recoil black-eye is – and squeezes.

The round he favours is a semi-jacketed hollow

point. It combines accuracy with high wound potential. The round has a feature adapted from armour-piercing shells, a small disc of jagged copper at the base of the cavity. As the round flares open and slows, the button detaches and ricochets within the Target, causing a second wound channel. The resulting mayhem is called a copper kiss.

The Target staggers as the bullet hits; a mixture of blood, bone and brain clouds the air behind him. The neck muscles spasm in shock, the jaw sags open, the eyes roll. He is dead already.

Hooper works the bolt and fires again. The flesh ripples under the impact, and there is more blood this time as the round tumbles through soft tissue, gouging a massive channel. The swaying Target still stands and Hooper whips back the mechanism to get a third round in. He smiles as he sees the knees buckle, and he can almost feel the ground shake as 1000lbs of well-bred stallion hits the earth, raising a cloud of vegetable matter, the lips trembling as air explodes from the lungs. The legs give one last feeble kick, and then the horse is still.

Hooper pulls away from the 'scope, blinks, and surveys the larger scene. Already he can see someone running down the lane, towards the field where the animal lies dead.

Hooper places his cheek back against the rest and

lines the person up in the graticule. It is a young girl, perhaps thirteen or fourteen. She is almost a kilometre away from him, but closing fast on the downed horse, arms and legs flailing inelegantly as she runs. He estimates the shot, lets his finger tighten on the trigger an almost imperceptible amount and says, 'Boom'. He pulls out the protective wads from his ears, snatches up the three pieces of brass from the leaf litter and zips them all into his breast pocket. He crawls backwards for a few yards before he turns and runs, crouching, through the trees. A scream of youthful horror, of innocence killed along with the animal, reaches his ears over the crisp rhythm of his tread. There'll be shock, disbelief, and then the hunt for the madman who could perpetrate such a heinous crime.

Time for a little E&E.

Five

'Come on, ten per cent of the subs and a consulting role on the movie. For what? A few scribbled notes at the end of each day. We'll do the rest.'

Roddy is pacing the floor of Sasha's apartment at Butler's Wharf, which comes with a mesmerising view of Tower Bridge. It is very far east for a West End girl, but perhaps she likes to keep business and pleasure separate. It is late afternoon and a soft winter darkness, tinged with fog, has settled over the city. The car lights on the bridge seem diffused, as if viewed through gauze.

Sasha is sitting on a cream leather sofa, her long legs tucked under her. Her voice is less polished than normal, with more warmth. Perhaps, he thinks, she feels she can let her performance slide down a notch or two in his company. Her face is scrubbed of make-up, and she looks glowing, healthy and innocent. Knowing what he knows about her private life, it is a heady combination, but he has to keep his mind on business.

'I don't know, Roddy,' Sasha says eventually. 'Celeste will kill me.'

'No, she won't,' he says with what he hopes is sufficient conviction. 'Because she will see there is no harm in it. Look.' He reaches into his Vuitton briefcase and brings out a cassette recorder. 'You could just speak into this.'

Sasha fixes him with a doe-eyed stare. 'Roddy, do you think I can't write? I have four A-levels.' She points across the room to a glass table, on top of which is a silver laptop. 'I could even e-mail it to you.'

Roddy tries to suppress a smile. She's nibbling. 'Well, that would make things easier.'

'You said about pics. I looked at some of the other sites. *Claire's Bedroom* – do you know that one, Roddy? I have a tame Professor who sees those parts of me . . .'

'Pure porn,' he says sternly. 'None of that.'

'You know, you get guys who sometimes turn up with these ideas and names. Cream pies, double anal, snowballs. I used to wonder where they dreamed it all up.'

'Internet,' he says.

'So I see. They think this stuff is what regular people do.'

Roddy tries to break the next part to her gently. 'You're not regular people, Sash.'

She studies him for a minute before she says, 'I'll assume you meant that nicely. So if there are no gynae-cological extravaganzas, then what?'

'Silhouettes. Mock-ups. Doesn't even have to be you,' he says quickly. 'Forget that. It's the idea of these four beautiful, funny women doing, um, what you do, that will get people salivating.'

Sasha wrinkles her nose. 'Funny? I'm not sure I can do funny.'

'I'll do funny for you.'

'The thing is, each of us girls are different, you know,' she says.

'Physically?'

'How we source clients. I work through agencies like Boardroom Exclusive and Hobson.'

'Really?' Roddy tries to keep the surprise from his voice. Hobson, named after a smooth, unflappable English valet in some movie or other, was set up by two friends of his. It is an on-line concierge service where, for a fee, members can have their path through life smoothed twenty-four hours a day. Roddy had been given the chance to invest, but declined, thinking it was too crowded a marketplace. Hobson boomed. 'And Natalie?'

'One of the big international escort agencies. She's mostly corporate. Because she's a bit . . .'

'Older?'

'More sophisticated, I was going to say. Timmy is on the books of a high-end tour operator, incoming from Europe mostly. Top end, of course. And Celeste is a Jilly.'

'A what?'

'Jilly Cooper. It means she keeps a regular stable. On contract. Very clever, if you can do it.' She smirks and her cheeks dimple in an attractive way. 'If a little predictable. So, we're all different.'

'Well, the variety makes it interesting. Gives you all individual character. And between you, you must have done some things, slept with a few celebrities and the like.'

'Well, you know when you read in the *News of the World* about a TV presenter love rat doing coke in Mayfair hotels with one-thousand-pound-a-night hookers?'

Roddy's eyes widen in anticipation. 'Yes.'

'That's never us.'

'Oh.'

Sasha looks at the large Omega on her wrist and jumps up. 'Too early for a glass of bubbly?'

'Never too early,' says Roddy absent-mindedly.

She returns from the kitchen with two full champagne flûtes and hands one to Roddy, who sips.

'The thing is, we all know some who do.'

'Do what?'

'You know, thousand pounds a night, TV love rat, that kind of thing. It wouldn't be hard to lift some of the stories.'

'That's the spirit,' he beams. 'But surely you must have had someone well known . . . I mean, I bet you're not cheap.'

'Is that also meant to be a compliment?'

Roddy laughs. 'I suppose it is. Sorry.'

'It's OK.' Sasha thinks back. There was a footballer once. She mentions him by name and Roddy's brow furrows.

'Christ, where is he now?'

'I last heard of him playing for Yeovil. It was a brief stay at the top.'

'I'll say.'

'And I once dated—' She stops herself, remembering her promise. She shouldn't even refer to it obliquely. 'No, nobody you'll have heard of,' she says quickly and changes the subject. 'So, Roddy. When I get the chance, why don't I do a dummy diary entry or two and e-mail it over to you? See what you think.'

'That would be super. Thanks.'

'You know, I never told anyone this before, but I always fancied being an author. Nothing fancy. More Barbara Cartland than Monica Ali.'

Roddy feels his heart sink. The last thing he needs is a Mills & Boon *manqué* with bodice ripping and the like. The punters will want something more for their money than that.

A shrill east wind is blowing between the luridly coloured buildings that look as if they are part of a child's construction kit and across the stagnant waters of the old docks. Piper wraps his overcoat tighter as he and Jacqueline Fletcher pass from the warmth of the foyer into the outside. London has one of its ceilings of cloud in place, withholding the sun from the city, allowing it only a grey, unsettling light. The glow of neon tubes fills the windows of the surrounding glass-fronted towers, even though it is only midday.

'There you are,' she says. 'The SOCA Report Unit.'

'Where?' he asks, glancing round the mix of old warehouses and the garish new apartments and offices.

'There.' She sticks out a finger.

'Those, um, shacks?'

'Portakabins,' she corrects. 'Or TOA – Temporary Overspill Accommodation.'

'Shit.'

They had been painted dark blue once, but most of that has been scuffed off as the prefabricated structures have been transported from one location to another. There are the remains of various stencils on the side, but none recent, other than one that suggests these were once mobile classrooms for a school in East London. Now they are forlornly sitting on the water's edge, as if waiting for the container ships that will take them away from all this.

He turns and looks at Jacqueline Fletcher. She is a striking woman, just over forty, tall and slim in her pin-stripe two-piece suit, who deploys a deft combination of grit and charm. At least, he remembered her as striking. She looks tired today: there is grey in her neglected roots, and the skin under her eyes is disfigured by dark crescents.

'You OK?' he asks.

She flashes an empty smile and strides across to the nearest Portakabin, pulls the door open and steps in. He follows. The inside is bare and dusty, the walls scarred by thousands of pin and tape marks. Only one poster is left, warning against sharing needles. The wind finds its way through cracks around the perished windowframes, making the mournful sound he feels inside. It is a long way from the comfort of overheated FBI classrooms.

'Jackie, I'm no prima donna, but did I really fly

the Atlantic to sit in a couple of containers dock-side?'

'No.' She runs a hand through her hair and makes a face. 'No, you crossed for a suite of offices at New Scotland Yard. Then, when they became unavailable, a nice room in there,' she indicated the building behind them. 'Then, suddenly, it's this.'

'Why?'

'Because SOCA is all about politics. Which is why we are continually shunted around, and why they have someone lowly like me heading up Stage One. Big guns aren't rolled out, in the shape of a Deputy Commissioner, until Stage Three. By which time, there will have been a general election.'

'They're stalling?'

She nods ruefully. 'They are that. It just might end up being another government's problem, you see.'

'And why me? Why did you bring me over?'

'They specified we should consult outside experts who knew what they were talking about. You had your Case Analysis Course at Quantico, also I knew you were pretty hot on FBI history and organisation.' Another smile, this time imbued with more warmth. 'Besides, I missed our little chats.' When they had been at APPLE, they had met at least once a week to discuss who had been doing what to US citizens, or, occasionally, what bad things Americans had been up to.

Piper traces a sine wave in the patina of dirt on the floor with his toe. 'It doesn't look like this is going to be so much fun.'

'Oh, I dunno, pet,' she says in an exaggerated Geordie accent. 'I like a good scrap, me.'

Through the grimy window he watches a jet heading for City airport drop from the cloud base with a whine, its wings wobbling in the crosswind funnelled between the tall office blocks. 'So you have some reading for me?' he asks.

'No. I have a lot of reading for you. Forget Christmas, m'lad. And by the time you see this place again,' she throws her arms open, 'it'll be something J. Edgar Hoover would be proud of.'

The talk of Christmas reminds him that he hasn't been through all the social niceties. 'How's the family?'

Fletcher surprises him by shaking her head. 'Messy.' Another one of those grins that fails to light up her face. 'Never trust a glamorous new PA.'

It takes him a second to realise she means her husband's PA. It clicks into place. 'Sorry. I didn't know. The kids?'

'He's got them for now. It's . . . ach. C'mon, buy me lunch and I'll tell. I know you Yanks are all scandalously overpaid.'

As she places a hand on his arm and guides him out into the first tentative flurries of snow, an unchivalrous thought crosses his mind: he hopes he has been brought over for his detailed knowledge of old FBI cases, and not for some other, more personal reason. That kind of complication he could live without.

'So, I mean, what . . . how does this work?'

Celeste looks at the man to her left, and places a hand under her chin, pretending she has no idea what he is talking about. They are in the Grosvenor House Hotel, in the midst of The Lakers, a tedious travel awards ceremony. The winner of the fifth award – Best Long Haul Airline Owned by Richard Branson – is making a toothy speech.

Celeste is on a table occupied mostly by wealthy resort and hotel owners who have come over to pick up a gong or two. Sebastian DeKrom, the man she has been paired with, is a partner in a hotel in London (Laker for Best City Newcomer) and another in Mauritius (Runner-up, Best Indian Ocean Beach Resort). He is South African, mid-thirties, with a mop of carefully ruffled dirty-blond hair, tanned and fit-looking. But then, he spends half the year living in a villa attached to his hotel in Mauritius playing tennis, so he should be.

The speech finishes, and the MC, a former stand-up turned chat-show host, makes a few industry in-jokes from a well-researched script, and announces the next category: Best Bottle Opener.

'What did he say?' asks Celeste, thinking this might be getting a tad too specialised.

'Best Bar Opening. Kommanch, New York,' Sebastian says.

'And the winner is, Kommanch, New York.'

Celeste leans back slightly as the untouched plate of chicken before her is removed by the staff. 'Do you know all the winners in advance?'

'Well, you can tell by who bothers to turn up. What's the point of flying halfway round the world to watch a competitor waltz off with the prize?'

'Dessert, madam?'

She shakes her head at the waiter and sips her water. The food has been palatable, but not much more: she is loath to waste calories on anything so humdrum. Sebastian accepts a fat slice of chocolate cake but refuses the cream.

This is not her normal milieu. Celeste is slumming it as a favour to Natalie, who is across the table, laughing at the lines fed to her by the Irish owner of a hotel on Jamaica (Best Caribbean Boutique Hotel). She is grateful to Celeste for leaping into the breach when one of her regular associates dropped out. It happens, and they oblige each other where they can. Natalie (Best Use of Diamond Pendant to Accentuate Cleavage), is by some way the most beautiful woman in the room, thinks

Celeste. Best Caribbean Boutique Hotel doesn't appreciate how lucky he is.

Sebastian clears his throat. 'So, as I was saying . . .'

'How does this work?'

'Yes.' He leans forward to exclude the rest of the table from their conversation. He has been drinking steadily, but it doesn't really show. There is just the merest hint of a flush on his cheeks, but his speech is unslurred, his eyes still bright. 'I know, roughly, about Michael's little arrangement . . .' He inclines his head towards Natalie's date. 'I just wondered if we could come to some similar understanding.'

'Just for tonight?'

'Just for tonight. And who knows . . .' He drinks some of the wine before him, and smirks before he puts on a showboating accent. 'It could be the start of something beautiful.'

Not really, she thinks. He doesn't smell right. He has used a light, citrus-y aftershave – one of those unisex numbers, she reckons – but under it she can detect something sour, slightly disturbing. And she always trusts her nose.

Applause fills the room for Best Business-Class Cabin. The cabin, apparently, cannot be here in person, so some rotund little man in an over-tight DJ bounds onto the stage to accept it. 'Afraid not, Sebastian. Tonight, and for one night only, I'm just a Cinderella plus one.' He raises a querying eyebrow. 'One hour after midnight, the meter stops running.'

'And then it says *Not for Hire*.'

'It does, surprisingly,' she agrees. 'Sorry.' She is about to add that she isn't that kind of girl. But, she remembers, she is that kind of girl, just one with a different niche. One she is determined to stay in. Natalie, Timmy and Sasha do hire out by the day, hour and week. There is nothing wrong with that; quality escorts have, in the last two years, become an accepted feature of the London social scene. Hardly anyone is shocked any more, not since the first wave of gorgeous super-Natashas appeared from the Ukraine three or four years ago. It simply isn't the role she has fallen into, except when she is doing a favour, like tonight.

'Ah well,' he says philosophically. 'You can't blame a boy for asking.'

The final award, Best Long Haul Tour Operator, is won by someone who has long hauled all the way from Chester.

'No. You can't,' she says pleasantly.

He reaches under the tablecloth and touches her knee. She catches Natalie's eye; her friend winks, and then Celeste glances at her watch. Eleven-forty. She gently lifts Sebastian's hand from her leg, where it is squeezing a mite too hard. He hasn't taken her refusal as a final 'no' yet, and he thinks treating her thigh like pizza dough might bring her round.

'So, how about we double your normal rate?'

She closes her eyes for a second. It is going to be a long eighty minutes before she can leave.

Hooper is staying in a small anonymous business hotel across the river, not far from Arlington Cemetery. He has chosen it because it has a rear entrance, with stairs up to his room, so nobody sees him coming or going. He has been to see Sol Cotton, the best gunsmith on the East Coast – or at least, the best unlicensed one – who has addressed a few issues on the rifle for him. The action had seemed a little 'snicky' to him during the third shot into the horse. What did Sol think? Sol has stripped it down and filed and greased it, and let him run twenty rounds through it and it seemed fine.

It is dark now, after the 200-mile round trip, and Hooper parks the car at the back of the hotel and sits for a moment in the lot, squeezing his eyes. He doesn't feel he has yet woken up to the fact that he is free, is no longer in prison, no longer has to shower and shit with twenty or more other guys. Perhaps it is because he isn't free. He has walked right from one kind of jail to another.

He gets out of the car, collects the guncase from the

trunk and walks wearily up to his room. He hears the music as he reaches the landing. He cocks his head, to make sure it is coming from his crib. It is. From a side-pocket on the guncase, he takes a Smith & Wesson revolver and listens at his door. He strains his ears, but he doesn't recognise the tune. Whoever is in there doesn't mind him knowing he has a visitor.

For a second he thinks it might be his wife, Renee, but the surge of hope dissipates when he realises she doesn't know where he is. Nobody does. Except one person.

He steps inside, his guard down. 'Hello, Kolski—'

The fist hits Hooper square in the face and he is rammed back against the door. He instinctively drops the guncase to raise his arm to protect himself. A second punch hits his chest and he wheezes the air from his lungs. He snatches at the pistol in his waistband, tries to bring the weapon to bear, but his wrist explodes into hot needles of pain and his fingers open. The gun drops onto the carpet with a muffled thud. He is against the wall now, and his assailant is pressed close to him. He can smell cigarette smoke on his breath, and the tang of stale alcohol. The words hiss into his ear, and a stubble of beard grazes his cheek, like coarse sandpaper.

'It was you, wasn't it?'

'Shit, Kolski, whatchadoin'?' he manages to gasp as the elbow tightens across his throat.

'It was you, wasn't it?'

'Urrgghh,' is all he can utter. 'Aggggomp.'

Kolski releases the pressure and steps back, breathing hard. 'You sick fuck.'

'What? Jesus.' He bends down and picks up the gun. 'I oughta—'

Kolski takes a defensive step forward and Hooper tosses the gun onto the threadbare sofa and rubs his wrist. Kolski was always good at the unarmed stuff. Hooper opens and closes his fingers, but there seems to be a time delay between the message leaving his brain and it reaching his digits.

'You'll be OK.' This time Kolski has ditched the ex-military gear, and is dressed head-to-toe in Gap and Banana Republic, apart from grubby Nike sneakers. It was never clear what he spent his considerable fees on. Not high fashion, that was for sure. 'It was you?'

'What was me?'

'The goddamn horse. You killed a fuckin' horse.'

Hooper shrugs. 'Maybe.'

'The paper says a sniper took out a poor, defenceless horse and disappeared without a trace. They are shitting themselves that an animal version of the Washington sniper is—'

'Hey.' It is Hooper's turn to step forward, to get angry. 'Whoa. *Whoa*. What the fuck do you care?'

Kolski runs a hand through his thinning hair. 'It was . . . inhuman.'

Hooper laughs. 'We spend our lives killing people—'

'Keep your voice down.'

'—and you are upset by the death of one of the dumbest creatures on God's earth. Wasn't like I shot Seabiscuit.'

'People think we're monsters, doing what we do.'

'Yeah? Your point being?'

'We do what has to be done for the good of this country,' he says. 'That's why we sleep at night.'

Well, Hooper thinks, everyone rationalises it in their own way. It's as good a schtick as any. 'If you say so.'

'But using animals for target practice – that's real sick.'

'You'd rather I used the little girl who owned him?'

'No, you dumb fuck. I'd rather you used Coke cans.'

'Not the same, Kolski. And you know it.' He flexes his hand again and winces at the burn that runs along his tendons. 'You sure you haven't broke anything?'

'Yeah, you'll be able to jerk yourself off OK, don't worry. Hey, Hooper, look at me. No more animals, eh? It makes me want to puke.'

'Right.' The dog must have affected him in more

71

ways than one. He sure never had Kolski down for the Animal Defence League.

'Sure?'

'Yeah. No more animals. I'm all set anyway.'

'I got a beer from your mini-bar. Want one?'

Hooper nods, the pain receding as he massages his hand. 'Why not, if I'm payin'.'

Kolski tosses him a Miller, which Hooper catches with his left hand. They pull the tabs in unison and drink. 'You OK?' asks Kolski, a sudden concern in his voice.

Hooper nods. He remembers this edge of irrationality in this guy from their previous work together. It never affected the job, not really, but he could get agitated by the strangest things. Again, it was probably just one of the coping mechanisms they all possessed. 'How'd you get on?'

'I sniffed around the Hill.'

'And?'

Kolski takes a large mouthful of beer and swallows before he says calmly, 'You were right.'

'About what?' He had aired some of his misgivings with Kolski, but that was all.

'We're being suckered, bro'. Big time. With bells on.'

Six

The stables for Hyde Park are situated in mews across the Bayswater Road. As is their habit, Natalie and Celeste meet at six in the morning for their weekly ride. It is an unholy hour for both of them, and the park's grass glistens with a severe frost. Both human and horse breath comes in dense clouds, and muscles shiver to generate heat. Still, it is the only time when you can let the horses really gallop – or at least canter – on the bridleways, with little chance of running down joggers or nannies and their charges.

In the gloomy stables, the chill air musky with the scent of equine bodies, Celeste selects Echo, a sixteen hands eight-year-old grey. He is not the most even-tempered creature in the string, but he has a cute snip, a white area on the muzzle that somehow lends him an air of bemusement. She spends fifteen

73

minutes grooming him and checking his hooves, just to wake him up gently. Then she slowly tacks up.

It is close to six-thirty as they mount up, with Captain Eades, the stables' owner, taking the rear, and clop over the cobbles towards the park. Celeste has to work hard to keep her horse in line. Despite her intimate and painstaking attentions, Echo is skittish and grumpy. Well, she can't really blame him.

'You know, one of these days I'm going to move to the country and get my own horse,' she says to Natalie, her voice echoing with the hoof falls from the white-washed walls of the cottages that flank them.

'One of these days . . .' says Natalie. 'How many times have we said that? I am sorry about that guy the other night at the Grosvenor.'

'Oh, don't worry, he wasn't too hard to shake off.'

Sebastian had made a couple of concerted efforts to change her mind, promising, if not the world, then a first-class ticket round it. She had resisted, and gradually the verbal and half-hearted physical attacks on her resolve had faded, until she poured him into a cab and bade him goodnight.

'He likes you. Asked if he can see you again. Interested?'

She remembers that scent in her nose and shakes her head. 'Fully booked.'

They cross over the main road, the commuter traffic

thin enough that they don't have to pause, and pass through the gates into the park, the horses, familiar with the routine, already eager to break into a trot.

'One of these days . . .' repeats Natalie wistfully. 'I am thinking my one of these days might be here.'

'Why is that?' asks Celeste, surprised.

'My son – I'm missing him. He thinks my mother is his mother half the time. I should go back.'

Celeste doesn't understand what kind of pull a son must have. The attachment to Roddy is strong enough. If that is anything to go by, the physical longing for a child you gave birth to must cause real pain. 'What will you do?'

'I have savings. I shall go back to Beirut and buy a shop, perhaps. A little business.' She smiles. 'Maybe find myself a husband.'

They let the horses move up a gear, and Celeste and Natalie rise and fall in unison in their saddles. Celeste is unsettled. She has never heard Natalie talk about such topics. For the past few months she has been aware of a shadow lurking in her own thoughts. 'A husband,' she says. 'That would be a thing.'

'What about you, Celeste? Do you ever think of—'

'No,' she says too quickly. 'Well, sometimes.' The shadow stirs, and she tells it to be still.

'Like after the other night?'

'Like after the other night.' The shadow emerges

into a half-light. 'Well, more than that. Two years ago I thought I had the business plan for my life. Now . . .'

'You're not too sure.'

'That's right.' She smiles at Natalie. 'But for the moment, this is what I do. I hope it works out for you. It isn't easy to walk away, so I hear. We're spoiled.'

Natalie shakes her head, dismissing the thought that freedom is a difficult path to take. 'I can do it.'

'Ready for a gallop, ladies?' asks the Captain as he overtakes them. Ahead is an empty Rotten Row, the ice in the puddles still opaque and pristine.

They both nod, and the subject of leaving the life is temporarily forgotten in the invigorating sting of cold air on their faces and the surge of powerful muscles moving effortlessly beneath them.

Roadworks in London are always perfectly timed for maximum chaos, thinks Piper. Just as Christmas approaches, the streets of the West End resemble those teeming cutaway beehives you had in science class in High School, men with striped tents and drills set up at every major road junction, creating havoc on the roads to match that on the pavement.

He is walking west from Regent Street, heading for the bank on the corner of Hanover Square and St George Street. From there he will hit Old Bond Street and find something small in Tiffany or one of the other stores to send to Judy. A peace offering and an apology all in one for his desertion – cowardice, perhaps – at the cemetery.

And something for Fletcher, to cheer her up? Clearly her personal life is a mess and her professional one could go that way with the poisoned chalice she has been handed. Was he being ridiculous, thinking she had a personal agenda with him? Maybe. But perhaps he should hold off on the gift, just in case.

He passes Vogue House and a group of workmen arguing with a policeman about the siting of their cones. Cars are jammed up on all the approaches to the Square, and are squeezing past the obstruction in single file, the drivers mouthing frustrated obscenities. Piper thinks maybe he should get out of Town with his stack of reading. The only Christmas spirit on offer is mean-spirit.

Piper tries to shut the cacophony of horns out of his head. Tempers are flaring now, and he can see people stepping out of their cars. Road rage is as imminent as rain from the low clouds above. In the sky, he can hear the whine of a traffic helicopter, the pilot doubtless frustrated by the lack of visibility. Just ahead of him, two Santas are also arguing, poking each other in their amply padded chests – a dispute over a pitch, by the look of it. Gift sacks at dawn beckon.

A young blonde girl in a much briefer Santa outfit is on the opposite corner, smiling bravely even as she hops from foot to foot to generate some heat in her cruelly exposed legs. She is outside SPLIT, a multi-floored dining club and bar, and yet another place flying various Russian flags in honour of the group who – currently – have the most disposable income in London.

Behind the Girl-Santa, the club's doorway is guarded by two barrel-chested men in time-honoured security mode: dark suits, ear-pieces, hands crossed in front of their groin the way soccer players do when they are about to defend a free kick.

Piper finds the ATM machine in the wall of the bank, and inserts his card. He checks the balance. His salary is paid in dollars, then converted to pounds. This is not doing him any favours, and he down-grades Judy's gift from Tiffany to something less ostentatious. He says yes to another service and selects *Cash withdrawal*.

A little 'alert' flag goes up in his brain, the way it used to in the old days, when he was an active field agent. It tells him something in the immediate environment has changed.

As he waits for the cash, he turns and surveys the Square once more. The noise level has dropped a notch, because the road drills have fallen silent. The argumentative policeman is nowhere to be seen, and the two Santas are packing up, their differences settled.

He presses the button marked *Other amount*. He needs more than £100.

The two Santas are crossing the road towards SPLIT, carrying one of their sacks between them.

He punches in a request for £200.

As the machine clicks and whirs and tells him to take his card, he glances about once more. The hairs on the back of his neck prickle. He doesn't understand why, but experience tells him it is because his higher centres haven't fully grasped the information that, at a subliminal level, his brain has already processed.

Something is about to go down.

A limousine, a stretched Mercedes with blacked-out windows, is pulling to a halt in front of SPLIT. The Girl-Santa is bending down to open the door, her welcoming smile, as false as her breasts, pasted firmly in place. The two heavies are talking into their microphones, heads swivelling in anticipation. One steps forward, puts a hand on the door handle, the other takes up a flanking position, ready to move along any curious pedestrians. A white delivery van has pulled across the exit from the square behind the Merc and the driver gets out, leaving the van in an extremely inconsiderate position. The horns start baying for blood once more.

Piper unbuttons his jacket and moves to the kerbside.

The two Santas are on the central strip that divides St George Street now, weaving between the parked cars. They are wrestling with their sacks. The door of the limo has opened.

Piper unclips the leather retaining strap on his holster, freeing his automatic pistol.

One of the two heavies has also noticed the strange behaviour of the St Nicks. He gently moves the Girl-Santa aside, just in case. The air around them is juddering with vibrations from the unseen police helicopter above the cloud base.

Piper clears the Sig from his holster and moves into the road.

There is an unusual present in the sack. It is a mini-RPG, a rocket-propelled armour-piercing grenade. One of the Santas hoists it onto his shoulder, and aims it at the limo.

A second white van screeches out of position, blocking the road to the front. The limo might be armoured and bullet-proof, but it is trapped, hemmed in by the Transits. And the Santa has a weapon that could open it up like a can of tuna.

Piper raises his weapon, hesitating to shoot Father

Christmas in the back, when a wave of glass and metal breaks over him, followed by the boom of the shotgun. He staggers back and hits the wall, sliding down to the pavement. There is another shot which sprays mortar and brick from above him. The van drivers are armed and, it seems, very dangerous.

Piper looks to his right. The workmen who have dug up the approach roads also have weapons and are waving them at drivers, forcing them to abandon their cars. One brave man tries to speak into his mobile phone and is smacked in the face with a gun butt.

How many of them? Piper asks himself. Four or five workers, two van drivers at least, a couple of Santas. Nine or ten. He is outnumbered. He needs back-up. But if there is a Trojan unit, one of the Met's armed response cars, then it will get snarled in the gridlock they are creating. London is full of Heckler & Koch-carrying cops, but most are stationed at airports, embassies, Buckingham Palace, rail terminals – not Hanover Square.

But if the police can't get in, surely these guys can't get out?

The question is whipped away by the repeated low bark of shotguns – six, seven, eight discharges. People are running past him now, the slap and slither of leather on stone filling his ears. Another round is fired and a hail of glass showers over the Square. They are shooting at the TV cameras that are bolted to the lamp posts.

From his position down on the pavement Piper still can't see the actual heist taking place – just people and cars. He can only surmise they are after whatever is in the limo. They haven't fired the RPG. Yet. He hopes whoever is being threatened by the thieves co-operates, because he has seen what those things can do to an armoured vehicle, the way they split open and how that copper wadcutter rattles around inside, slicing into flesh and bone.

As he stands, buffeted by fleeing drivers and pedestrians, he shakes his head to clear the after-hum of the shotguns. It doesn't go. It isn't, he realises, the sound of buckshot zinging in his ears.

He knows how they are getting out.

He holsters his gun and runs, crouched right down at floor-level, using his hands to help him scuttle along. He looks, superficially, like any other panicked motorist, albeit one who has lost his sense of direction. He hugs the wall, all the way round to Vogue House, and forces himself through the revolving doors, where onlookers have crowded. The foyer is full of pretty young girls and burly security guards.

'FBI,' he shouts.

A bearded white-haired guard steps in his way as he approaches the barrier. 'You can't—'

He flashes his Creds. 'Eff Bee Fuckin' Eye.' He jumps the barrier, ignores the lifts and runs up the central staircase. Think about the layout, he tells himself.

He takes a left on the second-floor landing and finds himself facing a locked door. Next to it is a numerical keypad. The lift opens behind him and he grabs one of the wide-eyed women clutching paperwork. Pages flutter to the floor as she raises her hands to her mouth.

'What's the code here?' Piper demands. 'FBI, ma'am, I need the code.' He can see the disbelief and terror in her eyes. 'FBI London office,' he tries again. 'There is a robbery in progress.'

'Two thousand and ten,' comes a male voice from the back of the lift.

He lets go of the woman's arm, hoping he hasn't bruised her too badly, and punches in the numbers, yanks the door open and runs through to a warren of offices and corridors piled high with clothes and boxes, the usual to-be-reviewed detritus and gifts for the Editor.

The Editor. They always have the best office, with the best view.

Piper holds his badge up for anyone to see. 'FBI. Where is the Editor?'

Someone laughs, thinking this is a joke, perhaps a spoof Strippergram. He pulls out the Sig, raises it as if he is about to fire into the roof and shouts: 'Vincent Piper, FBI London office. There is an armed robbery is progress outside. Now where the hell is the Editor's office!'

Most people have frozen, mouths agape, their limited experience of the real world meaning they are unable to cope with such an outlandish situation. 'Through there.' One of the secretaries points down the corridor.

'Thank you, ma'am,' he remembers to say.

He is vaguely aware of the PA standing in horror outside the door, glaring at him, mainly because FBI intervention isn't in the appointments diary he guesses. He runs by her and bursts into a room where glossy pages are laid out on the floor and four men are stroking their chins over them. Not even Armageddon outside can distract this lot from choosing their front cover.

One of the men, dressed in a sharp pin-striped suit, takes a step forward. He is taller than Piper, lean and quite trim, but he is no threat. 'Who the fuck—'

Piper puts an elbow to his throat, then sweeps his feet from under him. The man goes down on top of the proofs, crunching and scattering them. The others feel they should assert themselves, but Piper points his gun at the nearest, whose eyes widen beneath the mop of greying hair. 'Get out. You are in danger here

– and not from me. Call the cops if you like. Someone should.'

The trio quickly help their fallen colleague, who seems most distressed that he has lost a cufflink, and retreat, slamming the door behind them.

The room is silent. Piper lets his breath out in a slow stream and forces himself to make three deep, slow inhalations. He has to take things down now. Why is it so quiet? He lifts the Editor's desk and swings it out of the way, scattering a variety of awards over the floor, to give himself more room. He rips down the vertical blinds, covering himself in dust, then peers down at the street. He can see mouths moving, but hears nothing. He examines the window. The room is triple-glazed.

He slides back the double-skinned inner pane, then cracks open the window to the outside, and is assaulted by the racket. There is yelling and traffic horns, but the firing seems to have stopped. He can see that the Santas have persuaded the limo people to open the boot, which is gaping wide. Now, with one still waving the RPG, the thieves are heading for the Square. The other is heaving a large black box or suitcase along. It is clearly heavy. It obviously contains whatever they came for.

Elsewhere the workmen and van drivers are also backing away from their stations for crowd control, making for the central patch of green. He can hear the whine and whistle of the helicopter, feel the blades making the air throb.

It is coming to get them.

Its belly appears first, shocking red against the ragged grey cotton wool of the clouds. That's not a police helicopter, thinks Piper.

More warning shots are fired to keep heads down. Piper kneels down at the window, and considers his options. Firing blindly into a crowded London street is never a good idea, and he has trouble getting a decent bead on either of the Santas, who keep on weaving.

More of the chopper emerges, its bulbous snout pointing right at him, and he can see the writing across the front.

Virgin.

It is the London Air Ambulance. They have hi-jacked the city's flying rescue service.

Piper adopts a twin-handed grip on the pistol, resting it on the sill. He hears the door open behind him and yells, without looking, for whoever it is to take a hike. The door closes sharpish.

The chopper is clear of the clouds, the trees in the Square are bending under the rotor wash, and the agitated air slaps Piper's face. The room fills with its metallic chattering. What to shoot here? The pilot?

Does he want to bring a helicopter down in this small Square? There are still people lining the pavements, flattened against the walls, hidden in doorways, terrified, but with their natural curiosity almost overcoming that terror. Some are taking shots with their phones, and he can see at least three video cameras in action. Imagine the carnage as the helicopter hits the ground spinning, the blades slicing through flesh and shearing off as they hit trees, the hot slithers whirling through the air.

No. Don't kill the pilot.

The Air Ambulance is feet above the grass now, swaying slightly as the first men bundle aboard, taking the armoured box with them. The high-pitched screech of the engine is too loud for him to shout an audible 'police stop' warning to the characters streaming on board, and he knows the local cops would frown on anyone who does not advise that they are about to start firing. In the States, he'd take a chance. Here, his finger stays tense on the trigger, but does not squeeze. 'Motherfucker,' he mumbles to nobody.

He leans out of the window, scanning the streets for police, but there is no evidence of them. He runs his eye along the rooftops. No SO19 marksmen are in place up there either. *It's down to you, Piper.*

Already the robbers are inside the body of the Aerospatiale and he can hear the strain in the chopper's engines as it starts to rise. Too many men, too much weight. This French model was meant for five or six people; it probably has a dozen on board. Still, even if it is sluggish, it'll make it. Once it is into the clouds, it will be lost for ever, able to fly in any direction it wishes, below the radar, out of sight of any aerial pursuit by the Met.

Make it come down, that is the solution. Not fall down, just create a situation so it has to make a controlled descent. He needs to nick a fuel line or a coolant tank or a gearbox cog.

Piper lines up on the bulge of the engine cowling and squeezes. The recoil jars his arms over the sill, snagging his overcoat. He pulls off the coat, flings it across the room and re-aims, his ears already ringing from the single shot.

He squeezes, five rounds well grouped, but for one which hits the rotor, sparking and flashing as it is batted away.

The helicopter is rotating on its axis now, and he can see the men huddled in the doorway, hanging onto straps and internal bracings. He fires four more shots. Now he's really glad he opted for the 9mm – there are thirteen rounds in the magazine, as opposed to twelve in the other calibres. Every one counts. Three are left, but the chopper is still rising. Is it his imagination or is it climbing more slowly?

There is a commotion in the open doorway of the helicopter. One of the Santas is standing there, and even from this distance, Piper knows the man behind the skewed beard is staring right at him. They've seen the muzzle flashes. They know where he is. Santa is aiming the RPG right at his window.

His instinct is to turn and run, but he knows he'll get a rocket up the ass anyway. As Santa flicks up the range-finding sight, Piper wonders for a second if the guy has got the moxie to do it, but the odds are you bring an RPG to the party, you want to see what that baby can do.

There is a thin plume of vapour bleeding from the cooling vents of the chopper. *Bingo.*

The RPG steadies on him, and Piper stands for his own shot, and takes it fast. He fires two in quick succession, and he knows he has hit right away, because the needle-nose of the rocket lurches upwards. He fires one more for luck, and the slide stays back. Empty. There is a glow of flames in between the huddled figures, as the propellant trail bursts out of the chopper at a wild angle, streaming heavenwards.

The rocket disappears from view and the entire building shudders as it detonates somewhere high above, and a curtain of debris rains down in front of him, splattering onto the windowsill.

He steps back into the room as pieces of brick and

concrete and a whole sheet of glass go whistling by. Beyond this curtain of falling masonry, the helicopter has banked away from him slightly and is climbing, still trailing puffs of white smoke. He slots in the spare mag, raising the weapon for a parting shot, as the window erupts around him, flinging him back over the Editor's desk, a streak of hot pain bursting over his face and eyes, and one ridiculous thought filling his head.

He's forgotten to pick up his cash from the ATM.

Seven

As dusk thickens into night, a weary Colonel Henry Logan Wallace Junior (retired) walks the four blocks from the meeting place in Georgetown to the underground car park where he has left his Acura. He had parked the car and spent thirty minutes on what he calls SER – the Standard Evasive Routine – to make sure there was no tail. He then kept his appointment at the private dining room in the rear of the James Monroe restaurant, where he had mostly listened for three hours, only speaking when his opinion was sought and to make a progress report on Operation Palimpsest.

Now, after performing a second SER, he is facing a drive down to Charlottesville, and a lonely dinner for one in a house too large for him. His wife died eighteen months ago, and their son is in Iraq, enduring the aftermath of a war the Colonel once wholeheartedly supported. In fact, as a member of the office of the Deputy Chief of Staff for Operations and Plans at the Pentagon he had helped initiate it.

His forced retirement – he was one of those who had insisted that the planning for post-Saddam was woefully inadequate, and who, embarrassingly, had been proved right – coming so soon after Margaret's death, had left him rudderless. His hobbies of golf and painting had seemed like empty time-fillers. Which is why he welcomed the chance to get back in the covert saddle, to work in the areas he had excelled at before his desk job at the Pentagon. OK, so the parameters were slightly different, but the moral centre was there. Working for a better America. As long as that was the strategic aim, he was happy.

He walked past the entrance to the garage and kept going, stopping on the corner to admire the display in a jeweller's window, then the realtor's next door. The price of apartments was criminal; you got zilch for your money anywhere half-decent inside the Beltway, it seemed. He checked the time on his watch against a clock on the wall inside, and glanced around. He was pretty sure it was all clear. Still, you couldn't be too careful. He took a lazy stroll around the block, just to be on the safe side.

Palimpsest. A stupid name, he thinks. Too damn clever by half in one sense, on the other hand not clever enough. It was insisted on by Jerome, the investment banker. He is one of those stalwarts of Davos and G8 fringe meetings and the Bilderberg Group who are occasionally thrown into the limelight by Anti-Globalisation groups as a prime example of a puppet-master, a person who pulls the strings that make economies and governments dance. They aren't far off the mark: the man is a regular Geppetto.

Even Geppetto needed customers though, and a cash flow, and Palimpsest is mostly financed by another patriot, out on the West Coast, whose interventions, erudite and forceful, come via a scrambled teleconferencing link. If there is one driving force, one vision, it comes from that old man on a computer monitor.

Like the Colonel, like Jerome and the other dozen people on the Committee he has just left, the old man believes in a strong United States, but one which will no longer be drawn into opportunist wars like Iraq, where too many of America's boys come back in flag-draped coffins. The thought makes Henry shiver, as he thinks of his own son, Dwight, an Electronic Intel specialist. *Please let him come home safe*, he prays, even though he doesn't believe.

The night has folded around him, and he stops his evasive measures as he feels the icy wind spring up.

The shops are closing, the restaurants opening up, the bar across the street suddenly looks inviting. It is that twilight lull between shoppers departing and diners arriving. He reaches the garage and takes the elevator to the sub-level.

Please let him come home safe.

They jump him as he steps from the elevator. The bag is coarse canvas, and it scratches his face as it slides down over it. The wire garrotte is round in an instant, throttling off his cry. Colonel Wallace, though, was with the 1st Special Forces Group (Airborne) at Fort Lewis, WA, and served at the US Army Jungle Operations Training Battalion in Panama. He isn't an easy take.

He reckons there are at least two and, as he lashes out, is aware that he has mere seconds before the blood supply to his brain is cut off by the tightening wire. In a flurry of punches and kicks he connects five, six times and is gratified to hear a curse.

The pain in his thigh is sharp and hot, and that leg starts to collapse under him. Whatever has been injected into him is fast-working, so he stops struggling. They clearly don't want him dead yet. Save the fight till later, he almost manages to think before he folds down onto the chill concrete of the garage floor.

The last words he hears are spoken into a radio or cell phone. 'Target acquired.'

* * *

ENTRY TEN

*I met the man I shall call Michael Y at a charity party,
the day of the Cartier Polo Match at Guards (Mexico
won by a goal). The party, at XXXX House, was quite
a glamorous affair – think the Hickses, the Guinesses,
the Von S's and the Fennells – plus a couple of Earls
and a Count or two. I was actually there with a friend
of Michael's, whom we shall call The Hon. J., who had
asked for a blowjob outside in the car park, while the
other guests were filing in. That element of risk again,
I suppose (see Entry Six). Anyway, I said it would
really mess up my make-up – would he settle for a
handjob? Well, he did, and it was quick and fine, but
he sort of lost interest in me after that, even though
he had spent £3000 to have me for the whole day and
night. I knew full sex wouldn't be on the cards, but I
had become all moist in the meantime and I definitely
wanted a good shag that night . . .*

Sasha clicks on the Save button and rereads what she
has written. She had thought this would be fun, but
every time she sends a blog entry over, Roddy sends
it back with suggestions and corrections. *More raunchy.
Stronger hint about identity of X. Stop being coy.* It is hard
work. Furthermore, he wants to take some photos,
and she just isn't in the mood.

She scans the letter that arrived that morning once

more, trying to decode it for hidden meanings. An 'abnormality' has been found, it says. *Nothing to worry about* and *just routine*, her doctor has written, the kind of palliative phrases that are always trotted out. She will ring him the next morning, get the truth.

She moves to the kitchen and pours herself a glass of white wine. For ten minutes she stands, looking over the river to Tower Bridge, wondering if all the trappings she has worked so hard for – the flat, the car, the clothes – are about to be snatched away by a clump of bandit cells. She returns and sits in front of the computer screen, sipping, trying to put herself in a 'raunchy' frame of mind. The phone rings and she lets the answerphone click on.

'Hi, Sash, it's Timmy. Can you pick up if you are there? I wondered if you wanted to come out tonight? There is something on at Aura. I've got a client, and he's got a friend.' Don't they always, Sasha thinks. 'He's loaded. Bit of a . . .' she struggles with the word, 'Twit my man says, but harmless. And rich – did I mention that? Well, it could be fun. Look, I'll try you on your mobile. Bye.'

Sasha waits a few moments and hears her mobile trill, before it switches to answering service. Does she want to go out? She presses Exit on her laptop, saves the entry so far and heads for the bathroom, planning a nice long soak, a magazine and bed. She just isn't in the mood for Aura, or for a client's chinless wonder of a friend. And she certainly isn't in the right frame of mind to start raunching-up for Roddy.

As Colonel Henry Logan Wallace Junior comes to, he can hear voices, distant and metallic, as if refracting down a long steel tube. He can't make out the words, they are just cadences and rhythm. Question and answer. A female and a male. He can smell cigarette smoke, and a long-forgotten craving for the comfort of nicotine surfaces. He ignores it.

Colonel Wallace is sure he is lying down, probably on a bed judging by the softness under his face. Certainly not a floor. He moves his arms and legs as slowly as he can, just a few centimetres in each direction. As far as he can tell, he has not been bound. This is a good thing. The voices begin to gain clarity.

'You, Hugo, are the Weakest Link. Goodbye.'

Television. He is hearing a quiz show on the television. He keeps his eyes shut, hoping to ascertain as much as he can before whoever is holding him captive realises he is awake. This isn't too difficult, because the drug has left him woozy. His throat is bone dry and scratchy, as if he has swallowed a twig, and his head feels like he has consumed half a bottle of Scotch.

Who would have taken him? The Committee he works for might have some interesting methodology, but so far, they have committed no crime. Nor will they countenance one, at least not on US soil. Well, there was the old man in San Diego. But that was almost a mercy killing.

However, if someone in, say, the NSA, the National Security Agency, or the CIA has got wind of what they are up to, well, perhaps they have decided it comes under their remit. In which case, they will want him to talk. It has been quite some time since he underwent an anti-interrogation techniques course. He hopes he is still up to snuff. Assuming they don't physically torture him, in which case the training is useless. Everyone breaks under torture, if it is done properly. And the CIA and the NSC can lay their hands on some decent practitioners of that black art.

A lavatory flushes and someone enters the room.

'He awake yet?'

'Yeah, but he's pretending he's not. Aren't you, Colonel?'

He opens one eye. Hooper, the one who has just come out of the bathroom, is standing next to Kolski, who is sitting in front of the TV, a cigarette in his hand.

He has been kidnapped by the very men he hired for the paint job.

Professor Winslott's consulting room is situated in a relatively modest house at the top end of Harley Street, near the Marylebone Road. The chintzy country-style waiting room, which is shared by all the medical people in the building, is full of *Country Life* back-issues, and the walls are hung with hunting scenes.

The Professor's room, in contrast, is stark and modern. The fittings, including the examination couch, are in Italian black leather and steel. The colours are plain and neutral; the only pictures on the wall are of the sleek boat he keeps at Cowes – one of the perks of being among the country's best gynaecologists.

The Professor is a big man in all senses – six foot three, seventeen stone, happily corpulent, with an avuncular presence that makes him impossible to ignore. Today, though, he isn't smiling. He has his glasses on the end of his nose, reading Sasha's notes once more. He knows what she does for a living. In fact, he has almost a dozen clients in the same profession. He knows there is a continuum in the sex industry, that runs from the snot-faced bags of bones who still infest the fringes of Kings Cross, through to the kind of girls who would slot right into *Jennifer's Diary* or the *Bystander* columns. This is not only the oldest profession, but also the most widespread. And prostitutes need a good gynaecologist.

'It's a small patch of cells. Tiny.'

'But spreading?'

The Professor takes off his glasses. 'No. I said *pre*-cancerous. It is just an early indication that they might

99

become something unpleasant.' He smiles. 'At the moment all we have is threatening behaviour. Nothing malicious has actually happened yet.'

Sasha feels sick to her stomach. 'You know I lost me mam to breast cancer.'

The Professor nods. She has reverted to her flat Northern vowels, as she always does whenever she mentions her mother or her father, who is still alive and running a pub in Barnsley.

'This is not related. The best thing for that is regular mammograms and self-examination. As we discussed.'

She shudders at the memory of what her mother endured.

'Sasha?'

'Yes?'

'Are you all right? You've gone quite pale. Would you like a drink?'

'No, thank you. I'm fine. So what happens now?'

'We cauterise the little bastards,' he says with feeling. 'Very simple procedure, won't inconvenience you too much.'

'When?'

'Whenever you wish. My secretary can book you in today.' He consults the desk diary and turns a few pages. 'I have some time free next Thursday . . .'

'Is it that urgent?'

'That you do it right away? Probably not. Why?'

'I have a busy few weeks coming up and—'

The Professor leans forward. He senses she might be about to go ostrich on him, pretend it is nothing. 'My dear, you can never be too busy to do this. It isn't something that is dangerous at the moment, but it might be in the near future. I bet you are always busy. Make arrangements – book a little holiday. We should do this within a month. Also, a couple of your blood markers are up slightly. I think we might do a few other tests while we are at it, keep you in overnight – just to be sure. Think of it as an MOT.' His voice takes on a sonorous quality, and she feels as if she is before a particularly stern headmaster. 'Do you understand, Sasha?'

'Yes, Professor.'

It is Kolski who worries the Colonel. Whereas Hooper was the tracking expert, Kolski had two skills: abduction and interrogation. He was one of the freelance interrogators used at Abu Ghraib prison near Baghdad.

Colonel Wallace knows he has to take control of this situation. He slides up the bed. As he does so, he can see there is a pistol on the table next to Kolski. His own Beretta. Next to it is his cell phone. 'So, you compromised the mission already?'

Hooper shrugs. 'How do you figure that?'

Wallace has to work hard to enunciate his words because his tongue feels like it has been borrowed from an affectionate puppy, lolling around in his mouth. 'You must have used a third party in the snatch. There were two of you at the elevator, and I heard the Target Acquired call. So, there are three of you at least.'

Kolski stubs out his cigarette. 'Thing is, Colonel, I haven't been banged up like Hooper here. I didn't get rusty doing time. I kept my hand in. That was all me. Although you cracked my shin pretty good.'

Kolski smiles his cadaver's grin. He is a cold one, thinks the Colonel. No wife, no family, just a place in upper Michigan that was snowed in for half the year and a career moving around casinos.

'What the hell is the point of taking me down?'

'The point of the exercise,' says Hooper slowly, 'was that you haven't been entirely straight with us, Colonel.'

'Ex-Colonel,' adds Kolski.

'Yup, retired. Never thought to mention that?'

Wallace says nothing.

'Plus,' continues Kolski, 'I have trailed you for a week now. You made no official government contacts at all.' He picks up the cell phone from the table. 'No Pentagon or NSC numbers dialled. You are out, Colonel, but you're acting like you're not.'

'We are only concerned because, although we appreciate we have always operated on a total deniability footing . . .' Hooper begins.

'. . . We always had back-up. Local CIA, whatever,' Kolski goes on.

'If we are playing cold calling . . .'

'. . . Then we'd like to know why,' finishes Kolski.

'Yeah. What gives, Colonel?'

'Quite the double act,' Wallace manages to sneer.

'That's why you hired us,' shrugs Hooper.

'Not so you can play at being the Smothers Brothers. Can I get a drink of water? My mouth feels like a chicken died in it. What was that shit you put in me?'

Hooper goes to the bathroom and he hears a tap running. Kolski says: 'One of Abbey Labs' newer formulations. Don't worry, it's got excellent elimination characteristics. Be out of your system by tonight.'

Wallace takes the glass of water and gulps it down. 'Another.'

Hooper obliges, while Kolski just stares at him. After he has drained the second tumbler, Wallace says, 'I should be furious at you two. Of all the thick-headed, crazy—'

'Spare us, Colonel. We just need to know whether we are cold or hot.'

Wallace hesitates. He had hoped to get through this mission without having to elaborate on the small print. It looks as if he had underestimated the comfort blanket of knowing that Uncle Sam is willing you on from the wings, even if the audience can't see him. 'Tepid,' he says. 'Not official, but with some friendly support.'

'So how do we get into England, for example, without being tagged? Because if we aren't going through Company channels . . .'

'You think we didn't address that?' Wallace snarls at them. 'You go in on a KC-135 Stratotanker into Mildenhall in Suffolk. It's an RAF base, not subject to the usual bureaucracy. We have an, uh, arrangement, for infiltration and exfiltration.'

'So, we need to know why this target is so goddamn important.'

The Colonel shakes his head, regretting it when the little hammer starts up in his temple. 'I don't think so. You know the score. The less you know, the more secure the mission.'

Hooper walks over and stands, peering down at him. 'Yeah, that works. But only when the mission is sanctioned. Look, Colonel, we don't have to tell you the difference between official and unofficial paint jobs. On the one hand, you are ultimately working for the President, on the other . . .'

'Ah, but you will be.' Wallace decides it is best to come at least partially clean, or they'll be here all night.

'What?'

'Working for the President of the United States.' Hooper and Kolski exchange glances as Wallace adds: 'Just not the current one, that's all.'

Eight

In the centre of the swirling monochrome light-show that passes for his vision at this moment, Piper is aware of a human shape moving. Another visitor. He opens his eyes and tries to focus. The room sharpens and the aurora borealis patterns retreat to the periphery of his retina.

'Hi, Vince. How are you?'

How is he? His chest hurts, he still feels as if someone has dropped an anvil on it. The skin on his face prickles, and he is very, very tired, especially after two lengthy interviews that morning.

'I brought you some coffee.'

It is Jackie Fletcher – here, he hopes, as a friend rather than to quiz him any more about the previous day's events. He has gone over and over his actions, and what he saw, until he is beginning to doubt any of it is true. Half the time he had been working on instinct, performing as he was trained to do. It's not his fault the FBI are drilled in a different methodology from the Brits. He pushes himself up the bed and blinks the moisture away from his eyes.

'How do I look?'

'Interesting.'

'Thanks.' Although his face has missed a lot of the blast – that was taken by his chest and his upraised forearms – the doctors have picked out a few shards of glass and a couple of pellets from his chin. His arms, though, will always have a pattern of pepper-pot indentations.

'You made CNN,' she says.

'I heard. Did I look good?'

'Couldn't tell. Most of the footage was filmed by someone who liked that cinéma vérité style. Either that or they had Parkinson's. You are just a shadowy figure in the window.'

'Good.'

There is a pause before Fletcher says quietly, 'Hardly. Have SOCA been to see you?'

'Yup. Twice.'

'They tell you about the chopper?'

'Found on the Hackney Marshes? Empty?'

'Not entirely. Scene of Crime finished with it an hour ago. There's blood in the cabin. A lot of blood. You hit someone, Vince.'

He should feel bad, but the news gives him a warm glow inside. Like he's said to the SOCA guys: you start running around with guns, you better be prepared to take the consequences. One of which might be, someone out there is a better shot than you. 'But no sign of who it was?'

'Do you want this coffee?'

'You have it.' If it is anything like the other cups he has been brought, it is no great loss.

She takes a drink. 'No, they had ground crew to get them away. The chopper is pretty banged up. We haven't got much of a flying ambulance at the moment.'

'Sorry about that. Maybe they could dock my expenses.'

'Richard Branson is going to pick up the tab.'

'Nice of him.'

'Yeah. Never one to miss a photo opportunity. If he asks you along, say no.'

'I don't even want to be identified.'

'No. The newspapers are sniffing around, of course. Half of them have you mixed up with Batman.'

'Batman never uses a gun. Except, I believe, in one issue, back in . . .' He sees her eyes glaze over. This wasn't the time to trot out his juvenilia. 'Colt forty-five auto, as I recall. What about the other half?'

'The *Daily Mirror* reckons you are the bastard son

of Charles Bronson and Michael Winner.' He raises an eyebrow. 'Remember *Death Wish*?'

'I remember Bernard Goetz. This was hardly that. What is the official line?'

'You are, I quote, "A law-enforcement officer legally entitled to carry a concealed weapon" who, for security reasons, cannot be identified. For the moment. If someone managed to snatch a better picture of you . . . well, the papers will print it and half of London will say: "Isn't that the guy who shot up the US Embassy a couple of years back?"' Piper's picture had been in the *Evening Standard* in the aftermath of the bomb at the Residence in Regent's Park.

'That's not fair. It was Winfield House, not the Embassy, remember?'

'You think the public know the difference, or care? Either way, you'll be ID'd.'

'Do we know how much they got?'

'SOCA didn't tell you?'

'SOCA made it clear that they asked the questions. I think it amused them to be grilling an FBI man.'

Fletcher stands and moves to the window, looking out onto the rush-hour traffic, snarled back from the Westway. This sixteen-bedded private hospital is a favourite of embassies and the security services. It isn't unusual to find armed police at the door. Now, though, she can see someone on the roof opposite, probably an

SO19 sniper. No telling whether they are up there for Piper or not. The number of security alerts and protection details in London has reached dizzying heights.

'It was mostly white diamonds,' she says, moving away from the glass. 'A few dozen items, each one worth between a hundred grand and one point five million. They were meant for a showcase for visiting Russians. The club across the road had been closed for the private event.'

'So the total would be?'

'There will be an insurance claim for between ten and fifteen million. Pounds, not dollars.'

'Jesus. Any leads?'

'A thousand, all tied up in one great impossible knot.'

'You start with the chopper.'

'It's SOCA's case,' she reminds him. 'But, yes, start with the chopper, then the security arrangements on the diamonds. Look for the weak link.'

'Inside job, for sure. Wouldn't you say? You don't hijack a helicopter on the off-chance.'

'Yes.' Fletcher comes back and puts the cup down on his bedside table. 'Why didn't you just stand and observe? Did you have to play *Gunfight in the Wild West End* again?'

The hurt in her voice surprises him. 'You're pissed at me?'

'I'm pissed off, if that's what you mean. For Christ's sake, that RPG only dented the Condé Nast building. You were damned lucky it didn't kill anyone. Including you.' The glass and debris had hit the pavement without causing serious harm. The worst injuries – shock, cuts, lacerations – were to a bunch of smokers on the roof. She always knew cigarettes were bad for the health.

'I couldn't just stand there, Jackie.'

'No? There were three armed officers in that crowd, all of whom thought it prudent to hold their fire. Not to provoke a firefight in the centre of Town. They simply noted down everything they could.'

Piper feels himself reddening. Was this why the SOCA boys had been so aggressive in their questioning? Because they thought he'd acted like some kind of cowboy on their territory? Or were they ashamed that their own guys hadn't been quite so pro-active? 'Which was what, exactly?'

'More than you got looking down the sights of your gun. Better descriptions, makes of weapons, possible age – that kind of thing.'

'I thought it wasn't your case.'

'Yeah, well, you head up an enquiry into someone's very existence, they tend to be very nice to you.'

So she's read the SOCA interviews already. Piper reaches up to scratch his face and she gently grabs his wrist. 'Don't do that. You'll infect them.'

'I was only doing what I thought was right. We aren't trained to be passive observers.'

'Do you mean the FBI or the United States?'

'Both.'

She sits down on the bed and he shuffles to make room. He can feel the heat of her through the thin sheet, but tries to ignore it.

'I just can't believe it, after what happened last time you were in the country. Lightning striking twice isn't in it.'

'I guess. Look, I'll be out in a day or two and—'

'And on your way home.'

'No, I can go straight back to work. I'll have the paperwork sent over. Do some of the background reading.'

'No, you won't.' She is businesslike once more. 'The thing is, you are now part of a SOCA investigation.'

'A witness, that's all.'

She laughs. 'A little more than that. Look, Vince, you are off the working party.'

'Why?'

'Why? Because you have been subject to questioning by them – a process that is far from over. They may choose to get forceful with you.'

'Forceful?'

'You know what I mean. Aggressive questioning. I've been told, Vince, that this is the way it is. Like I said, if you are part of an enquiry, they tend to be nice. Well, they don't want that constraint. They don't want to muddy the waters, colour your vision and a dozen other platitudes. It all comes down to the same thing. You're out.'

So that is why she is so snitty to him. She has lost her tame FBI expert. 'Sorry.'

'Me too.' He yawns and she smiles at him, although the usual warmth is absent. 'I'll let you get some rest.'

Fletcher turns to go, then remembers something. She produces an envelope from her bag.

'What's that?' he asks sleepily.

'A party invite.' Another smile, this one sardonic. 'You're a celebrity now, Vince.'

The forward end of the Stratotanker, behind the bulkhead shielding the pilots, has been tricked out with seats and berths. It is comfortable enough, but it is hardly First Class. The lack of soundproofing means that the whine of the engines is very audible and highly fatiguing, and the air is tinged with the sharp odour of petrochemicals.

Hooper is slumped in his chair, watching Kolski with envy. He is fast asleep in one of the bunks, as is the only other passenger, a civilian who made it clear he didn't want to talk, give his name or the time of day. That is fine with Hooper. The man is restless, tossing and turning under a thin blanket, occasionally mumbling to himself in that incoherent dream talk we all have, with its odd emphases.

Kolski, on the other hand, looks calm and peaceful and untroubled. The guy always could sleep anywhere, anytime, as if he was storing it up for those occasions when he needed to go seventy-two hours without any. Hooper has seen him do that, too.

Hooper's feet are resting on his case, which contains a collapsed rifle, a handgun and several knives. He hopes the Colonel has, as he promised, smoothed things out at the other end. Any metal detector would probably explode at the hardware he has in there. The Colonel has assured them they will be met and whisked through without any formalities. As far as any official agency, Brit or US, is concerned, they were never in the country. Unless something goes wrong.

Wallace has given them two names for back-up. They usually work with a minimal safety net, but in this case, it is good to have a couple of fall-backs. He hadn't been in London for more than a decade, and he'd like to catch up with it. He's heard you can eat some of the food these days. Restaurants could wait until some other time, though. They expect to be back on this noisy old tanker in less than a week.

One of the crew comes out with a coffee and Hooper

takes it. Through the open door behind the guy he can see the pilots' heads and, between them, the blackness of a sky punctuated by jewel-bright stars. It is a good night to be at 40,000 feet; the air outside is calm, with the tanker hitting barely a ripple. 'Excellent service. Better than flying United,' Hooper says.

The young crewman smiles at the feeble crack and indicates the pair who have bedded down. 'You should get some sleep.'

'Nah. My jokes aren't any better after shut-eye.' He raises the polystyrene cup in salute. 'Thanks for this.'

The crewman returns to his post and Hooper sips at the coffee. He is too unsettled to sleep. He saw his wife, Renee, before he left, and although it went OK, he could sense the distance between them. He had hardly touched her: just held her hand in the coffee shop, kissed her cheek when they parted. He had suppressed every other urge, even though they were uncommonly strong. He still loved her, wanted her. He made sure she understood that from his words, not some hasty, clumsy actions. Then he had explained he was going away, that he had work to do, and she made him swear it wasn't something illegal. He had, and the damned thing is, he isn't sure whether or not he lied.

The Colonel had convinced them that night, after they had snatched him, that all they were doing was helping the democratic process along, re-balancing the scales a little. Furthermore, he told them, they were just one of three missions. Only theirs included a foreign paint job. He'd called on the spirit of JFK a lot, although Hooper is too young to have experienced the golden glow of Camelot first hand. All it is now, is a mythical age, a time when giants walked the earth, before they were all cut down.

A judder runs through the plane, as if it, too, was suddenly nervous about the future.

Kolski opens one eye. 'How long I been out?'

'Three hours, give or take.'

He nods at the coffee. 'That fresh?'

'Yup.'

'Is there a stewardess button?'

'I reckon you have to knock on that door.'

Kolski swings his legs onto the cabin floor and rubs his face with both hands, as if trying to iron out the wrinkles the thin pillow has left on his cheeks. 'I'll go and freshen up.' He stands and puts a hand on Hooper's shoulder. He clocks the furrows in his partner's forehead and the downturned mouth, both of which quickly disappear. Not fast enough though. 'Hey – you're not worried about this?'

'No.'

Kolski glances over at the civilian, who is snoring through an open mouth. He could be faking it, but the rivulet of drool that has formed at the corner of his lips looks authentic enough.

'I meant, you know, ethically. Morally. Scrupulously – is that a word? From a scruples perspective. Whatever you want to call it. You always did think too much about such things. It's to finish a house next to a lake, that's all. Don't worry about whether it's a mortal sin, f'Chrissake.'

Hooper laughs loudly, and their snoozing companion smacks his lips and rolls over. 'We're a little beyond that, aren't we?'

'Yup. You and me. Beyond redemption.'

Kolski heads off to the can and Hooper finds himself wondering if that is true. Can he do this one job, go back to Renee, finish his house, and find some kind of peace? Not redemption, perhaps, but he'd settle for a little inner calm.

The civilian screams, a nasty guttural sound of real terror, and sits bolt upright, his forehead glistening with globules of sweat. 'Jesus,' he says, then remembers where he is. He looks away and composes himself, before hurriedly getting out of the bunk and following Kolski to the lavatory. One thing is for sure, thinks Hooper, I don't want to end up with that man's dreams.

Piper sleeps fitfully that night. His various pains have subsided enough for him not to want painkillers, but the aches still keep lifting him into half-consciousness. As he drifts in and out, he wonders if Fletcher was right. Should he have done nothing, sat on his metaphorical hands? The reel of the robbery runs over and over, from several points of view, sometimes with him being more decisive, others less so. It is as if he is trying to create a definitive director's cut.

After Fletch had left he had received a message from Roth, saying he would be in tomorrow to discuss the enquiry that will convene to pass judgment on his actions. Oh, and to make sure he is OK. Enquiry? Well, discharging a weapon in the line of duty was tantamount to dereliction of that duty in some people's minds.

At three in the morning he wakes fully, goes to the bathroom and, upon his return, swallows two tablets which the nurses said might help him sleep. Within a few minutes a warm glow starts to spread through his veins and he finally leaves this world thinking that, no matter what some chickenshit enquiry decides, he did right. If he had his time over again, he'd still shoot at the bastards in the helicopter.

Colonel Wallace looks at his watch. His boys will be on their final approach to the RAF base by now. He pads across the darkened living room, opens the cocktail cabinet and pours himself a rare but welcome three fingers of Jameson's twelve-year-old whiskey. He returns to his place in front of the TV, watching the silent pictures, the highlights of the previous night's football game.

He raises a glass to the twin pictures sitting in identical gilt frames on top of the Sony. One is a snapshot of his wife, Margaret, taken fifteen years previously, before she slid into middle age, still whippet-thin and vivacious. It was taken on their wedding anniversary weekend at The Point, the swanky hotel up in the Adirondacks. The buildings are converted from the extravagant log cabins of the old Rockefeller summer camp, and you still have to be robber-baron rich to afford it. It was worth it though, to see her sitting on that polished mahogany motor launch, the wind whipping through her hair as they were taken off to some remote lakeside spot for a picnic.

The other photograph is of Dwight, his son, in full military gear, next to an Abrahams tank, smiling and proud to be serving his country. Wallace hopes he gets in touch soon. With Margaret gone, he has become all the more precious. When Dwight's tour of duty is over, he'll see if he can't lean on a few old friends to help secure him a desk job, close to home.

The phone makes him jump. He picks it up. 'Wallace.'

'Yes, sir, this is DHL. Sorry to call so late. We need

to deliver a priority package. Will anyone be home tomorrow a.m.?'

'Yes. Before eight.'

'Before eight. That's fine. We'll see you then.'

'Thank you.'

'You're welcome, sir.'

His boys have landed, ahead of schedule. He sips at the whiskey. He thinks about the way they took him and humiliated him. It was a stupid thing to do. He had had misgivings before about the finale of their mission, especially about Hooper. Kolski, he had no qualms about. Hooper, though, still had a spark of decency left in him. Not as much as before he went inside, but it was still discernible. But after the kidnap they pulled on him? Such a dumb-ass stunt. Now, he was glad neither of them would make it out alive.

Nine

'The biggest mistake in the last war was insisting on unconditional surrender from the Germans.' US Ambassador Jack Sandler raises an eyebrow, daring Piper to disagree with him.

Piper knows that World War Two is Sandler's pet subject, that his father had been a USAAF long-range fighter pilot based in the UK for part of it. They are in a corner of the main reception room at Winfield House, the Ambassador's Residence in Regent's Park. The last time he was here, Piper had been involved in a bloody gunfight. He hoped this pre-Christmas drinks party would be less eventful.

He has been invited because Sandler had made it his business, once he'd heard rumours of US involvement, to find out who the lone gunman at the Hanover Square robbery was, and he'd been secretly delighted it was the man who had saved his life. Sandler tends to overlook the fact that it was Piper who put it in danger in the first place.

Piper sips his champagne. He is rationing it. It doesn't do to get drunk at these things. There are plenty of other folks to play that role. 'With all due respect, Ambassador . . .'

'Yes?'

'That's bullshit.'

Sandler hops from foot to foot, as he always does when he is excited. He is a little shorter than Piper, with a big square sincere face and a thatch of dark hair. He is very young for an Ambassador and also, thanks to his family, very rich. This cocktail of power, money and relative youth is a heady concoction. Piper knows that many people think Sandler is wasting his time serving overseas, that he should be in the Senate or running for Governor somewhere. 'How so?' he asks.

Piper, who has a tenuous grasp on the subject, nevertheless produces the arguments he used to hear thrashed out over steaks in the yard by his father. That Russia, after she had been so devastated, would have accepted nothing less than total dominance and submission from the countries she had over-run.

When he has finished, Sandler shakes his head. 'I

can so rip that apart,' he says with a smile, 'but I have
to circulate or the Protocol people will have my ass. I
can show you some contemporary writings that prove
you are wrong. Jensen, Roosevelt's adviser . . . anyway,
later. Before I get swamped, there's someone I'd like
you to meet. And I forgot to say well done for the
other day.'

'Not everyone thinks the same way – that it was
well done.'

The Ambassador slaps him on the shoulder once
more, a habit that could become irritating. 'Yeah, well,
that really *is* bullshit, Agent Piper.'

A hand grabs Piper's upper arm. It is Brewster, the
Secret Service man, now on permanent duty at
Winfield House and the Embassy as London Security
Adviser to the Ambassador and State Departments.
There was a time when there was only a Secret Service
presence in the city when high-level dignitaries came
through. After all, as its core business, the Service is
responsible for permanently guarding fewer than
twenty lives – the current and ex-Presidents and their
families. However, since credible intelligence from
multiple sources suggested an attack on the London
Embassy a few years back, there has been a permanent UK staff of eight agents. The attempt came in
Paris, but here they remain.

Brewster is only slightly taller than Piper, but his

broad shoulders and wide chest make Piper feel tiny next to him. 'Excuse me, Mr Ambassador, can I just borrow Eliot Ness here.' Brewster pulls Piper to one side.

'Eliot Ness was one of yours,' Piper reminds him.

'I know that. It's a compliment. I just wanted to say, I was with you on what you did with the helicopter.'

'Thanks.'

'But I have to ask you if you are carrying tonight?'

'No. Your guys made me turn it in. It's like Dodge City here, isn't it? "You can pick up your gun when you leave, cowboy".'

'Better that than another *Gunfight at the OK Corral*. No offence.'

'None taken.' More Western analogies. Piper wonders if he really does have a reputation for being a trigger-happy gunslinger. Brewster, he knew, had history in that department too. It had been when he was assigned to the previous First Lady, when he let someone into the Zone, the protective area thrown around the protectee, to present flowers. The guy had veered from the script, produced a pen for an auto-graph. Someone had yelled, 'Gun, gun!' and Brewster had blown away the flower guy's knee-cap. Rumour has it he was really ashamed about it at the time. He'd been trying for a body shot.

123

'Good. Have a nice evening.' Brewster turns and shoulders his way through the crowd, something he can achieve quite easily, because most people who see him coming wisely step aside.

'Everything OK?' asks Sandler.

'Yeah. I guess he's frightened I might think I have to fire my gun every time I see you.'

Sandler smirks, but adds: 'He's a good man, Brewster. You know he took the enquiry into security here pretty hard, when it said there were substantial failings.'

'I hear he offered to resign.'

The Ambassador winks. 'I intervened.'

He places a hand in the small of Piper's back and steers him expertly through small clumps of guests, as if they are icebergs in a hostile sea, sometimes just nodding hello, other times saying he will be back in a moment.

'You like B-17s, Vince?'

'The cocktail?'

'That's a B-52. No, the real one.'

'The Flying Fortress?'

'Yes. They've found one in North Norfolk, or think they have. A birdwatcher . . . what do they call them?'

'Twitchers.'

'A twitcher found a piece of one in the mudflats. Gave it to the local aircraft archaeological society. They say they can't tell which one it is. Quite a few went down over Germany and the Channel with no witnesses. You seen the glass memorial wall to missing US planes at Duxford?'

'No, sir.'

'You should do. It's impressive. There is a very low tide on the weekend of the twenty-first. A good chance to take a look at this lost B-17, if that's what it is. Every plane tells a fascinating story. You should come up.'

Piper can think of plenty more exciting things to do on a bitter December weekend than wade out into North Sea mud in search of what would by now surely be mere fragments of a plane. Still, he knows that people with an obsession can be just as exercised by fragments as the whole thing. Maybe more so. 'I'll check my diary, sir.'

Sandler gives a little laugh at his transparent lack of enthusiasm. 'Liar.'

The Ambassador guides him to a space on the right-hand side of the terrace doors and says, 'I think you two know each other.'

The woman in the well-tailored grey suit turns and Piper blinks to make sure he isn't seeing things. A stone drops into his stomach, and for a second he has the desire to turn and walk away. A dull ache starts in one temple, reminding him of the painful memories about to be unlocked. In the end his dry mouth manages to let him say: 'Celeste.'

After an uneventful passage through minimal formalities at Mildenhall, Hooper and Kolski have been transferred to a house on a gated estate near Colchester, often used by the Army and GCHQ. It is nicely private, blandly furnished with Ikea furniture and cream paint, and the fridge and freezer are well stocked with provisions. They spend the first day shaking off jetlag, watching CNN and eating pizza, although Hooper does assemble his rifle and check it, despite it never having left his side for the entire journey.

On the second day, Eric DeCesare arrives. DeCesare is their London liaison, another of Wallace's old boys. Except he is an even older boy than them, his pedigree stretching back to the later stages of the Vietnam War. He must be in his mid-fifties but, apart from the steel-grey cropped hair, it doesn't show, except when he smiles and the face puckers into a thousand lines. Perhaps that is why he doesn't smile much.

DeCesare accepts a cup of coffee and parks himself on the sofa, placing his attaché case next to him. He eyes up Kolski while Hooper fixes the drinks. 'Good trip?'

'We got here,' says Kolski, stretching to show he doesn't consider a Stratotanker appropriate transport, 'with a few stiff muscles.' He nods at the case. 'That for us?'

'Mostly.'

'You got photographs?'

'Yes. We are using a local guy called Martin Billing for surveillance. Either of you know him? No? I'll give you his cell. He knows the city, and the people. I've used him a lot over the years.'

Hooper hands DeCesare the coffee and asks: 'How much do you know about this operation? I mean really know?'

'What do you mean?'

'Just that this isn't a paint job in the old sense. It's more like—'

DeCesare's eyes flash with anger. 'Hold it there, soldier. I know about as much as I need to, no more. And I don't want to know what you know, either. Jesus. The Colonel said you were pros.'

'We are,' says Kolski, 'which is why we don't like being treated like saps.'

DeCesare puts the coffee down on the badly assembled table and stands. 'Gentlemen.' He bends to pick up the case.

'Hey,' says Hooper. 'Who put a rocket up your ass?'

DeCesare points a finger. 'You two. You make me nervous. I don't like to be nervous. If you got some beef, you shouldn't have brought it here. You should have sorted it Stateside. I can replace you two in less than twenty-four hours, but the Colonel said you were good. Specialists, he said.' DeCesare turns a corner of his mouth up in disgust. 'Specialist assholes, maybe.'

Hooper raises his hands in supplication. 'Whoa. Just calm down here. It was a dumb thing to say. I didn't mean nothing. I was just going to ask about the level of official back-up.'

DeCesare prods a finger in his own chest. '*I'm* your back-up.'

Kolski takes a deep breath. He isn't intimidated by many people, but DeCesare seems like he is about to go critical. He can tell from the way he is tensed. He wonders if the man has a weapon in the attaché. 'This could have started better,' he says slowly.

There is a half-laugh from DeCesare, recognising the truth in that.

'Shall we begin over?' asks Kolski.

'Maybe we should,' says Hooper. 'Maybe we haven't kicked the jetlag yet. OK. We do this thing, we go home. End of story. C'mon. Sit down. Coffee is getting cold.'

The older man resumes his place. He unclips the case and opens it. Onto the table, next to his mug, he places a buff folder. 'Everything you need to know about the Target.'

He takes a second folder and extracts from it a

stack of six-by-eight glossy black and white photo-graphs. 'These are Billing's surveillance photographs from the past few weeks.'

Kolski reaches over and sorts though them, nodding. 'Some looker this one, eh?'

He holds up the picture of Celeste Young snapped at the Wolseley and passes it to Hooper, who nods in agreement. They don't notice DeCesare shake his head in dismay. It won't be difficult to waste these two jokers once it is done, he thinks.

'Hey. Isn't that what you Americans say to each other? "Hey!" I've seen it on television shows. You know, when two people haven't seen each other for a while, or have something difficult to say, they normally start with a—'

'Hey.'

Celeste realises she has been gabbling, so she just adds: 'Yes.'

Sandler has left them; they are hemmed in by the crowd, pressed against one of the fluted pillars next to the mahogany French doors. Beyond her, through the glass, in the halos thrown by the garden lights, Piper can see flurries of snow dancing across the lawn.

'What are you doing here?' he asks.

'Oh, Jack invites me to most things. He has this daft idea I saved his life.'

'Jack?' he says sarcastically. 'He's Jack to you, is he?'

She raises her eyebrows. 'It's not like that. He's a happily married man.'

'With three kids. I know. You did save his life.'

'I also wrecked my car.'

'Did the United States ever buy you another one?'

She shakes her head. 'I got a nice thank-you letter, though. I bought the Mini myself.'

'Trading down?'

'It stops me from being tempted to drive over concrete barriers. But it's a Works model.' There is a hint of pride, or perhaps challenge, in her voice.

'I'm guessing that's not, like, the slowest in the range. Right?'

'Right.' She sips her champagne. 'How long have you been back?'

'A few weeks.'

It is Celeste's turn to flirt with sarcasm. 'A *few*?'

'Two or three.'

'I see. Forgot my number, did you?' He can see colour in her cheeks. Clearly, she thinks she should have been next stop after Heathrow Customs. She might have a point.

'I was going to get round to it.'

'You certainly took your time.'

'Celeste,' he re-emphasises. 'I was going to get

round to it.' He has a feeling that the actual reasons for his reticence, the baggage she brings with her, wouldn't go down too well. 'I'm sorry. Really. It was remiss of me.'

'Yes, it was. Is it because of Martha?'

He laughs as if that is the most ludicrous suggestion he has ever heard. 'No. God, without you . . .'

'But I remind you of all that, don't I? Of Martha and that woman and of Monroe – of you having to shoot your lover?' There is a pause, which grows past the point where he can deny she has touched on a truth. He is sure his face gives him away. 'I understand.'

She turns to go and he grabs her upper arm, trying to judge the pressure, firm without bruising her. 'Stay.'

'No. It clearly hurts too much.'

He pulls her in closer to him. Some other guests watch them with a mixture of anxiety and curiosity, unsure whether a full-blown row is about to erupt. 'It's worth the pain.'

Celeste gives a wan smile. 'I doubt it.'

'Please? I am sorry. Now I've seen you . . .'

He has raised his voice, and she is aware of the eyes on them. 'Shush. Enough,' she chides him. Then: 'And may I please have my arm back before I get gangrene?'

Piper lets go and she flexes her bicep. 'Hold this.' She passes him her glass and reaches into her handbag. 'I have brought you a present.'

131

'You knew I was going to be here?' He sees the twinkle in her eye. 'Jack told you,' he guesses.

'Jack told me he'd invited you. I wasn't sure whether you would come, though. Here.' She takes her drink back and hands him a CD. It is by a band he has never heard of, The Bad Plus.

'Thanks. Is it . . . ?'

'Jazz – of a kind. Someone gave it to me, thinking I would like it, but as far as I am concerned, it sounds like a psychopath taking a large hammer to an innocent piano. Right up your street.'

'Thanks.' He pretends to study the sleeve. 'You know, I haven't really listened to music since the last time we met.'

'No?'

He shakes his head, thinking of all those unplayed Miles and Chet and Coltrane CDs gathering dust. 'I can't. It seems as if it is part of another life.'

'That's sad. I always feel sorry for people who don't have music in their lives.'

He tries to think how he can explain that the emotional attachment you need to engage with music is no longer there. It is as if that part of him has been pumped full of novocaine. He hopes it will wear off, one day. 'Don't feel sorry for me. It could be worse. I might have got to like country music.'

'"Lord, you gave me nothing",' she twangs. '"Then You took it all away". True.'

She sees the flash of pain as the joke falls flat, reminding him that God and a couple of crazed women did take everything away from him, almost. She reaches up to touch his face and he moves his head.

'Oh, sorry.'

'No, it's just that it's still a bit tender.'

'You look fine. You look good, Vince.'

'You, too.' He can feel the thaw starting. The ice caps aren't melting yet, but it's warmer. Yes, he should have called. But he thought Celeste was in there with Coltrane and the others – just another pathway to the re-opening of old wounds. He is pleased to find she isn't. He asks: 'How you doin'? Really?'

'Really?'

'Yeah, really.'

'Do you fancy getting out of this place? Going somewhere we can talk properly?'

Piper just nods, so she takes his hand and leads him out through the gathering, dumping both their glasses on a passing waiter. They collect their coats and head out into the swirls of flakes joining the white blanket settling across Regent's Park.

Ten

The Four Seasons Biltmore Hotel at Santa Barbara thoughtfully provides small sachets of solvent for washing off tar picked up on the beach. Colonel Wallace wonders why, until he sets out to jog along the beach, north towards the town and its pier. It is only a little after dawn. He came in late last night on a flight from Washington to LAX, and then took the commuter airline up the coast. Running, rather than driving, to his appointment will clear his head, he thinks. Besides, it is a joy to feel warm air after the needle-sharp winds of Washington DC.

The reason for the sachets becomes clear when he sees the flames dancing on the horizon, vivid against a milky streak of cloud shading the barely risen sun. Oil rigs, dozens of them. Nobody seems to mention that when Santa Barbara is discussed as a millionaires' playground, wall-to-wall Kevin Costners and Rob Lowes. He is surprised they don't do something about this blight on their view. And the dark stains on their Nike soles.

The Southern California sun finally drives away the haze, and the sky lightens as he plods along the sand, eyes peeled for any globs of tar that might adhere to his own pristine white trainers. Pelicans are patrolling the shoreline, almost mocking him with their effortless flight, skimming inches above the waves, just the odd, lazy wingbeat to keep them going, while he is puffing and sweating. He nods a comradely hello at a tan, muscled woman who powerwalks past him in the opposite direction, arms pumping, but he isn't sure she even notices the wheezing old man.

He stops and drinks at a water fountain, watching the early dog walkers exercise their mutts, all religiously pooper-scooping, while he catches his breath. Colonel Wallace checks his watch. He is early, but he is sure he can get a coffee while he waits for his employer. Santa Barbara has almost as many coffee shops as it does offshore oil rigs.

As he sips a tall latte, aware of his heart-rate finally falling and the sweat cooling on his brow, Wallace watches the parade of pelicans lined up at the end of the pier, patiently biding their time until the first tourists or fishermen arrive and they can begin a new day of scavenging. He shades his eyes and sees the shiny-black shape of a dolphin break through the water to his left. Then another arched back, and a third. A small pod, heading out to sea.

Behind him he hears the rumble of rubber wheels on the timbers and turns to see Charles Pearl heading swiftly towards him. Like many paraplegics, Pearl has an enormous upper body, developed from years of wheelchair marathons and pumping iron; not for him a chair with an electric motor. Even now, in his seventy-third year, he looks as if he could take on the Governor of California at arm wrestling and win.

He stops the chair next to Wallace and holds out a hand. Pearl reminds him of Paul Newman, those same boyish good looks, somehow slowly fading out of focus rather than aging conventionally like the rest of us. He takes the hand, which closes in a surprisingly gentle grip.

'Colonel.'

'Mr Pearl.' The old man never invites him to call him anything other than 'Mr Pearl'. Theirs is very much an employer-employee relationship. Pearl has brought him out of retirement, pays him good money, and doesn't want him to forget it by becoming over-familiar, Wallace guesses.

'Walk with me.' The voice is a shade softer, weaker than he remembers it from their last face-to-face meeting three months previously. Pearl is the only one of the think tank known as the American Future Democracy Committee who doesn't travel to Washington DC. He either uses the secure link or, as it is mostly his money bankrolling it, he can afford to have Wallace come out West. Usually, they meet in LA at the Beverly Hills Hotel or the Fairmont in Santa Monica. This is the first time Wallace has been close to Three Pines, the old man's fabled ranch and vineyards in the San Ysidro Valley. 'Or rather you walk, I'll wheel.'

Pearl pushes himself forward and Wallace falls in at his side. 'You ran here?'

The Colonel suddenly feels this might have been insensitive: jogging to see a man who hasn't even walked in twenty years, ever since a heli-skiing accident. 'I needed to blow away the cobwebs.'

'Good, good. I envy you that.' He slaps his dead legs. Before Wallace can reply, Pearl says, 'Wonderful sight, eh?'

The Colonel isn't sure at first whether he means the pelicans or the fast-disappearing dolphins, but then realises he is referring to the oil rigs. 'Yes, sir.'

'My family got rich making platforms like those, you know.' He is Pearl as in Pearl-Carlsson, the global engineering company set up by his father. 'I got us richer by diversifying into pipelines and then entertainment. You have any kids, Colonel?'

They had been through this when they'd first met, but perhaps Pearl's memory is going. 'A son. On secondment in Iraq.'

Pearl raises his eyebrows. Even though the Iraqis now nominally govern themselves, it is hardly a secure posting. 'He OK?'

'So far.'

'No, I mean – is he OK? You like him? Trust him?'

Love him, Wallace almost adds, but he guesses that isn't high on Pearl's list of priorities. 'Yes. I'm very proud of him.'

'My son is a prick. My daughter, she's little better than a slut. You've heard about the video, I suppose? Everyone else has.'

Wallace looks down at the pier's ancient planking, embarrassed. 'Yes. Look, sir, it seems to be some rite of passage that women these days let a boyfriend film them—' He stops. It isn't his place to defend someone he hasn't met. And he can tell by the grinding of teeth, Pearl doesn't want him to. His heart isn't really in it anyway. The girl probably is a slut.

'Film them doing *that* with another woman?' The old strength is back in the voice. 'Is that today's idea of fun? All over the internet? Well, she's out now. I'll make sure she knows she won't have enough money for going to movies, let alone making them. Maybe if Richard gets his nose out of those drugs . . . I have a Dr Pepper back there, would you get it for me?'

Wallace undoes the cool-pack hooked over the rear of the chair and hands Pearl the can. There is a hiss as he lifts the tab and he gulps some down. 'Want one?'

'No thanks, sir.'

'They always say that the first generation makes the money, the second spends it and the third loses it all. Looks like the Pearls are holding good to that last part.'

Wallace says nothing. The kids are young, they might come around. Probably not until their father has gone, though. It is that kind of slap in the face that will wake them up, when it's too late for the old man. Perhaps, thinks the Colonel, this is what Operation Palimpsest is all about. A legacy for Pearl to be proud of. Although there is a better-than-evens chance he won't live to see Palimpsest come good either.

'So, three projects on the slate.'

'Yes.' Wallace is used to speaking in movie-making metaphors now, and slips into it easily. They reach the unfenced end of the walkway, and Pearl rolls forward so his wheels are close to the edge before he applies the brake. Below, the sea laps languidly against the heavy piles. Bulky gulls squawk at him from their posts, as if he is encroaching on their personal space.

'You think they will all be green-lit?' asks Pearl.

'I have no reason to doubt it.'

'And the budgets?' asks Pearl. 'The bottom line?'

'Acceptable. Only the overseas one is on the high end.'

'Domestic crew?'

'US-sourced.'

'Expensive. Points?'

'We are just paying them scale.'

'Scale?'

'Mexican scale. Just below-the-line expenses to cover.'

Pearl nods. He knows what that means. Mexican scale is when you don't intend to pay anything if you can help it.

'Our studio has a movie opening next month,' Pearl says suddenly, taking Wallace aback. He is talking about a genuine project. 'One hundred and fifty million dollars.' Wallace knows he must be referring to *Bounty!* – the musical remake of *Mutiny on the Bounty*, which has already been slated in some quarters. 'Right cast, great script, wonderful locations, fantastic book, some of the best songs since Rodgers and Hammerstein. It'll tank, though, because for some reason the industry wants to see it fail. You can't predict anything in the movie business. Are we doing something similar?'

Wallace nods. 'Yes. But if you don't do something, you end up doing nothing.'

Pearl laughs, recognising his own quote from when he sold the whole idea to Wallace. 'Of course, I might not be around to see the results.'

'Nonsense. Of course you will.' He tries to sound confident, but suspects it rings hollow.

'I'll be eighty-two.'

'Someone has to be,' says Wallace.

Pearl switches tack once more. 'We've got closed sets arranged on all three?'

'Very closed.'

'Which one do you think is most likely to be a success?'

Wallace lowers his voice as a fisherman appears and begins unpacking his gear. 'That's not my department.'

'Gut feeling?'

'London.'

'Yeah, I think that. London.' He carefully lets off the chair's brake and backs away from the edge. 'Look, why don't we go up to the ranch. You can stay for lunch. We'll stop by the hotel and pick up some clothes for you.'

'Yes, sir. I'd like that.' Wallace, a man who has had

the ear of Colin Powell, Sandy Berger, John Podesta, John Poindexter, Donald Rumsfeld, Dick Cheney and others in his time, is slightly ashamed to feel so thrilled at the prospect of seeing Three Pines at last.

Hooper walks into the living room, brushing his teeth, getting ready for bed. Kolski is still going through the Target's folder. Kolski, after all, is the strategist. Hooper is better at tactics. Kolski looks up from his reading. 'Turning in already? It's only nine-thirty. I thought we could go out.'

'We go out when we get back Stateside,' Hooper says through a mouthful of foam. 'What you got?'

'I've got bad news for you.'

Hooper stops brushing. 'What's that? We gotta see that prick DeCesare again?'

'No. You probably won't need your rifle.'

'OK.' Hooper shrugs. He doesn't much care what method they use. He just wants to get back to building his house. He feels it was a mistake coming. They should have pulled out when they discovered that Wallace was working for a non-governmental agency – that this is what is known in the trade as an NJA, a Non-Judicial Action. 'Why?'

Kolski throws the folder onto the coffee table. 'All laid out for us in there. Acquisition and Elimination will take a phone call and a credit card.'

'Then we can go home?'

'Then we can go home and spend the money. Unless you want to stay and shove your rifle up DeCesare's ass.'

'You know, I'd almost consider doing that for free.'

'Almost.'

'Yeah. You wanna give me some of your share to do it? I'll let you watch.'

Kolski grins. 'Don't tempt me, Larry. Wanna beer?'

'Uh-uh.'

Kolski fetches a Grolsch from the refrigerator. When he returns, Hooper is reading the folder. 'It struck me earlier, there is an assumption here we can't be certain of.'

'If anyone else knows?'

'Right.' He taps the folder. 'This assumes pretty much a hundred per cent containment.'

'Which is rare.'

'Which is very rare.'

Kolski nods his agreement. 'In which case there'll be a lot more painting going on. The first Target will just be an undercoat.' He laughs at the analogy. 'Perhaps this puts a different gloss on it.' Another snigger.

Hooper has heard all the decorating jokes before, and doesn't crack a smile. 'Which means a renegotiation of price.'

Kolski takes a large pull on the can. 'Of course. Don't worry about it, Larry. It's not our problem. We've been told to do one, we do one. Let the Colonel and his pals worry about containment.'

The main ranch dates from 1890. It has been extended over the years, with guest rooms located in small bungalows in the hills, a fully equipped gymnasium and pool, and a modern wing that was constructed of aged wood, so it is hard to know what is original and what is relatively recent. The well-tended lawns slope down towards the ocean, where you have a view over the coast, the freeway and the melon and artichoke fields, perfectly framed by the three eponymous pines, now tall, gangly and probably in their senescence.

Pearl gives Wallace the guided tour on the smooth-surfaced tracks that zig-zag across the property, explaining how the ranch's horses are kept on the paddocks to the west of them – the Colonel is welcome to ride after lunch if he wishes – and the small vineyard that produces mostly pinot is to the east.

He finally stops at a small lookout, an hexagonal wooden belvedere with a domed roof, enclosing a metal table and chairs, where the Colonel can gaze down over the highway and watch the rollers fall onto the beach. Or, if he wishes, can count the number of oil rigs he can spot from up here. Wallace stops at fifteen.

Pearl asks: 'Would you care for a glass of our cider?'

Wallace, who has changed from Footlocker gear to sports jacket and slacks, and is feeling the unfamiliar heat, nods.

'Lovely, cloudy and unfiltered. The orchards are over yonder, over that hill.' The old man presses an intercom built into one of the lookout's pillars and barks an order for two glasses of cider.

'So, how do you like it?'

'The ranch? It's pretty impressive, sir.'

'Yes. Notice the security?'

'I did.' Even now, he could spot figures lurking on the perimeter. The main gateway had been tougher to get through than Langley.

'I have my own security firm. And a team of private investigators.'

A golf cart approaches and a young, crisply turned-out Latino hops out and places a tray with a jug of straw-coloured liquid, two glasses and some potato chips on the table. 'Will there be anything else, Mr Pearl?'

'No, thank you, Carlos.'

When the lad has gone, they both sip for a while, Wallace wondering where this is going. He smacks his lips in genuine appreciation. 'Delicious.'

'Isn't it? Strong, though. Kinda creeps up on you. Anyway, it so happens that when my team were checking my daughter's indiscretions, they came across something else.'

From the side of his wheelchair, the old man produces a clear plastic envelope. Inside are print-outs of web pages.

'Our friend the Governor from the Midwest. Slate number two.'

Wallace nods. This is one of the men Pearl wants to 'groom' for higher office. Having despaired of his own family, this is the role the old man has chosen for himself, an *éminence grise*, a king-maker. With Wallace doing the dirty work.

'Yes?'

'I think we may have to reconsider. It seems trouble runs in the family.'

The Governor had been a tricky one to groom as a candidate all along. His father had done prison time, and had become a bum. Even though he had fallen off the grid, they had been sure that, were the Governor to make a move towards running for executive office, some newspaper hack would dig up the old man and expose the truth: would-be President's dad a Cisco-drinking down-and-out calling himself Hank Porter. Which is why Wallace had sent a team to eliminate the old hobo in San

Diego. Nobody missed him, and that trail was now cold. 'Not just the father, then?'

Pearl shakes his head. 'The Governor's father was a degenerate. Now it appears the Governor's son runs a few websites. My team came across them while they were running down my daughter's little escapade. I can't remember the titles offhand. "Young and Hairy" or "Young and Hairless" or maybe it's both of the damn things. "Extreme Fucking" is the other one. Here.'

Wallace doesn't need to look, but he glances at the material anyway. He knows the kind of thing. 'I thought we'd checked the son out.'

'So did I, Wallace, you son of a bitch. So did I.' There is real fury in the voice. His hand is gripping so tight, Wallace worries the glass might break. 'And a piece of goddamn luck brings us this.'

'Well, if we only found it by chance . . .'

'Then someone else will. Jesus, you know the level of scrutiny we are talking about down the line. Look what they threw at Kerry, and that man was pretty squeaky clean. Furthermore, it seems the Governor knew about his son's endeavours. Didn't approve, of course.'

'You spoke to him?'

'Damn right I did. I told him what I thought.'

'So he's off the slate?'

'Oooohhh, yes,' Pearl says with emphasis. 'We are down to two.'

'Right.' This wasn't good. The odds of getting any one of them through to the finishing line were pretty astronomical, which is why they had wanted a whole stable of projects.

'Wallace, I want you to go back over the remaining pair with a finer-than-fine toothcomb. No fuck-ups. Nothing that will bite us in the ass later.'

'Yes, sir.'

'I want to do this right.'

'Yes, sir.'

'And if it goes wrong, I shall blame you and those other knuckleheads in Washington. I include Jerome in that – I could buy and sell him tomorrow. Understood?' Wallace nods and Pearl presses the intercom once more. 'Can you bring a car round for Colonel Wallace. He's leaving now.'

The Colonel is so shocked, he forgets to ask what happened to lunch.

Eleven

Celeste edges the Mini through the new two-metre-high concrete barriers that have been installed at Winfield House to create a choke point and the little car judders over the metal prongs which are angled to prevent people who are up to no good from driving in through the Out gate. She turns onto the Outer Circle of the park, the wheels spinning and finally catching on the ice-glazed surface. The snow is streaming through the yellow cones of the street lamps, bouncing the headlights back into their faces.

Celeste flicks on the heating and the fan, and Piper tries to relax. He always feels European cars are too small, too close to the road or the guy in front if you should tailend him. He still mourns the passing of muscle cars, of bonnets that you could play table tennis across.

She weaves the aggressively growling Mini through the thin traffic and turns north, over the canal.

'There's a gastropub between Primrose Hill and St John's Wood. Nothing fancy.'

Gastropub. How he hates that name. It sounds like the kind of place salmonella hang out and drink in.

'Unless you want to go into the West End?'

'Nothing fancy is fine.'

He leans forward and ejects the CD – Bantock, someone he has never heard of – and slides in The Bad Plus CD. It begins with frenetic, take-no-prisoners drumming, quickly joined by the pounding piano, which does sound like it is being disciplined for some misdemeanour, the player occasionally picking out a surprisingly delicate melody, before resuming the attack.

Celeste floors the accelerator, working the six gears, and he is pinned back in his seat. 'Shit,' he breathes.

'You're tapping your foot – you like it?' He smiles and nods. He is actually trying to work a non-existent brake pedal.

She moves round a gritting lorry with one twitch of the wheel.

'Yeah, it's got enough of the Keith Jarrett thing to keep me interested. They don't seem to have much between off and full-on, though. Might get a bit wear—'

The word is cut off as he is jerked against the seat belt when she brakes suddenly and slithers into a parking space. They are outside a brightly lit pub, its steamed-up windows full of illuminated Christmas angels. 'Dinner,' she announces. 'On you, as a punishment for not getting in touch.'

He steps out into the weather, sleet driving into his eyes. 'They take credit cards?'

She grins. 'Oh, yes. Anything but American Express. And before you say that's all you have, Roddy knows the owner. For me, he'll even take an IOU from you.'

'The best I've got is a Taurus – a Police Ultra-Lite. You know them? Five shot. Thirty-eight calibre. Very tasty piece of work. Brazilian. Came from a bust of some Colombians – Custom and Excise, but don't worry, it's not traceable. Geoff told me why you wanted this. Fair enough. Now excuse me for being blunt, but you don't seem like the vengeance type. If you bottle it, and it gets back to me . . . well, do I have to spell it out? I mean, you could get Geoff or . . . oh right, it's personal, I get you. Cheers, another pint will do nicely.

'Thanks. As I say, as long as Geoff says you're OK, I don't mind. I suppose all the other stuff I got for them is all gone now? Right. Which canal? No, don't tell me. I hope it's a deep 'un. Don't want no kids fishin' for frogs bringing that lot up. So all we need now is a price and we have a deal. How does six sound? No, not here, we can do it at the Turk round the corner. The baths, not the

restaurant. In the changing room. Ten o'clock? Good.
Cheers, then. And best of luck. Give the bastard one for
me.'

Piper and Celeste are shown to a table at the rear,
near the fire, but also close to the lavatories, for
which Saul, the owner, offers effusive apologies.
Celeste tells him not to worry. It's Christmas. She
orders a gin and tonic to freshen her tastebuds after
the champagne. Piper has a Scotch and water.

'How is everything?' he begins. 'How's your brother?'

Before she can answer, her mobile rings.
Apologising, she stands and walks away, taking the
call out of earshot. She is back within a minute.

'Talk of the devil. That was Roddy.'

'How is he?'

She pulls a face as she accepts a menu from the
young, highly decorated waitress. 'Same as ever. You
remember what he is like? Forever after money for
some daft scheme, then tapping me for a loan when
it goes belly up. The thing is, I could give him the
cash, but what good would that do?'

'Salve your conscience?'

'I don't have a conscience about Roddy,' she says
defensively. 'Why should I? He just has to realise that
he hasn't got an ounce of entrepreneur in him. Get
himself a job, perhaps.'

Like you? he almost asks, but he holds his tongue.

'Can I tell you about the special?' asks the waitress.

'Does it involve turkey?' Piper shoots back.

'Well, yes.'

'No, that's OK. We'll be fine.'

The waitress walks off rattling her piercings and Celeste says: 'You rude bastard.'

'I don't know what you do to turkeys in this country, maybe it's some kind of genetic modification, but how do you get old shoe leather to grow where the breast should be?'

She smacks him on the head with the laminated menu. 'It'll be very nice here.'

'Good, you have it then,' he says with a smirk.

Nat King Cole comes over the speakers, his syrupy voice crooning 'O Little Town of Bethlehem'. Waste of a great piano player, Vince thinks.

'What will you do for Christmas?' Celeste asks.

'The way things are shaping up, I'll probably be back in the States, having decent turkey with my mom, seeing as how I missed Thanksgiving.'

Celeste's eyes narrow. 'Your dad?'

He shakes his head.

'I'm sorry.' She reaches across and briefly touches his hand, the sensation warm and soft on his skin.

'Yeah.'

'But I thought you were assigned here?'

'Assignment terminated. You shouldn't go letting off your weapon in public. *Shit.*'

'What?'

He bangs the table. 'I left my Sig at the Gun Cage in the Embassy. Damn. What was I thinking?'

'My fault. I shouldn't have hustled you out. We can go back and get it later.'

'If we can get in. I think we make everybody at that house jumpy.'

Celeste hits him with a full-beam smile, and he begins to remember how it had been with her, even among all the garbage that was going down at the time. 'Can you blame them?'

'No, I guess not.'

The illustrated waitress appears. 'Are you ready to order?'

'Yeah,' he says. 'I'd like to try your deliciously moist turkey.'

The waitress hesitates, not knowing if he is being ironic, but assuming from his accent he can't possibly be.

'With the works, please.'

'I'll have the monkfish,' says Celeste. 'And can we have a bottle of the Kumeu River Pinot Gris.' The waitress starts to check the list, looking puzzled, and Celeste says; 'It's not on there, but I know Saul has some.' She whispers to Piper, 'He's got a case of the ninety-seven Chardonnay as well, but we won't get that out of him. I know you like French, but try this. You'll be surprised. Where were we?'

'Christmas. Me going home. My gun.'

'Right. Shame you have to go back so soon.'

'It's the way the cookie crumbles. I was there when the robbery went down, I felt I had to do something, then afterwards I'm told I should have pulled out a pad and started taking notes. Maybe make the odd sketch. Go figure.'

'When you should be a hero?'

She is mocking him. He shakes his head. 'No. Under the Federal Employees Protection Act, they aren't even supposed to release my name, not to Jack Sandler, although they did, and not to you. I don't want to be a hero. That was my dad. I just want to be able to finish the job I started. Otherwise, reading close to a thousand pages of boring shit is wasted.'

'Would you like to taste the wine?'

'Please.'

The waitress unscrews the Stelvin top and pours Celeste a couple of centimetres. She sniffs it and nods, then checks the temperature of the bottle. 'It's a little too cold. We'll leave it out of the ice bucket for a while.'

'What about you?' he asks her.

'I'm positively frigid.'

'You know what I mean.'

'Christmas? Oh, I'm going to friends in the country.'

He repeats it, putting an unwelcome emphasis on the word. '*Friends*?'

'Don't start, Vince. Old family friends.'

'But you're still, um . . .'

'Yes, I'm still a professional um.'

Piper throws his hands up in the air in irritation. 'I wasn't going to say it. It always comes back to this, doesn't it?'

She nods and takes a sip of her wine. 'Pretty much, I suppose.'

'Why do I always end up apologising?'

'Because you always end up getting flustered and behaving like a pillock?'

Piper laughs and points a finger at her. 'That could be it.'

'You know, the other day . . .' she begins, remembering the horse ride.

The food arrives, and they wait while plates are placed before them. Celeste orders a second bottle of wine and Saul comes over to mockingly complain that he can't see the point of a secret stash of booze if everyone knows about it. 'Enjoy your food,' he says.

Piper takes a mouthful of turkey and prompts her: 'You were saying?'

'What?'

'That the other day . . .'

'Oh, nothing. How's your turkey?'

Piper considers for a moment, rolls his eyes heavenward, swallows and takes a sip of wine. 'Delicious,' he finally says.

Sasha and Timmy are the last customers at the BodyBliss Day spa in Kensington. They are lying in the relaxation room, following their various combinations of scrubs, peels, waxes, hot stones and algal wraps. Soft, plinking music bleeds from the Minipod speakers. Lulu, the spa's star masseuse, glides in with hot towels and silently lays them next to the beds where the pair recline.

'Mr Chow's?' asks Timmy, naming the restaurant just across the road.

'Drinks, Mju first,' says Sasha. 'Then San Lorenzo?'

'Launceston Place.'

'Foliage?'

'I was there last night. One-O-One?'

The list goes on, a verbal joust with nearby restaurants, until they settle on Zafferano.

Timmy rolls onto one side, her elfin features puckered in concern. 'Are you OK, Sash? You seem a little . . .' She struggles for a word. Her English accent is near-perfect now, but her vocabulary occasionally gives out. 'Distant. Preoccupied. Is that what they say?'

'That's what they say.' Sasha reaches over, wipes her face with a soft towel and sips her water. 'Sorry.'

Timmy watches as she slumps back. 'Are you going to tell me?'

'I was, over dinner.'

'Tell me now.'

Sasha lets out a big sigh. 'I have to have a . . . procedure. That's what the Professor calls it. A procedure. So much less threatening than operation.'

There is a wariness in Timmy's voice, a little flicker of anxiety about what the answer to her next question might be. 'What kind of procedure?'

'I have to open my legs while they stick a laser beam up my cunt.'

Timmy shudders. 'What?'

'Not a laser beam. Something that can burn precancerous cells away.'

'Oh God, Sash.'

'*Pre*-cancerous. Not cancerous. Just a precaution, the Prof says. It's just not a very nice thought. You know nuns don't get cervical cancer? What hope have we got?' She laughs, but there is a bitterness there, and Roddy wouldn't recognise it as the usual deep and sexy number. 'Have you had a smear recently?'

'Last year, I think. When do you get this done?'

'Soon. Next week.'

'Oh. If there is anything I can do, Sasha.'

It is Sasha's turn to raise herself on one elbow. 'Actually, Timmy, there is.'

Twelve

On the way home from the gastropub, Piper calls US Embassy security and tells them he'll be over for his weapon in the morning. The duty guy promises that they'll try not to lose it, in a voice that is very punchable. Piper lets it go. He doesn't want to spoil the mood.

Aware that she might be near the limit, despite switching to water and letting him polish off most of the second bottle, Celeste drives very sedately through the whitened streets. Piper leans back and closes his eyes, letting an unfamiliar happiness wash over him. He is well into the comfort zone.

In far too short a time, Celeste pulls the Mini to a halt outside the door to his apartment block. There is an awkward silence for a second. 'Want to come in?' he asks. 'It's kinda impersonal, but I have booze and I have coffee.'

She flashes a regretful smile. 'Can't, sorry. No more booze and coffee'll keep me awake. Early start tomorrow.'

'Client?' he asks testily.

'Riding. Of the horse kind,' she adds hastily.

'Right.'

'I had a good time tonight, Vince.'

'Me too.'

She leans over and kisses his cheek. He struggles with the door catch. 'You have to flick it twice, remember.'

'Yeah.' He steps out. 'See you again?'

'Don't forget your CD.' She presses the eject button and hands it over, along with the case.

'Thanks. I will play it.'

'Just not when I'm around, please. Phone me,' Celeste says. 'If you can bear it.'

He adopts a grimace of pain. 'I'll grit my teeth.'

He slams the door and watches the little car pull out into traffic and zoom off like a go-cart. He is still standing when the icy sleet starts to fall again, stinging him into action, and he goes inside.

He puts the CD on the player, keeping it low, and pours himself a splash of Scotch. Best not overdo it. He realises how tired he is and begins to strip off. A shower and bed, that will be just the ticket. He moves through to the bathroom and fiddles with the shower attachment. He swears he can spit at a greater volume than the water pressure here manages.

He steps into the shower, pulling the cheap plastic curtain across, drowning out the percussive piano-playing from the other room, and looks down at himself. He has lost a few pounds since he was last in the UK, and looks better for it. Some of the hairs on his chest have become hard, wiry and grey. He pulls one out and regrets it. Tough little bastards, too.

Piper knows he has lost his way. A career trajectory that was smooth and predictable has, in the past few years, started jerking like one of those ECG traces. His superiors don't really trust him. Even his actions the other day proved to be a double-edged sword. Yes, some people thought he did well, but others pointed out that the guys still got away with the loot. That's as maybe, he says to himself, thinking of the blood in the chopper, but not scot-free. That was something.

So will he play out his final years in the FBI in front of a whiteboard, going over and over the same half-dozen cases, highlighting the good, the bad and the incompetent? He supposes there are worse things, but a niggling feeling in his brain tells him he will go stir-crazy as a tutor. Talking about field operations, but not being able to take part – like watching pornography with both hands tied behind your back.

Piper grimaces at the analogy and turns off the water. Must have sex on the brain. He stops and listens to the music, wondering if the CD has jammed or if the pianist is inordinately fond of the phrase his left hand is picking out.

He walks into the living room, towelling his hair, and is aware of the movement behind and to his left, but he is too slow, too weary, too drunk. Something heavy wraps itself around his neck, and he goes down, naked and vulnerable.

Hooper and Kolski have moved into their London base. It is in Clerkenwell, a loft-style apartment in a block where neighbours won't notice or care who comes and goes. In fact, they have seen neither hide nor hair of any living things since arriving. Someone empties the ashtrays in front of the elevators, occasionally there is the sound of distant dance music, and lights certainly blaze in a few of the dwellings, but they feel pretty much alone. Which is the idea.

The flat is sparsely furnished. Two white sofas, a large plasma TV and DVD, a steel kitchen that looks ready for open-heart surgery and a Bang & Olufsen stereo. It is a movie-set designer's idea of a yuppie apartment, but neither man is impressed. They think it cold and uncomfortable.

Hooper has gone over everything in the Target

folder, and realises that Kolski is right – his particular skills are unlikely to be fully utilised. There will be no 'painting'. It means he can relax – Kolski has the lion's share of the work. So he suggests something out of character: 'Maybe we should catch a movie?'

Kolski looks up from the magazine he is reading. 'We can watch a DVD. That thing is as big as a cinema.'

'Nah. I'm gettin' a little antsy. Let's go out.'

'What, like on a date?'

'Fuck you, Kolski. I'll go by myself.' He fetches his jacket from the twisted sculpture that they finally figured out was a coat-hook. 'You comin'?'

'No.' He looks at his watch and leers at Hooper. He reaches for the phone and shows Hooper the cloned credit card he has in his left hand before affecting a good-old-boy accent. 'I'm just gonna confirm ma booking for some ripe poon-tang.'

'Confirm?'

'Yup.'

'Where?'

'Suite One-oh-seven.'

'Tomorrow, then?'

'Tomorrow.'

Hooper slips off his jacket and rummages through the DVDs next to the player. If it's tomorrow, he'll just hang loose. He pulls out a case and holds it up to Kolski. '*Scarface*?'

163

'That'll do nicely.' The phone connects, he shows Hooper his palm to quieten him and his voice changes register. 'Hello? Yes, I'd just like to confirm a reservation for tomorrow night. Yes, I do have a credit card . . .'

For the second time in less than a week, Piper finds himself coming around, wondering where the hell he is. His first sensation is one of deep cold, and he is aware that his teeth are chattering. Not only that: they hurt, too. Pain is shooting from the sockets, flaring around his temples, the hot spots so painful he has to keep his eyes shut.

Piper moves his hands and feels the smoothness of the apartment's oak floor. He is still in his living room. The music has stopped. How long has he been out? He risks flicking open one eye. He can see a lampstand, lying on the floor parallel with him. The TV is on its side. There is no music playing because the CD player has been stomped on: it is next to the TV, its casing twisted and burst.

The place has been turned over; or there has been a struggle. Not one involving him though. They took him real easy.

He rolls over and has trouble identifying where the worst agony is coming from. The back of his neck crossed the line first, with his ribs and jaw a photo finish for second and third. Shit, Piper, he thinks, this is going to hurt no matter how you do it. He hops up onto his haunches and stands, steadying himself against the wall as his head spins. The room oscillates for a few seconds and then decides to be still.

His whisky has been thrown up the wall. The glass is smashed. Magazines, cushions, books and anything else not screwed down has been dumped in the middle of the room.

He walks through to the kitchen, where plates and cups and more glasses have been reduced to shards, as if in some kind of frenzy. His juicer is broken, coffee grounds are splattered everywhere, including the ceiling. If someone was searching, they seemed to be doing it by using King Kong. And what was there to find?

In the bathroom he pulls on a robe and splashes water on his face before he examines himself in the mirror. There is a nasty yellowing around his neck, and a livid mark on his temple, possibly where he hit something as he fell. His ribs are rebruised, the fresh marks livid on top of the older ones from the shotgun blast.

Piper fetches a Coke from the fridge, clears a space on the sofa and dials his boss to tell him the bad news.

'What is it with you, Vince? Is it the city? The jetlag? You must be over the goddamn jetlag by now.' Stanley

Roth is sitting on the sofa, his face back to lugubrious. It is gone one in the morning and he is not happy to have been called out of bed because Special Agent Vincent Piper has put a foot up his own ass once again.

'I don't know, Stan. Ow.'

Piper sits on the other sofa, dressed only in sweat pants while Doc Turner from the Embassy goes over him. He has taken his blood pressure, checked his eyes and ears, and is prodding his ribs. 'I don't think anything is bust. You must have a rubber skeleton, Vince,' he says.

'That's not the only thing that is made of rubber,' adds Roth.

'Lock was picked.' It is Brewster, the Secret Service man, also bleary and bad-tempered at the end of a fifteen-hour day. Roth had known he was still on duty, and had pulled him in rather than disturb an FBI man. Piper wishes he hadn't. 'Don't you throw the mortice?'

'Only when I go to bed.'

Brewster shakes his head at what he considers to be a serious breach of duty. 'Anything missing?'

'Not that I can see as yet,' Piper admits.

'Well,' says Roth, 'nobody's going to take that crap you call music.' You grouchy bastard, thinks Piper, but says nothing.

Brewster sneers: 'Good job you left your gun in our

care, eh? Otherwise we'd have an armed perp running around London.'

Doc Turner turns his attention to Piper's skull, moving his head this way and that, his fingers gliding over the marks on his temple. 'You might need an X-ray.'

'They won't see anything up there,' says Roth.

'Stanley, knock it off, eh?' Piper snaps back. 'It's not my fault.'

A silence descends. The three other men don't know how or why, but they all reckon that somehow, it *is* Piper's fault.

'I'll get a team in here, clear this up,' says Brewster.

'I can clear it up myself,' retorts Piper.

'An SOC team,' corrects Roth. 'Then a set of cleaners to put it all back. And we'll tell the Brits. By the book, Vin.' He shakes his head once more. It's going to come loose soon, thinks Piper. 'The sooner you get back Stateside, the better.'

'Yeah.'

'Meantime, I want you in a hotel.' Piper opens his mouth to protest, but Roth overrides him. 'A hotel. On the firm. But not Claridge's, eh?'

'Jesus, Stan. It's a simple burglary. Aren't you over-reacting?'

Doc Turner steps back. 'It's lots of things, Vince, but it isn't a simple burglary. That mark on your temple?'

Piper instinctively touches it and winces. 'Someone held a gun barrel against it and pressed. Very hard. Seems be a circle about nine mil in diameter.' The doctor holds up his thumb and forefinger, indicating a small distance. 'My guess? You were this far from being shot in the head.'

Piper looks at Roth, his jaw open in disbelief.

'Not Claridge's,' repeats Roth.

Hooper and Kolski venture out for a late dinner. It's a slight risk, they know, but not much of one. Who is going to recall two quiet Americans, soberly dressed and polite, and associate them with a senseless murder?

There is a vast choice of bars in Clerkenwell, but many of them are too young and too loud, so they are in the Zetter, a local hotel, eating T-bone steak and veal chops. The crowd, mostly local office workers, is thinning, although the bar has received a second wind with the advent of a younger group, who look as if they've stopped over on the way to a club.

'How is everything?' asks the waitress with the multi-hued hair and a winning grin.

'Good,' says Hooper, indicating the slab of lightly grilled beef. 'Best piece of meat I've ever had in this town.'

'Good. More water?'

'Yeah. Thanks.'

'And you are still OK with beer?'

'Sure.'

'Cute,' Hooper says to Kolski when she has gone.

'Yeah. Kinda.' His taste in waitresses is more straightforward: loud and blonde, not streaked and cool.

'You OK about tomorrow?' Hooper asks his partner. He means about the delineation of roles. Kolski is the point man.

'Yeah. You?'

'Not much to it.'

'Left arm, buddy.'

Hooper looks down at the table and smiles sadly. His left arm is curled like a fat anaconda around the plate in the standard defensive stance you adopt in the joint, just to prevent another con from coveting your grub. He slides it back. 'Thanks. Force of habit.'

Kolski takes a swig of beer and leans back in his chair. 'Did you think you'd come back to this when you came out of the house?'

Hooper, still ploughing through his steak, signals the waitress who bounds back over. 'Actually, can I have a glass of red wine to go with this after all?'

'The Mendoza?'

'Whatever. Thanks.'

When she goes, Kolski reaches over and takes his

partner's beer and pours it into his glass. 'Waste not. Did you hear what I said?'

'Yeah, I heard. It's not what I would've chosen. It chose me, I guess. I ain't qualified for much else. Construction, maybe.'

'Don't pay,' says Kolski, as if this is a serious option. 'And it's too seasonal.'

Hooper's wine arrives, he takes a sip to approve it, and returns to attacking the steak. 'What about you? You cut out for anything else?'

'If I am, I ain't found it yet. Wanted to be a racing driver once. Indy Five Hundred. Tried a little stock cars once. Not too shabby, but I ain't no Gil De Ferran either.'

Hooper shrugs to show the name means little. 'I don't follow motor sports. I wanted to play ball. Same thing as you. I might have made the minors, but I'd never have made the cut. So that's us then, stuck with what we do.'

Hooper carries on chewing, savouring the flavour of the T-bone. The conversation has skirted around the core topic people like him and Kolski never like to discuss. When are you too old? When does your luck run out? When does the knowledge of what you do start to disgust you? And you never say you are doing one last job, even if you think that.

Kolski lights a cigarette and inhales, holding it for

thirty seconds, then letting the smoke leak from the corner of his mouth where it hangs like cotton candy. 'Being able to smoke in a restaurant,' he says with a little shudder of pleasure, 'without some cunt yelling in your ear about giving her cancer. How cool is that? Want one?'

Hooper shakes his head. He didn't even smoke inside, simply used the cigarettes as currency. It was better if you didn't have too many habits and cravings in there. Sooner or later the Aryan Brotherhood or the Mexicans or the Crips would find a way to exploit you. The first few months were hard, of course, like basic training. But you quietly broke a finger here, poked an eye there, faced down some numbnuts in the yard, paid – with smokes – for someone to watch your back when you were exposed, made sure there was no mileage in you for anyone, and it settled down. One shop-made shank in the back, that was his score-line. Not bad at all.

Hooper finishes the food, pushes the plate away.

'Dessert?' asks Kolski.

Hooper shakes his head and signals for the bill. 'No. Let's turn in. Big day tomorrow.'

Thirteen

Vincent Piper sits amid swirling clouds of steam, listening to the strident voices of two cabbies, discussing at great length the stupidity of something called the Hackney Carriage Office. He has his head in his hands, letting the accumulated sweat plip onto the tiled floor. This is Porchester Hall Baths in West London, one of the last great Turkish and steam baths in the city.

Piper massages his temples, pressing gingerly on the place where, according to Doc Turner, there is the impression of a gun barrel. But whose? Who would have ransacked his place and come within a few millimetres of killing him? Roth thinks there are two possibilities. A connection to his helicopter escapade – which, they both agree, is unlikely – or, more sinisterly, a hangover from his last sojourn in London. That had been a mother-and-daughter team. Both were now in Federal prisons, but what if there was a third member? A son or brother or lover? There had always been a questionmark over how the pair had obtained explosives. Roth is re-checking the files, to see if they had missed an accomplice. Meanwhile Piper is holed up in an upmarket guesthouse – nice, but not Claridge's – while Scene of Crime go through his apartment.

The steam whooshes around him as the door opens. The two cabbies leave, and a single person takes their place. He hears the slap of flesh on the tiles, and the ritual clearing of nasal passages.

He is aware of the man leaning forward, peering through the fog. 'Piper? Vincent Piper?'

'Yeah.'

The man crosses over, lays out his towel and plonks himself down next to him. 'It's Roddy. Roddy Young.'

He holds out his hand and Piper takes it. 'Of course. Forgive me. Hi, how you doing?'

'Christ – what happened to you? Did my big sister do that?' He chortles at his own joke. 'She charges extra for that sort of thing.'

'I fell down some stairs,' Vince lies feebly.

'Yeah. FBI do that a lot, do they? Fall down stairs?'

'Only some of us.'

'I hear you fell down some stairs the other day, too. Near Hanover Square. Maybe you ought to buy a bungalow.'

'Christ, is there anyone who doesn't know about that?' Piper asks with genuine anger.

'Celeste told me, when she was off to that party at the Ambassador's house. Said you were that masked man.'

'Not much of a mask.'

'Mum's the word,' Roddy says chirpily. 'I won't tell. So you saw her, my sister?'

'You know I did. You called when we were in the pub.'

'You were there? She didn't say. How's it going, if you don't mind me asking.'

'I do,' Piper says petulantly.

'That good, eh?'

'Look, Roddy, I've got a headache. I'm not being rude, but . . .'

'No, OK, understood.'

Roddy makes to move and Piper feels bad. 'Look, I don't mean . . . What are you doin' now? How's the internet business?'

'Well, we have a couple of nice little things coming to the boil. If you've a few bob spare, there are worse investments.'

'I don't have a few bob to spare, Roddy.'

The other man stands and wraps his towel round his waist. 'I'll leave you to it.' He leans in close, so close Piper can see the moisture squeezing through his open pores. 'I know I joke about her, but don't upset my sister, eh? Celeste's a very special person.'

It's more likely to be the other way around, he reckons, but says: 'I know that, Roddy.'

'You mustn't judge her by what she does.'

'I don't judge her.'

'People do – all the time. I mean, I wouldn't want to have to send my friend Lennie round to sort you out.'

He'll have to join the fuckin' queue, Piper thinks. 'I remember Lennie. He won't have to come see me.'

Roddy's voice is low, hoarse. 'That's good. I'll see you around.'

'Probably in the plunge pool.'

Roddy laughs mirthlessly and Piper relishes the cool blast as he leaves the room. He returns to massaging his temples. Well, at least Roddy reminded him of one thing: he'll have to see Celeste, tell her he's definitely leaving Town. Again.

Special Agent Brewster stands impassively in Jack Sandler's office and the Ambassador rips open the wrapping of the package that has arrived for him. Summoned by the mail room, Brewster has had it X-rayed, suspicious about the contents, but Sandler knows exactly what it is.

'There. A one-seventy-second scale model of a B-17

Flying Fortress.' He holds up the box, which shows Lucky Lucy over Westphalia, with Focke-Wulfs and Me 262 jet fighters filling the sky around it, the lurid panorama criss-crossed with tracer bullets.

'Very nice,' says Brewster impassively.

'Japanese kit. How ironic is that, Lee?' He lifts the lid off and sorts through the hundreds of tiny plastic parts.

'Your father fly in those?'

'Lockheed Lightnings. Bomber escort. Before that, P-40s. You don't get all this, do you?'

For once Brewster cracks a grin. 'No, sir. It was a long time ago.'

Sandler sits down at his desk and pours himself some water. Brewster shakes his head when Sandler indicates the second glass. 'It was. How old are you?'

'Thirty-five.'

'Well, what a difference a decade makes. I was brought up on this stuff and Korea. In my day, war still had a glamour and a moral certainty. People who only know Vietnam and Iraq, they are more ambivalent about it.'

'With respect, sir, it isn't that.'

'Oh? What is it?'

'In the Service we feel it is more important to fight and win today's battles, rather than reliving yesterday's.'

Sandler bursts out laughing. 'You know that makes you sound like a horse's ass?'

'Yes, sir.'

'Because you can do both. Here.' He pushes a sheet of paper across. 'A rough breakdown of my movements before the holidays.'

Brewster picks it up and studies it, nodding. 'This trip to Norfolk.'

'Personal trip.'

'I'll send someone.'

Sandler waves a hand. 'No need.'

'My assignment is to—'

'Yes, yes. But you can't come to the can with me, and you can't come up there.'

Brewster is silent for a moment, his brow furrowed. He finishes reading the itinerary, satisfied with everything else. 'I'd like to lodge a complaint about that, sir.'

You know where you can lodge it, Sandler almost says, then relents. The man is only trying to do his job. Since the attempted assassination of the US Ambassador in Paris, everyone is jittery and overwound. 'OK, send one of your interns.' He smirks, knowing the Secret Service in London has no such thing. 'But I warn you, all I'm doing is reliving yesterday's war.'

177

Brewster nods his thanks. Neither of them fully realise that they have made a decision which means that yesterday's and today's wars are about to converge.

Fourteen

A silver mist has rolled through the streets of London, blurring the edges of the city. Visibility is down to about twenty yards, which means Hooper has to park closer to the hotel than he would like. He taps the wheel on his hired Ford in time to an old U2 track playing on the radio. Across the road, in Suite 107, Kolski is probably emptying the mini-bar down his throat, psyching himself up. Good for him. He hopes Kolski enjoys this, because this is their swansong as a duo: he won't be working with him again.

Over the past few days he has dared to decide that this is it. He knows that when the Colonel asked him in the diner if he still had the moxie for painting, he should have said no instead of pulling that bullshit trick with the Beretta. Pride, vanity, that's all that was.

It isn't that he has suddenly got a conscience, that

179

he thinks the Colonel is a renegade idiot – which he just might be – or that killing people is always wrong; it's simply that the game doesn't juice him any more. Not once, not even when he downed the horse, has he had that buzzing in his brain, that sub-orgasmic rush he used to have. It's like the loss of libido – nothing he can do can bring it back. He doubts there is a Viagra equivalent for painters. Face it, Hooper, prison did change you, he thinks. It performed some kind of lobotomy. It took out your desire to kill.

So, he's only in it for the money now, and he is sure there are better ways to earn that. When he gets home, he'll talk to Renee. They'll work out a new way forward. And he'll have the fee from this in his back pocket, give them a little cushion to sit on for a while.

He keeps all this from Kolski, of course. He wouldn't understand, he'd think it was bad karma. He can see in his partner's eyes, that it is still there for him. Particularly when it comes to a set-up like tonight. That's right off the hook for him. He probably has a hard-on right now.

The taxi draws up noisily, its gritty exhaust spiralling up to add to the thin blanket of fog. Hooper sits up as he sees the Target emerge. He speed dials on his cell and says just one word: 'Acquired.'

'Understood.' Kolski hangs up.

As the Target enters the hotel, Hooper starts the

Ford, puts on the lights and heads east. It is going to take him longer than he has allowed, thanks to the weather, but that is not really a problem. It isn't as if the Target is going anywhere.

DeCesare lets himself into the Clerkenwell apartment, wrinkling his nose at the smell of stale bodies, spilled booze and unwashed crockery. He flicks on the lights and shakes his head at the stash of cans and cigarette stubs on the coffee table. Although he knows Hooper and Kolski will perform an excellent disinfecting job on the place before they leave, the evidence of their carelessness irritates him. He sits down next to the phone and dials the USA. Wallace answers on the second ring.

'It's me.'

'What's happening?'

'It's a location shoot. Tonight.'

'Good. There has been one change.'

'Yes?'

'The slate is down to two. And the studio thinks London is the one. How are the talent?'

DeCesare hesitates. He pulls the jacket away from the weapon under his arm, the one he was going to use to execute Hooper and Kolski. 'Abbott and Costello? Yeah. They're there.'

'There may be an increase in budget.'

181

'How big?' asks DeCesare.

'Whatever it takes. We don't want to have to do any re-shoots or send a second unit out for pick-ups at a later date.'

'So let me get this straight . . .'

'Hmm.'

DeCesare knows he has to be careful. 'You basically want an option on anyone who has read the script?' Which means anyone who might have an inkling of what the Target knows.

'An option, no. Total buy-out.'

'That could be expensive.'

'Find out how much. If it is unfeasible, get back to me.'

There is irritation coming down the line. Wallace just wants it done. He is telling him that he doesn't mind how many people die, within reason. What is within reason? thinks DeCesare. Six? Ten? A dozen? Twenty? No, surely not. 'I'll run a budget on a shooting script. How is that?' *Shooting script*, he likes that, although he is aware that 'shooting' is one of the prime words, like terrorism and bomb that might wake up an auto-listening word-filtering computer somewhere.

'Fine. Tomorrow?' asks Wallace.

'Same time.'

DeCesare puts the phone down and crosses to the kitchen to make himself a coffee and try to relax. Like a racehorse which has been turned away from the stalls at the last moment, he is jittery and disappointed. They might need Hooper and Kolski for more work. Looks like he won't be killing anyone tonight.

Hooper takes close to three hours to complete his assigned portion of the evening's work. His journey across London is slow, if uneventful, and he arrives back at the hotel where he saw the Target emerge from a cab at just on midnight. He parks the Ford around the back of the building and lets himself in through the service entrance. There is nobody about; the kitchen is closed, most of the staff gone. Just a few bodies remain prowling the corridors, collecting breakfast menus and shoes for polishing.

He takes the stairs to the second floor, where suite 107 is located, taps on the door and lets himself in with the spare electronic key. He hesitates in the small lobby, listening. A light is showing from the lounge door. He opens it and steps inside. Kolski is facing him in an armchair, a tumbler of amber liquid in his left hand, a small cigar in his right.

Kolski nods, then indicates the bedroom. Hooper can see the woman's feet from where he is standing and he has no desire to see much more. However, curiosity gets the better of him and he takes a couple of steps forward.

'Shit.'

She is laid out on top of the bed, her arms and legs splayed out and tethered to the bedposts with cords of leather. A large object of some sort – Hooper doesn't want to peer too closely – is protruding from between her legs. The sheets around her are specked with blood. She is blindfolded. Her mouth has had a large rubber ball forced into it, and a gag placed over the top. Her pale skin shows livid bruising and, across her breasts are the red tracks of teethmarks that have sunk deep into the flesh.

None of this really shocks Hooper. What makes him gasp is the brunette wig draped over the bed's padded leather headboard, and the woman's cropped blonde hair.

They have killed the wrong girl.

The bar is a mixture of dark woods, raw steel and halogen uplighting. The room is crowded, the lavatories need an instruction booklet to tell you what to do where, there is a DJ playing hip-hop and the average age is under-age. Piper and Fletcher are, by some margin, the oldest there. But she has asked to meet him for a drink, it is halfway between them in terms of distance, and this dive has a late licence.

She is drinking a vodka cocktail, Piper is sticking with beer. Fletch is, he realised quite quickly, some way ahead of him in the drinks league table. Judging from the rawness around her eyes, she has also been crying. 'Cheers. Thanks for coming out.' She has to raise her voice to be heard. 'So late. And at short notice.'

'Least I could do. You sounded . . .' She cocks an ear, but misses the last part. He, too, increases his volume. 'Are you OK?'

'Just another average day with my ex-husband.' She takes a small sip of her drink, just enough to wet her lips. 'No, I'm not all right. The kids are going to stay with him for a while, because with all this SOCA stuff going on he reckons I won't be able to give them my full attention. Doesn't want them with a child-minder twenty-four seven. As if I'd do that.'

'That's rough.'

'I miss them. They're nice to come home to.' She takes a large mouthful of the drink and her eyes widen as the alcohol bites her throat. 'Christ, that hit the spot. Look, Vince, I also wanted to say I was sorry for being so shitty at the hospital.'

'I filed it under "disappointed" rather than genuinely mad at me.'

'Well, that's where it belongs.' She reaches up to touch his head and he stops himself from recoiling. He isn't after physical contact with Fletch, much as he likes her. She turns out to be simply rotating it to catch the light better. 'What's that?'

He explains about his apartment and the impression left by a gun.

'Bloody hell, Vincent. This Brewster – who's he?'

'Head of Embassy Security, which includes all assigned staff, no matter what their agency. Like me.'

'He tell our people about what happened?'

'APPLE, I would imagine. Me being a US Citizen, I finally get to be a subject of our old outfit.'

'I'll check first thing what's going on. Christ, what is it with you?'

Piper shrugged. 'Roth said much the same thing. I'm beginning to think I am some kind of shit magnet. As they say.'

'You want to know what I think?'

He nods.

'I think you were bang on course to be a good FBI man. Then something happened. Your life went off the rails . . .'

'Thanks.' It was a little near the mark. She might be even drunker than he'd thought. 'How does that result in my apartment being trashed?'

She ignores that. 'I'd guess it was the marriage break-up.'

'You could be right.' Piper finds himself mildly irritated. If he wants a shrink, he'll pay good money for one.

'Then Martha, then your father . . . Jesus, I don't

know how you coped. My hubbie is playing away from home and I'm barely keeping it together.'

'You know I was offered trauma counselling – after Martha died.'

'And?'

'I didn't take it. Maybe I should have. I'm just thinking, you Brits are real screwed-up when it comes to asking for professional help. Talking to someone, someone who isn't in a bar, might help. Fletch, you have to be careful. I thought I walked away from all that free as a bird. Baloney. Nobody does.'

'So? How did it get to you?'

'Initially? Obsession that I knew who killed Martha.' He had pursued one man blindly, convinced that him being her killer was the only solution, when, in fact, it was far from the truth. That man had his own demons he was wrestling with.

'I know about that, remember. What about longterm?'

He takes a deep breath. He doesn't like admitting this to himself, let alone anyone else. 'I don't care as much now.'

'About what?'

'Anything. The job, music, people. It's like someone sandpapers the end of your neural system, blunting it.'

'I don't believe you.'

'Doesn't mean it's not true.'

'I don't believe you don't care. A man who didn't care wouldn't have got involved with that robbery with the chopper. Wouldn't have risked his life that way.'

'A man who was thinking straight might have done something differently. Being dumb doesn't mean you care. Maybe it was reflex. You told me I shouldn't have played SWAT.'

'Yes. I did say that.' She drains her drink. 'Another?' He indicates he still has most of his bottle left and Fletcher shoulders through to the crush and yells in the barkeep's ear for a refill. There is much fussing with blenders, fruit and brightly coloured liquids, before she gets her fresh cocktail.

'Anyway,' she continues when she returns, 'ignore what I said at the hospital. I think you care.'

A four-to-the-floor bass figure starts to vibrate through his chest. 'I don't care for this music.'

'Me neither.'

An ashen-faced girl with artlessly – but no doubt expensively – chopped hair, pushes by and heads towards the bathrooms, hand over her mouth to hold back the contents of her insides, too much sweet liquor in her young stomach.

'You seen your friend since you got back?' The word 'friend' is loaded with slurred innuendo.

'Celeste?'

'Yeah. She still a high-class tart? If you'll excuse the expression.'

Piper has heard worse. 'I guess you'd say that.'

'So, have you seen her?'

'Yeah. Once.'

'And are you . . . ?' She swirls her drink in a way that manages to be suggestive. 'You know.'

'No, we're not.' A new piece of music, this one with drums that are machine-gun fast. Piper's teeth start to rattle.

'Hey, you want to come back to my place when we have finished this? I have better music. Do you like Norah Jones?'

Piper takes a swig from the bottle as a way of giving himself time to think. There is probably no professional reason why he shouldn't go back with her, not now he's off the SOCA working party. But he recalls what happened last time he fell into the sack with someone in London. It was the wrong person. If, of course, that is what she is suggesting. Besides, he hates Norah Jones or, more precisely, the wave of tasteful jazz-lite that broke in her wake.

'Nice idea, but . . . Look, I don't mean to sound—'

Fletcher jumps straight in. 'No? OK,' she says lightly, dismissing the idea. 'Well, pet, you'll just have to stand there and watch me get pissed then, and fuck the music.'

* * *

'I knew it wasn't her as soon as she walked in,' says Kolski, clacking something like castanets in his hand.

'You could have let her go,' says Hooper, pointing over his shoulder at the slowly cooling body on the bed.

'I wanted to find out what the fuck was going on.' He says it slow, as if he is talking to a retard. 'How'd you do?'

'Laptop, diaries, letters, address books. All in the car.' He tries to keep the impatience out of his voice. Kolski is in the post-kill zone, where every sensation comes thick and slow. Hooper must remember the guy has just tortured a woman to death. It alters your perception of things. 'What did you find out?'

Kolski lights a cigarette, taking his time. 'Her name is Timmy Braniza. She is a friend of our Target. So close, they swap dates, fill in. Like substitute teachers.'

'Jesus. DeCesare—'

'Don't worry about DeCesare. I talked to him. Turns out he wants the works. A total rewrite, as he put it. Fee to be agreed.' Kolski nods towards the body. 'We'd've gotten around to little Timmy sooner or later, I'm sure.'

'But Sasha?'

'She's in hospital, having something or other cauterised.'

'Which hospital?'

'Timmy claims she didn't know.'

'You believed her?'

He nods. If she'd known, she'd have told him. She'd have told him anything he wanted to know by the end. 'It was just an overnight. So maybe she didn't spread it around. Might not have wanted visitors.' Kolski stands and fetches himself a beer. 'Want one?' Hooper shakes his head. 'The name of the clinic or doctor or whatever, it's bound to be in some of that shit you picked up. Maybe on the laptop. Don't sweat it, Hoop.'

'How wide are we going to have to go? Did she know, for instance?'

'Little Timmy? She told me that Sasha never disclosed her "special" clients. If she did, it would've been to her, or one of her other close friends.'

'Who are?'

'Remember the pictures taken at that swank restaurant?'

Hooper nods.

'That's the High Class London Whores' Quilting Circle. Or the equivalent. We start there. OK, we better clean the room, but good.'

Hooper inclines his head towards Timmy and asks: 'What about the body?'

'Some client freaked out on her. Tried the gonzo sex number, went too far.'

'You think they'll go for that?'

Kolski holds up the castanets he has been playing with and clacks them together. It is a hinged set of false teeth. 'Not only that, after they check out her tits, they'll be looking for a thirty-year-old male with an overbite.'

Three-quarters of an hour later, the two men leave the carefully 'disinfected' room, all trace of them gone. They miss by just a few moments the call to Sasha's mobile phone. It chirps, a half-dozen times, before switching to message. It rings again five minutes later, and then a text message beeps through. All, of course, go unanswered.

Fifteen

The cell phone rings and Piper grabs it on the sixth, just before it switches to message. He sits up in bed, fumbling for the lamp. When it flicks on, it is so bright, his eyes water. 'Yes?' he barks irritably, looking at his watch. 5.30 a.m. He can hear birds singing lustily in the garden square out back.

'Vince?'

He snaps awake, the combination of a familiar voice and the tone – a mixture of fear and exhaustion, the adrenaline lending it a tremor – is the equivalent of a splash of cold water to his face. 'Celeste?'

'Yes. I'm sorry to call, I didn't know what else to do.'

'What's happened?' Already he is out of bed, grabbing clothes from the chest.

'I've just seen . . . I've just identified Timmy.'

The language makes his stomach contract. 'Identified? As in identified a body?'

She tries to speak, but it comes out as a sob.

'OK. Look, stay there. Are you at home?'

'No.'

'You want me to come over?'

'Can I come to you?'

'No. I'm not . . . yes. But I'm in a hotel. Is that OK?'

'I need to see you, Vince.' He gives her the address, says he'll meet her downstairs in fifteen minutes. He turns on the shower, and while it is coming up to temperature, he lays out his clothes on the bed. And the retrieved Sig-Sauer, just in case.

He takes her to the all-night coffee shop on Westbourne Grove, sharing it with the usual detritus of very early mornings – cabbies, cleaners, cops and clubbers. He lets her gulp her way through a large latte before trying to get any more information from her. She looks younger, her face is devoid of make-up, and is panda-eyed from crying. Her hands shake, and he knows she is just a careless word or two from collapsing again. She has already explained that Timmy has been found dead in a hotel bedroom, but has not gone into detail. Piper has to take it slow, to work around it.

He tells her about events since she dropped him off, his mugging at the apartment and the gun imprint.

'Are you scared?' she asks. 'About what happened to you?'

'Spooked. Not scared. Don't worry about it.'

'I do.'

'Let's just get a few things straight about Timmy. Forget about me and my problems, I'm a big boy. Tell me some things.'

'OK.'

'Who contacted you?'

She takes a card from her bag and passes over a standard Metropolitan Police contact card, with the name of a DI he does not recognise on it.

'Tell me how they found you – the police.'

She looks surprised. 'Don't you want to know about—'

'Later.' He didn't need to know exactly how Timmy died. Not yet.

'The other girls work with several agencies, all good. Usually Hobson, sometimes Exclusively London. Tonight's was Boardroom Executive. They have a policy of calling girls with new clients to check they are OK—'

'It was a new client?'

'Yes.'

'Did he request her specifically?'

'The police asked me that.'

'Well?'

195

'Probably. The agency should have a record of that. To check for repeats.'

A thought strikes him. 'How would he know who to ask for if he was new?'

Celeste sniffs back the tears. 'Could be a personal recommendation. Or from the net. There are internet sites reviewing almost every girl in London, often with star gradings.'

'Really? Like restaurant reviews?'

'Pretty much. The client then looks at the picture on the agency's site and . . .' The next part comes out in a rush, louder than she intends. 'The thing is, she was Sasha.'

'What?'

'The client would have been expecting Sasha. It was her booking. Timmy was standing in for her. Sasha had cleared it with the agency, and with a dark wig on Timmy, they look pretty alike. They'd done it before.'

'And they found you how?'

'I'm on her agency card as an emergency contact. Regular mother hen.' She takes a tissue from her bag and blows her nose.

'So the cops think . . .'

'It was a scenario that got out of hand. Bondage, strangulation . . .'

'Shit.'

'They told me that more than seventy prostitutes are known to have been murdered in the UK since 1990.'

'Really?' Piper doesn't say what he is thinking – that it's not that high, considering the risk. Adjusted for population, it's probably three times that rate in the US.

'But not at our end of the game.' Celeste reaches over and grabs his hand. 'Thing is, Timmy never did that. Nor Sasha. Not the asphyxiation thing. A little light bondage maybe, but tying up the client. I always warned them about letting themselves be bound. You do that, the power balance shifts. Rule one, always stay in control. No gonzo stuff.'

'How can you be sure that they never did it?'

'You can tell. That stuff leaves marks.' She touches her neck. 'Believe me. Look, I'm not defending what we do, but we are the elite. Eighty per cent of girls working in this town are foreign, the vast majority trafficked in some way. Most owe a fortune to their pimps. It's nasty, degrading sex slavery and it is there that people die. Not us.'

There's always a first time, thinks Piper. The sex industry has changed. The search for ever-more extreme excitement is insatiable, until vaginal intercourse is too boring, money shots too commonplace, several partners too few, until you reach the wilder shores of gonzo, with no rules, no condoms and no respect. When things shift in the movies, real life isn't far behind. 'OK, let's think about who did the hiring. The client would have paid how?'

'Credit card. The agency will have that. They would also have checked that payment went through before authorising Sasha to go ahead – I mean Timmy. The police will trace him through that, surely?'

'Yes.' Unless it's a cloned card, Piper thinks, but doesn't elaborate. Chances are it was genuine, the guy panicked, and now there is one scared perp running around London, wondering how to get out of this shit.

'Where's Sasha?'

'The agency said she was booked into a clinic for a procedure.'

'Really?'

Celeste shakes her head, guessing what his tone means. 'Not that kind. Not an abortion – I don't think so. Sasha's fixed up in that department.'

'Which clinic?'

'I have no idea.' Then a thought occurs to her. She looks at her watch. It is still too early to call him, but within the hour it will be OK. 'But I know a man who does.'

Kolski used to have a longer name. At least, his grand-father did. His father chopped a consonant and a vowel off it, as if it sounded less Polish that way. Grandpa Kowolski had worked in the Pittsburgh steel mills. Kolski still remembered him, hunched over his food, shovelling spoonfuls of *bigos* stew into his mouth, his arms roped with sinews and criss-crossed with scars of many colours.

He told his grandson tales of the mills, of bare-knuckle fights during lunch-breaks, of hideous accidents with molten metal or unguarded presses, torn-off limbs, agonising deaths and the camaraderie of tough blue-collar lives.

Kolski's father was ashamed of the old boy with his Slavic accent and steelworker's habit of hawking and spitting wherever he damned well pleased. He moved the family to a prosperous dorm town, where he could commute to his white-collar job. Kolski Junior, though, as soon as he was old enough, would go into the city to visit his grandfather in his apartment in the decaying downtown. The one-bedroom fourth-floor walk-up smelled of sweat, urine and stale food, but Kolski didn't care. He brought *krowki*, toffees, from Lucyna's and fed them to the old man while he told stories of fighting the Nazis, coming to America, then fighting all over again for his place in the society.

It was clear that he despised his soft-handed son. Not that he wanted him to be a steelworker like him, but he thought it disrespectful to deny his roots. Kolski didn't care about earning the admiration of his father, but he did of the old man. When he enrolled in the army, it caused a rift with his mom and dad, one that had never healed. His grandpa gave him five hundred bucks he'd saved up and advised him to specialise. He'd done that all right, he thought, as he shifted his weight to stop the suppressed pistol beneath his jacket digging into his ribs.

He is sitting in the Ford, in a street just off the King's Road, watching the area slowly come to life as a milk-float whirs by and paper boys struggle with their sacks. The houses are glaringly white and uniform, their railings black and glossy, the parking entirely Residents Only. It could be the backdrop for a Masterpiece Theatre production, all horse-drawn carriages and top hats. Except, that is, for the yellow alarm boxes on many of the houses, and the diamond-shaped metal shutters on the lower windows.

Celeste lives at number 14. He has already been in the house, but has decided against waiting inside. He'll have more control out here, can choose his moment to kill her more carefully.

The streets of London remind Piper of one of those pulpy horror movies, where the hero wakes up and everyone has gone. *Day of the Triffids*, maybe. Sure, there is some commuter traffic, but surprisingly little, and the drive across to Celeste's home in the Mini takes minutes.

On the way, he calls the number Celeste has given him. Four rings and a cultured voice answers. If he is annoyed at being disturbed so early, it doesn't show. 'Yes?'

'Professor Winslott?'

'Indeed. Who is this?'

'I am a friend of Celeste Young. She's here with me.' He holds the phone and Celeste says hello. 'Look, I'm sorry to call at this hour, but we need to know where one of your patients is.'

'Sasha Zee?'

'How'd you know?' asks Piper.

'Someone telephoned about fifteen minutes ago. Same request. Claimed to be a friend.'

'Did he give a name?'

'Bob Andrews.' Piper repeats it to Celeste who shakes her head.

'What did he sound like?'

'Like you.'

'Like me? How's that?'

'American.'

Piper takes a breath, trying to gather his thoughts. 'American. Did you tell him where she is?'

'No.'

'Will you tell me?'

'No.'

'Professor, listen carefully,' he begins, unsure how much to explain. They are nearly at Celeste's place now.

'I will tell Miss Young. Put her on.'

Celeste takes the handset and listens for a moment. 'No, I'm fine, Professor. It's Vincent Piper – the FBI man I told you about? Yes.' She listens again. 'The Portman. Fine. Thanks very much indeed.' She hands the phone back to Piper. 'The Portman Clinic. I know it. I'll get changed and—' She sees the look on his face. 'What?'

'Nothing. I mean, something. But I don't know what it is.' He dials Fletch and she picks up.

'Hello?'

'It's Vince.'

'Ah.' He feels her gather her strength. 'Vince, about the other night . . .'

'Forget it. It's not about that.' Celeste pulls to a halt a few doors down from her house, behind the milk-float.

'Vince, I was—'

'Drunk. Look, you may find this hard to believe, Fletch, but I've been there. And back.' He covers the mouthpiece. 'Go and grab your clothes,' he tells Celeste. 'Freshen up. I'll just be a minute.'

Celeste nods and gets out, walking past the milk-float and into the field of vision of Kolski.

'Look, Fletch, I need a heads-up on a case.' He looks at the Met contact card. 'A DI McAllister is running something on a dead prostitute called Timmy Braniza.'

'Friend of yours?'

'No. Yes. That's not important. What is important is that he needs to get a protection detail over to the Portman. Another girl might be in danger.'

'Why not tell him this?'

'Because I'm outside the loop. How long would it take them to establish I'm not a crank? And by that time it may be too late. You got a pen?' He tells her Sasha's details and all he both knows and supposes. It doesn't take long.

'I'll get right on it,' she says.

'OK, I'll call later. Tell this McAllister we'll be over to the Portman soon.'

'Will do. Vince, I'm still sorry—'

'Just do this, we're quits,' he says brusquely. 'It'll never be mentioned again. Ever.'

'Right,' she snaps back. The line goes dead.

Kolski climbs out of the car and is taking his first step towards the house, when the girl backs out of it into the street. Her body language suggests something has alarmed her. He slows the second step. As the milk-float grinds away, he sees the guy getting out of her car. She runs to him, and he listens, nodding. He glances around, and steps slightly ahead of her, shielding her. He is a pro.

Kolski is back in the car before he is spotted, and slides down in the seat, still watching the guy, who undoes his jacket and flicks it to make sure his gun can slide free. He is armed. Shit. The man takes up position in the doorway of the house while the girl goes back inside, and Kolski curses some more. He can't get out of the car without arousing suspicion. He wouldn't make it across the street. He hopes Hooper is having better luck.

'You sure?'

'Of course I'm sure. I'm good with smells.'

'I can't smell anything.' Piper is standing in the doorway while Celeste packs an overnight case. He isn't really waiting for any more confirmation than the bad feeling in his stomach, but her unease confirms it. He is getting her out of there.

'That's because you're not good with smells. I could smell cigarette smoke. Someone has been in here. Someone who smokes.'

'No pro would smoke.'

'I didn't say he was smoking. I said he smoked. I can even get residuals.'

Piper loosens the Sig in the holster. 'OK, we'll sort this out later. I'll put you in a safe house somewhere.'

'No way.'

'What?'

She appears in the hallway behind him, flushed and breathless. 'I'm not being kept in some Godforsaken safe house somewhere in, I don't know, Hackney.' Her nose wrinkles at the thought. 'I have a full diary.'

'Cancel it.'

'Vin—'

'Cancel it.' There is no room for argument in his hard tone. 'Trust me. I may not be real good with smells, but something stinks here. Cancel everything.'

'A safe house?'

'You done?' He points down at the bag at her feet.

'Yes. I've seen movies, Vince. Safe houses are called safe because they aren't very.'

'Bullshit.'

'You have one in mind?'

He shakes his head. 'The London Legat isn't too big on safe houses. Fletch might help.' He grabs the bag and steps out into the street, still not looking at her as he talks, scanning the road, waiting for something to catch his eye. A thought occurs to him. 'You got anywhere you can go that's water-tight? I mean, rock solid, not a friend's place in the city.'

'No.' Then a thought strikes her. 'Yes, there is a place in the Cotswolds. Still being renovated, but it's habitable.'

'How far?'

'Hour and a half away.'

'And you think that would be OK?'

'Nobody knows about it. Just my brother.'

'You should go. I'll come down, too. Check it out.'

'Roddy has the keys.' Celeste double-locks her front door and they retrace their steps to the Mini.

'Then let's go see him.'

'Vince.'

'What?'

'Has this got anything to do with you being . . . you know.' She points to her temple, miming a pistol with her fingers.

'I don't know,' he says, but he's lying. Piper is pretty sure it does, he just can't put the pieces together yet.

As they climb into the Mini, Piper slings the bag on the back seat, and Kolski turns the key and starts the engine of his Ford.

Sixteen

Natalie Des Barres scrapes out the last of the expired logs from the fireplace of her home. She uses a dustpan and brush to sweep the grate clean, carefully putting the fine ash into a black bin liner. Satisfied, she turns and fetches the pile of paper and notebooks to her left. The loose sheets she crumples and uses to form a base. She tears handfuls of pages from the journals, balling those as well, until she has an irregular paper pyramid. Origami, she thinks, was never her forte.

The telephone rings and she lets it click through. Both the landline and the mobile have been squawking at her, but she has ignored them. She has come to a decision and, having made it, is looking only forward.

Natalie Des Barres has to die. And from her body will rise Salma Najimy, the name she was given at birth. She uses a box of matches to light the lower level of paper, and it browns and then catches, the flames pale yellow and weak. She strikes another match and touches four other points. Smoke rolls up the chimney. I am burning the story of this life, she tells herself, as the flames finally catch and little rafts of charred writing swirl upwards.

She moves across to the desk and organises the letters she has spent most of the night writing. Apologies to friends, instructions to banks, a to-do list for Kathy, her cleaner and confidante, who has somehow become her consigliere. She will miss her, the voice like balm, her calm commonsense a lifeline so many times.

She feels a hot tear roll down her cheek and gather at the corner of her mouth, a tiny salty puddle that she licks. She picks up the picture of her son, and smiles back at him, at that row of tombstone teeth, the impossibly beautiful face, so like his father, long dead, shot on a lonely mountain road while trying to negotiate a hostage release back in the days of madness.

Leaving all this behind, this so-called life, to see him, be with him for the rest of her life? Why the doubt? It is a good bargain.

She returns to the fireplace and pokes the thickest pieces, which are like large blackened crêpes, crushing them to tiny flecks. No going back.

Everything about what she did to whom, all those priceless contacts, all gone. She could have passed them on, of course, but that would have left her with some connection. It would be like a golden thread, an umbilical cord anchoring her to London, the way some people believe your astral spirit is attached to your earthly body.

Can you begin again at forty? Forty-three, she reminds herself. Can she ever really lose the stains on her soul, the memory of what she has done this past decade, first in Beirut, then in Paris and finally, as a piece of exotica, in London? Yes, she thinks. Caring for her son and her mother, that will cleanse her, that will be her penance.

She moves through to the bedroom and picks up her small suitcase. The luxurious gowns, the smart suits, the frilly underwear, they have no place in her new life. They would mark her out as what she has been. She is erasing all that, simplifying, downsizing and downsexing. And she is looking forward to it.

She places the case in the hallway and has one last look around, waiting for the wrench of parting to hit her, but there is nothing. She cocks her head to one side, as if trying to catch a faint sound, carefully examining her own emotions, but there is just a cool acceptance inside. The feeling that this is right.

She will catch a cab at the rank on the corner of

the road. Kathy will sell her car, keep a percentage of the fee, and forward the money to her account in Paris, the one that has been fattening like a goose all these years. Well, like a capon at least. There is enough there to keep her comfortable for a long time, even if she doesn't make it work for her. And she fully intends to do that.

Forty-three, and I am finally ready for my life to begin. Again.

She checks herself in the mirror and removes a number of small smudges, caused by ash from the fireplace. She makes sure that the fire is dead by dousing it with water from a vase.

The determination making her back ramrod straight, she grabs the suitcase and her keys and marches to the front door. She pauses to set the alarm and pulls open the door to the street.

The doorway fills with an unfamiliar body and she takes a step back. Hooper's hand clamps over her mouth, and the sliver of a blade slides in between the vertebrae of her neck as the door slams shut behind him.

There is traffic now, and Piper and Celeste make slower progress across town than earlier. Roddy has moved into a converted factory out near Bow, a little oasis of luxury (porter, gym, solarium, secure parking) in a sea of urban decay. It means they will have to drive right through the centre of London. And pay the congestion charge.

'Listen, it might be quicker to cross the river,' says Celeste. 'Go over Battersea Bridge, through Vauxhall—'

'Whatever you say. It's your fucked-up city.'

She shoots him a glance and turns south, at the same time pressing the activation button for the Bluetooth system. 'Natalie,' she says clearly.

The phone dials, and she hears it ringing and the message cut in again.

'Natalie's probably asleep,' she says.

'You think so?'

'I don't know what to think,' admits Celeste. 'Is your ladyfriend getting Sasha looked after?'

'I hope so. But she's not "my ladyfriend", whatever that means.'

'Just checking.'

'You OK? Scared?'

'A bit,' she says quietly. 'Maybe I was imagining that smell.'

Piper doesn't reply.

'I said maybe—'

Piper cuts her short. 'And maybe you weren't. There's a blue Ford behind us. There was one parked in your street. No, don't turn around. Just look in the mirror.'

Celeste guns the engine, the supercharger whines, and she makes to drop a gear. Piper grabs her wrist. 'Don't try and outrun him.'

'What then?'

'Let me think.'

They cross the bridge, the traffic moving marginally quicker heading south. The day has dawned bright, the sky no longer the lumpy grey it has been, but a hard steel blue, etched with a white weave of intersecting vapour trails.

'There's a Jeep pulled in between us,' says Celeste.

Piper twists in his seat. A woman and kids. Probably OK. Just in case, he says: 'There may be more than one.'

'You sure it's—'

'No. You sure there was someone in your house?'

'Yes.' She presses the dial button again. 'Natalie.' Again, the machine.

'We could be overcookin' it,' he suggests.

'What, both our places turned over?'

'Yours wasn't turned over,' he corrects.

'Violated, then,' she says softly.

They turn left, the Jeep carries straight on. The Ford is back with them, keeping its distance. 'Make a right.'

'I can't at these lights.'

'Whenever you can.'

He eases the gun out and places it across his knees. Celeste flashes him a concerned look. 'Vince . . .'

'He's turned with you?'

'Yes.'

'Make a left.'

'It's an environmental area. I can't for about four streets.'

'OK. As soon as you do, I want you to mount the sidewalk.'

'What?'

'Turn the car so it is across the sidewalk, on the left, with me nearest the car following us. You roll out your side, you got a whole car between him and you. Not much of one, but it's something.'

'No.'

'What do you mean, no?'

'I'm not putting you in the line of fire.'

'I'm supposed to be in the line of fire,' Piper insists.

'That's the Secret Service.' He flashes her a quizzical look. 'I told you: I see movies. I go to the Ambassador's parties.'

'Yeah. Well, as far as you are concerned, I'm in the line of fire. We're going to have to do something.'

Something in his voice makes her say: 'Shit.'

'What?'

'I'm never going to let you in one of my cars ever again.' She tries to smile, but it comes out all wrong. Now she is scared.

'Left here?' he says.

She indicates the school sign on the corner. 'Best not.'

'Right. Open up a gap.'

She puts her foot down and the Mini pulls away from the Ford.

'Next left. You can do this?'

There is only the slightest waver in her voice as she assures him: 'I can do this.'

The tyres screech as she yanks at the wheel; the Mini's body starts to pitch, but then steadies, and the tiny car flies round like it is stuck in tramlines.

'Clear!' Piper shouts, having checked for pedestrians, and his head hits the roof lining as the Mini bounces over the kerbstone. He yanks at the door handle twice and kicks it open, unfolding out of the vehicle in one smooth movement.

The Ford has turned after them and Piper, crouching, fires two shots into each front tyre, their popping louder than the weapon's discharge, and four into the engine, all the time keeping his eyes on the driver, waiting for the move that will force a kill.

Sparks fly as the tyres shred off and the hubs catch

the road, and the car slews to an ungainly halt. He can still see hands on the wheel, hanging on for dear life. Good.

Piper sprints around to the driver's side and pulls the door open.

'FBI!' he has time to shout before Mark Curtiss, forty-one, a sales agent for a domestic heating company, vomits all over his shoes.

Seventeen

The US Ambassador to the Court of St James leans over and whispers in the ear of his wife, 'That ceiling dates, apparently, from 1451.'

She looks up at the intricate panelling, and heraldic coats-of-arms at the centre of each one, thirty feet above her head. 'Devil to clean, Jack.'

'I wouldn't worry about it. We don't have to do the dishes either.'

They are on the top table of a grand banqueting hall in the heart of the City. Around them, liveried footmen are serving water and wine, while Sandler wonders how rude it would be to leave the soggy green vegetables, which are spoiling an otherwise decent meal. The occasion is the Marbury Address, a traditional lunch dating back to 1888 held twice a year by a conglomerate of London bankers. At each of the biannual events, a guest speaker talks on a theme of his choosing. Today, Sandler has chosen to talk on twin themes: holidays and money.

He is pleased to see the Chancellor of the Exchequer in the audience, with an uncharacteristic smile on his face, enjoying a joke with the tall, pale-faced man next to him, who is head of one of the City's traditional merchant banks. Discreet, anonymous, with impeccable manners, the man is a reflection of his own establishment. Not above turning a profit, but it would be too vulgar to be seen to put too much effort into it.

He scans the room, picking out a few fellow Ambassadors, the odd junior minister, and a sea of unfamiliar faces. At the back of the hall is Brewster, his good and faithful servant, the curly wire of the earpiece just visible. Every few minutes he speaks into his cuff, asking for an update on the security situation.

'My Lords, Ladies and Gentlemen . . .'

He realises he is about to be introduced by the man dressed in some ridiculously florid and frilly outfit, and misses much of what is said by way of introduction as he makes sure he has his glasses and his notes.

'Good luck, Jack,' says his wife, patting his arm.

He moves to the lectern, easing the collar of his starched shirt as he does so. He surveys the room.

'My Lords, Ladies and Gentlemen, Mr Chairman, Master of the Guild. I would like to extend my thanks to the Marbury Committee for choosing me, a damned colonial, as the speaker this year.' A ripple of laughter. 'I have checked the records, and in the last hundred years, there have been only two other US nationals asked to address this illustrious gathering. So I guess you haven't forgiven us yet.

'At least I can say we have eaten well. Unlike Walter Hines Page, one of my predecessors, who famously said of British cuisine: "They only have three vegetables, and two of them are cabbage".' More substantial laughter now. 'Well, I have two suggestions which I would like to explore today, neither of them are cabbage, and neither of them can be claimed as my very own. The first is about holidays. Now, I know most of you think you have too many, and I agree that locking up the country and throwing away the key for two weeks over Christmas is a little crazy, but I would like to suggest you add one more. Just don't call it a *Bank* Holiday. Everyone thinks you bankers are riding the gravy train as it is.'

He pauses to take a sip of water. 'What you guys need is a Thanksgiving.' A pause while they take this in. 'Think about it. All those holidays, most of them meaningless. May Day? Well, at one time all that skipping around had a context, but most of us would blush if we had to explain the reality of it to our children these days. Then the Russians took it over, but that hasn't been the same since the missiles got smaller in Red Square. August Bank Holiday? What does that commemorate? Oh, I know, probably the burning of the stubble or some such forgotten rural event, but, again, for most people there is no context. What you need is a day to give thanks. Now my wife, who loves this country, suggested that the British are far too cynical to fall for that. Give thanks for what? I'll come to that in a moment. Just a word of preliminary advice: don't have it in November. Two turkeys inside two months is too much.'

There is a small smattering of applause. The wine has helped smooth his reception, of course. This is the easy part. It is the monetary section that might raise hackles among the free marketeers. He knows he has a reputation as a pro-market non-interventionist, but he is about to put a state-controlled cat among the laissez-faire pigeons. He takes one more gulp of water, and ploughs on, surfing the goodwill while it lasts.

Eighteen

'They did *what*?' Colonel Wallace has to stop himself yelling down the line to DeCesare.

'The close-ups didn't come out quite right,' DeCesare repeats. 'In fact, it was the wrong actress.'

The Colonel begins to pace his living room, probably the only one in town totally devoid of any seasonal decorations. Christmas will not be celebrated here. 'Great. And what do you think the investors are going to say about that?' Wallace walks to the sliding patio doors and looks out over a lawn groaning under a thick layer of snow which was dumped last night. An animal's footprints are patterned across the surface, and it has excavated a hole in the centre. It looks like the work of a fox.

'Well, the investors did ask for back-up shots. Only the running order is screwed.'

'So the crew are still on the shoot? You haven't fired them?'

'Not till they make amends,' says DeCesare guardedly.

'Can they make amends?' The Colonel suspects that with the British police taking notice, things will have become more difficult.

'We're doing new footage as we speak.'

Wallace slumps down in an armchair and sighs. 'Make sure they do it fast.'

'Yes, sir.'

'Damn it, DeCesare—'

'I know. Leave it with me.'

Wallace clicks off the handset. Now he has to decide whether to call Charles Pearl in Santa Barbara and tell him there has been a hitch in the dailies. He laughs to himself. The dailies. The rushes. The close-ups. The film metaphors irritated him at first, but now he even finds himself thinking in them, as if he is Darryl F. Zanuck.

No, he won't tell his Executive Producer on the West Coast that there is a sequencing error. It will all come out in the final edit. In Wallace's experience, it is always better to deliver bad news with a sweetener of good. And DeCesare had better deliver something more positive soon.

He opens the sliding door to let some cold air

into the house, which always tends towards the stifling. Margaret knew how to set the controls just right. Wallace, on the other hand, always seems to have the place five degrees too hot or too cold, no matter how much he plays with the thermostat and boiler. Fresh flakes of snow are falling, see-sawing down to the ground. Already the fox's tracks are filling in. He hopes they can cover their tracks as easily.

He walks across the room, picks up the handset and dials the London number in order to tell his line producer that they might need to replace the director on this movie, as well as the two leads.

'I don't know what happened to you, Vince. You were a good agent once.' Stanley Roth runs a hand through his thinning hair, a sure sign of stress.

'I still am.'

Roth picks up the report on his desk and lets it drop with a thump. 'Yeah? Good agents do not try to shoot heating salesmen.'

'I was being tailed.'

Saliva spits out over the desk as Roth almost yells: 'By some poor sap who thought you'd found a new rat run.'

Piper leans back in the chair and spreads his arms. 'Up to a certain point, I am sure I was being tailed by a blue Ford. He picked me up in Chelsea. At some point, maybe, this guy slotted in . . .'

'And you didn't notice?'

'No.'

'A good agent?' he sneers.

'Yes.'

'You know, if this had happened in the States, Mr Curtiss would be suing us for the farm, the ranch next door and the mountains over yonder. As it is, he's happy with a brand new car on the US government. A BMW he's insisting on.'

'Dock my pay.'

'A six series.'

'Ah.'

'Right – way above your pay grade. Look, Vince, I'm sorry—'

'Hold on. I need to know what's happening with the girl in the hospital.'

Roth sighs. 'She's got a police guard. Very reluctantly.'

'And Celeste?'

He shakes his head. 'She smelled *smoke*?'

'Look, Natalie is also missing.'

'We had someone go round. Natalie Des Barres has gone back to Lebanon. She wrapped up her affairs. Left notes, instructions, money.'

'You checked the flights?' Piper asks.

'She has gone back.'

'You didn't check whether she actually boarded, did you?'

'Vince, this is insane. Ever since you met that woman—'

Piper stands up. 'Nope, don't pull that one on me. Ever since I met her *what* exactly?'

Roth smiles at his agitation. He knows he has hit home. 'Ever since you met that woman your career has gone down the tube. Look, I've seen her, she's cute, but you feel like you have to play Sir Lancelot every time she's around. It clouds your judgement. *She* clouds your judgement.' From his drawer he pulls out a blue document. 'Ticket back to Washington. One way.'

'Why would someone want to kill four friends?'

'There you go again. The Brits are convinced that the first girl wasn't murdered. The line is, it was an accidental killing during extreme sex games. She had a butt plug up her ass, for God's sake.'

'That proves nothing.'

'Does where I come from.'

'If four—'

'How'd you get four?' Roth snaps.

'I have three for sure. Timmy actually dead, Celeste tailed, Natalie missing, Sasha a target . . .'

'You have *one*, Vince. That's all. One.' The door opens and Roth's assistant enters with a coffee pot on a tray. She pours them one cup each, studiously avoiding Piper's eyes the whole time. Word must be out that whatever he has is catching.

'Thanks,' Vince says, and gets a nod in reply. He takes a sip. 'Look, just indulge me for a moment.'

'I'm doing nothing but indulging you,' replies Roth.

'We know what all four of them do for a living. What if this is to do with a client?'

'What, someone who didn't get his rocks off? Couldn't get a refund?'

'I don't know, Stan. I'm asking you to think about it. Get a list of all their customers, cross-check it.'

'Isn't there some kind of whore-client confidentiality?'

Piper doesn't rise to this. 'I can get Celeste's.'

'Where is she?'

'In the country.'

'You haven't got time for this.' Roth points at the American Airlines ticket before him. 'You gotta go.'

'You could check with the dead girl's agency, question Sasha.'

'That's the British police's job. Not ours. None of them are US citizens.'

'I am.'

'More's the pity.' Roth pushes the flight coupon across the table. 'Be on the flight, Vince.'

'You know the Brits won't do squat. Cops are the same the whole world over. They have a body, a motive, no killer yet, but hey, two out of three ain't bad.'

'On your way out turn your weapon in to the Gun Cage.'

'You're not going to do this for me?'

'I'll send someone along to see the girl in hospital. You get a list of clients from your girlfriend.' He raises his hand before Piper can object. 'Friend. Over the phone. I'll look it over.'

'And check Natalie got on her flight?'

Roth nods, his lips pursed. The words come through clenched teeth. 'OK, if it'll shut you up and put you on the plane.'

Piper finishes his coffee. 'Thanks.'

'It's nothing, Vince.'

'I hope not.'

'She smelled *smoke*.'

'I was tailed.'

'Don't forget to turn your gun in.' Roth busies himself with paperwork to show the meeting is over, and Piper leaves.

As he is closing the door, he hears a parting shot. 'Don't make me send Brewster and the Secret Service boys to carry you onto that plane, Vince.'

John Ditko smiles when he sees Piper coming down the corridor towards his Gun Cage. 'Ah, nice to see a satisfied customer. You are satisfied?'

'Very much.'

Ditko slides several sheets of paper over towards him beneath the wire mesh. 'Lots of paperwork when you return a fired weapon.'

'I've done all the paperwork. In triplicate.'

'That's the Bureau's DWP, the Discharged Weapon Protocol. This is mine. You can drop it off later.'

Piper takes the documentation and puts it in his jacket pocket. 'OK.'

'So. You turning it in?'

'No.'

'Once a weapon has been fired, I like to—'

'I cleaned it. It's fine. I just need some more ammo.'

'This is the second time you fired it.'

'And the second time I cleaned it. It's a gun, John. It's what they were designed for – firing. The ammo, please?'

Ditko hesitates then ducks beneath the counter, coming up with a box of 9mm shells. 'OK. Sign here.'

Piper does so.

'And here. Look, if you fire it again . . .'

But Piper has already taken the cartridges and is leaving. He raises the box over his shoulder in farewell and says: 'Don't worry. I won't be shooting anyone else in a hurry.'

He is wrong, of course.

Nineteen

Stanley Roth hates asking for outside help, but his entire team is investigating a credible threat to target a US trade delegation due to arrive in London in three days. He has nobody to spare for a wild-goose chase.

What's the point of questioning the girl in hospital, who is due out that morning anyway? No point. And Piper's random and unfocused surmises? She smelled *smoke*, for Christ's sake.

No matter how much the man protests otherwise, he knows Piper's brains have sunk into his balls as far as that woman is concerned. Piper is still a good agent. Roth admired his taking on the chopper, even if it was misguided. But shooting up a British citizen's car in broad daylight?

But what if he was tailed? What if he is right? Roth feels the instinct to cover his ass twitching. But he still can't spare any manpower. So, if he wants something done, he'll have to ask Brewster of the Secret Service for the loan of someone. Yet Brewster's boys are busy double-checking security for the delegates. That would leave AGA – Another Government Agency, as the CIA likes to be referred to. He'd rather drive hot needles through his eyes than ask Hansen, the station head, for assistance. He is sure Hansen feels the same.

Still, there is one thing he can do with minimum effort. He presses the intercom to his assistant. 'Mary?'

'Sir?'

'Can you contact the Metropolitan policeman who went round to the house in Holland Park this morning? It's logged on the action file. I just want to know what flight the woman was booked on. Then call the airline's communications office and check she boarded.'

'Yes, sir.'

'Thanks. Oh wait, before you do that . . .'

'More coffee?'

'Right.'

'Coming up.'

'The girl has a police guard in her room,' says Hooper. 'And I checked the sightlines from all the buildings. I can't paint her – not without being seen.'

The bare brick wall of the Clerkenwell loft has been covered in photographs and sheets of names, as if this were a police incident room. Hooper is pacing up and down, while a grim-faced DeCesare looks on from the sofa. Kolski is leaning on the steel counter that separates the living area from the kitchen, drinking a can of soda.

Hooper takes a marker pen and puts an X through two of the women photographed at the Wolseley.

'What about the Young woman?' asks DeCesare.

Hooper taps her face. 'She's got a friend. A pro, by the look of it. I followed him, but I think he made me. I pulled out.'

'I know who he is,' says DeCesare.

'Yeah?'

'Leave him to me.'

'OK. But we don't know where she is.'

DeCesare examines the people around the table once more. 'The man in the photograph?' he says, although he knows the answer.

'Is Roddy Young, her brother – the one who the e-mail blogs were sent to.' He indicates Sasha's laptop, which they have stripped of all information. 'There was a slight reference to our man, but no name. I don't think Roddy knows.'

'He'll know one thing, though.'

'Where his sister is,' says Kolski as he takes a final hit of soda. 'Yeah, we figured that. We have both his home and office addresses.'

'You'll pick him up,' says DeCesare, and it isn't a question.

'Yeah,' says Hooper. 'If he knows, he'll tell us.'

'Use Billing.'

'Why?'

'He has this little arrangement.'

'Who with?' asks Kolski.

DeCesare cracks an unpleasant smile. 'London Underground.'

The Evenlode Valley is categorised, according to Piper's guidebook, as an 'area of outstanding natural beauty', although why people have to be told this rather than using their own eyes, he can't be sure. Some way north of the M40, it is reached by a series of single-track lanes that criss-cross it, and it certainly deserves its status. There are a few hamlets of picture-book thatched cottages, undulating hills dusted with a persistent frost, the remnants of ancient woodlands, some very chilly-looking sheep, a lazily curving river, and the occasional farmhouse.

After the shooting fiasco, Celeste picked up the keys from Roddy and went on ahead to the country. Piper had to stay to make his excuses to Roth. He looks at the instructions he took down from Celeste, checks the large oak tree just ahead and makes a left, down an even narrower lane, the frozen tractor ruts in the mud bouncing his hired car on its soggy suspension. He wishes he'd opted for an SUV.

It is the day after he saw Roth, the day before he is due to fly back. He has spent it going over Celeste's house, looking for signs of entry that could corroborate her olfactory suspicions. He borrowed a Scene of Crime expert from Fletch, who drew a blank.

He checks his mirror. The Audi TT is still with him, also struggling with the ruts. It is Sasha, who discharged herself from hospital into his unofficial protection, and who is going to tear off her exhaust if she isn't careful not to mention what she might be doing to her insides. He slows down, forcing her to do the same.

Again, through the good graces of Fletcher, he had her delivered from hospital direct to his care with police escort. Fletch, too, thinks he is crazed, and he assumes that bank of favours is now empty. God knows what it'll take before it is in credit once more.

Roth hasn't come after him yet. He will, though. But Piper can't go back to the US until he is sure Celeste is not in danger. He owes her that and much more. Is that all it is? he asks himself.

No. Of course not.

The stable block is a long, low building of local yellow-ish stone with a slate roof capped with a squat clock tower, the dial missing its minute hand. The horses are long gone, and the middle section has been renovated into a dwelling. Three other units, in various stages of construction, share the shell of the building.

Piper parks the Vauxhall next to Celeste's Mini, and waits while Sasha pulls in alongside him before getting out. She exits the Audi and stretches. She looks pale and drawn; the horror of what happened to Timmy – what could easily have happened to her but for a rogue cervix – is etched across her face.

A flash of pain crosses her face, and she holds her stomach. 'I hope this is worth it.'

'Me, too,' he says. 'But they weren't going to give you a tame cop for life.'

'One of them was quite sweet. I wouldn't have minded keeping him,' she says, but the come-back is mechanical. There is little levity in her voice right now. Then: 'You think we'll be here all over Christmas?'

He shrugs. 'I'm sure we can rustle up a turkey if you are.'

The door opens and out steps Celeste, dressed in Earl jeans, a thick cable-knit sweater and Hunter Wellingtons. 'Hello, everyone. You're just in time for tea and scones.'

'Look at you,' says Sasha, who still has on an outfit, and shoes, more suited to a lunch at Harvey Nichols. 'Quite the country girl.'

'Everything OK?' Piper enquires.

'Yes,' replies Celeste, 'except I'd forgotten you can't get a mobile signal out here.'

'You got a landline?'

She points to the wires stretching from one corner of the building. There is a medium-gauge phone wire and two thick rubberised ones, which he guesses is the electricity.

'You'll live,' he says.

'And you don't mind, do you?' Celeste knows that Piper can't even switch his mobile on here, because Roth could use it to track him.

'What if someone wants to get hold of me?' she asks next.

Piper opens the boot of the car. 'You are here because someone might want to get hold of you. I have a present from Roddy.' He had been to see him to pick up a second set of keys, just in case.

'What is it?' Celeste asks.

He lifts the canvas bag out and puts it across his shoulder. 'A Benelli over-under.'

'A what?'

'Remember he went through a skeet-shooting phase?'

'Clay pigeons, yes.'

'I've brought his shotgun for you. Just a precaution.'

The two women exchange glances and Celeste

shudders at the reminder that this isn't just a jolly jape in the sticks. 'Come in,' she says glumly. 'I'll show you your rooms.'

She hesitates and Piper senses that her attention is elsewhere. He turns. There is a white cat sitting on the wall, almost lost in the snow, only its blue eyes and the dirty tips of its fur showing clearly. 'Shoo,' says Celeste. 'Go away.' The cat merely blinks, slowly, with a hint of disdain about it. 'It's been hanging around all day. I tried to bring him inside, but he just spat at me. Gives me the creeps.'

'It can't hear you,' Sasha says.

'Why not?'

'White fur, blue eyes. Nearly always stone deaf.'

'Great.'

'Can we get in, please?' says Piper. 'Just in case it can hear.'

The intercom buzzes. Roth presses the switch and Mary says: 'Sir, Agent Brewster to see you.'

Roth stops writing and reaches over. 'OK, send him in.'

Brewster enters and Roth rises from his desk. 'Lee. Thanks for coming in.'

'My pleasure,' he says in a tone that suggests there is no such thing in his life. He stands the way all Secret Service men do, legs apart, hands clasped lightly in front of him at crotch level. He also has that expression the Treasury stamp on their officers; the neutral almost-a-frown is designed to convey the message that this is a serious business. Whatever it might be.

'How's things on the third floor?'

'You know Jack Sandler.'

Roth thinks he detects a note of weariness, but it is likely that is because the Ambassador won't lock himself into a steel box and stay there for the duration. The Secret Service are at their happiest when that happens. 'What's he done now?'

'Jogging to work for one.'

Roth realises how difficult it is to set up a secure Zone around a jogger without closing streets and deploying SWAT. And that is hardly likely to happen. 'In December?'

'Which means we have to take turns jogging with him. Then, over the weekend, he is taking part in an excavation in Norfolk of a B-17 believed crashed in the sea. The site is uncovered at low tide.'

'My,' Roth says with an unsympathetic grin. 'You are going to get muddy. And cold.'

'We are that.' Brewster neglects to add that he hopes to detail someone else for this particular bone-chiller. He has a home in the US to go to.

'And for the holidays?'

'He's going Stateside, Christmas Eve. What can the Secret Service do for you, Stanley?'

'Tell your guys to be aware that Vincent Piper will be posted to fugitive status as of midnight tonight. If they see him or come into contact—'

'Whoa. What's he done now?'

Roth takes off his reading glasses and rubs his eyes. 'Apart from shooting up harmless commuters, you mean?'

'I heard about that.' Brewster thinks back to the day he blew off a flower-guy's kneecap. 'I heard it was an honest mistake.'

'I didn't know you cared.'

Brewster almost cracks a smile. 'I don't. Not that much. Just don't like to see . . .'

Roth nods. 'One of our own get posted. I know. Thing is, he should be catching an American Airlines flight to the US tomorrow but we can't find him.'

'Cell-phone trace?'

'It's off.'

Brewster considers this. 'Last known sighting?'

'He hired a car at Avis, using his credit card. He took three hundred pounds out of his account, so we guess he is using cash right now.'

'What's he up to?'

'Celeste Young,' Roth says simply.

'Oh shit. You watching her?'

'Disappeared, too. Somewhere in the country.'

'So they are together?' Brewster surmises.

'Best guess. He thinks there are people trying to kill her.'

'Are there?'

Roth tells Brewster the story so far.

'Circumstantial,' he says when Roth has finished.

'Yes, it is.'

The intercom buzzes again. 'Sir.'

'Yes?' Roth enquires.

'A DCI Jacqueline Fletcher is on line two.'

'Thanks.' He looks at Brewster. 'I should take this. Stay. Hello, Chief Inspector, Stanley here.'

'Hello, Agent Roth,' says Fletch. 'I have something that might interest you. You are aware that Natalie Des Barres never caught her British Airways flight to the Lebanon?'

'I am. I passed the information along.'

'I borrowed a forensic officer for an hour. A Scene of Crime specialist.'

'You're a good friend,' he says, unable to keep the tetchiness out of his voice. It was because of his good friends that Piper could get away with murder. Well, not that, not yet, but you never knew with him.

'I did it because I believed he might have something.'

'And?'

'There are the remains of a spray of blood up one wall, very fine. Most of it seemed to have been cleaned. They missed a couple of specks high on the paintwork.'

'Careless. We sure this isn't a nose bleed?'

'Well, it's not like any nose bleed you or I have ever had. Judging by its height from the ground, it would have to have been Olympic standard.'

'So what's happening?'

'We are opening a Missing Persons case on her. For the moment.'

'Meaning?'

'It might progress to murder once a full SOC team go in.'

'Keep me informed.'

'It's not going to be my case. I start a SOCA—'

Roth interrupts. He doesn't care about the SOCA review. 'Maybe not. But you'll take an interest.'

Fletcher pauses before she admits: 'I'll be copied in.'

'Like I said, keep me informed.'

Roth puts the phone down. Brewster hasn't moved from his 'alert' position. His only question comes in the form of a raised eyebrow.

'Piper's off the want-list,' Roth growls. 'Let him run.'

'Why?'

'It just got more than circumstantial.'

Twenty

Roddy slowly emerges into consciousness with a strange smell in his nostrils. It is a mixture of steel, asbestos and decay. A warm breath occasionally caresses him, a familiar sensation that he can't place. There is a pain in his back. He is lying on something, and it is digging in. He opens his eyes, but it is dark.

He attempts to move his arms, but they are tightly bound. His legs, too. He tries to remember how he got here, but his short-term memory appears to have been erased. The Colony Club, Mayfair, that is his last memory. He'd been drinking. Trying to forget. Well, that worked, at least. No, wait, he can recall walking down Shepherd's Market, heading for . . . ? No, it's gone.

He smacks his lips. When he swallows, there is a clicking sound. His throat is very dry, as if he hasn't drunk any fluid for days. Has he been drugged? He grunts as he tries to twist free.

The beam of light and the water hit him simultaneously. The former makes him screw his eyes shut and turn his head, the latter is like a thousand knives stabbing at his face, and it drives the breath from his body.

He spits out a mouthful of the vile-tasting liquid and says: 'Jesus. What the fuck is happening?'

The flashlight beam flicks away from his face, and through distorted watery vision he can see some shadows moving about, in front but somehow above him. He hardly has to tip his head up to see them. He counts three, but there could be more.

'Morning, Mr Young,' says one of them. The voice is London, not Cockney exactly, but Essex estuarine. He can see he is a big man, wide, although a lot of the bulk is an overcoat. The face looks ghostly, full of dark hollows in the torch beam. 'Comfortable?'

'No, I am fucking well not.'

The second batch of water burns his face, and again he shakes his head to throw it off. He is shivering now, the stale breeze he could feel against his face cooling him down rapidly.

'What are you doing?' he splutters.

'Conductivity.'

The torch picks out a film poster, and curved tiled

walls. He realises where he knows the foetid warm air and the smell from, and he feels his bowels loosen. He has to squeeze his sphincter tight. Roddy is as much and as little a coward as the next man. But the next man isn't tied across the live rail of a London Underground Tube station.

It is the time of two lights, the hour just before dawn when some people consider the world to be full of demons. Piper thinks there is never a time when it isn't full of monsters. Just that at this hour, with your body clock wound down, you tend to believe in them more. He is sitting in the living area of the cottage, a fresh cup of coffee in his hand, watching the sky lighten imperceptibly. Soon, the stars will begin to fade, and the demons will be driven away by the rising sun. If only.

He is thinking about his father, about the dream that has woken him. His dad had been young in this vision, muscular and fit in his bowling shirt and chinos. They were on the Blue Ridge Parkway, driving to one of the lodges for lunch and a walk in the woods. Just the two of them. His father had asked what he wanted to be when he grew up. 'A Federal Officer, just like you,' he replied. 'FBI.'

His father had shaken his head, as if to say, 'You can never be like me.' 'I can,' he had insisted. His dad began to laugh, louder and louder, until he was banging the steering-wheel hysterically, the car veering all over the road. That's when he had woken up.

The scene had never happened, to his recollection. They'd been to the Parkway, many times, but his dad was a little older then – he appeared to be around twenty-one or -two in the dream – and he had never asked Vince what he wanted to be when he grew up. Piper liked to think his dad knew all along where he would end up.

But would his father be disappointed in him? After all, that was what the dream was about. Yes, for sure, was the answer. His dad might have bent the rules a few times, but always according to what was acceptable at the time. Going renegade was never acceptable. He knew that Roth would be forced to post him for not catching the flight, that his details would be circulated to all arms of the security services, and to the British APPLE office. His old outfit would be hunting him soon. It wasn't a good feeling.

The creak of an ancient floorboard makes him turn, his hand reaching for the shotgun that is propped beneath the window as he does so. The door swings open and Celeste stands there, cinching a dressing-gown around her waist, backlit by a nightlight on the hall table.

'Can't sleep?' she asks quietly.

He lets the shotgun rest back against the wall, wondering if she has noticed it. 'No. You?'

'The pipes clank in my bedroom when you run the taps down here.'

'Sorry.'

She finishes tying the cord and reaches for the light switch. 'Don't do that,' he says.

'Why not?'

'Please. And close the door behind you.'

'OK. You think—?'

'I think I'm being paranoid, but indulge me. Want a coffee?'

'Please.' He busies himself in the tiny kitchen, working from the downlighter in the cooker hood. There is only a jar of instant granules, so he just has to re-boil the kettle. 'Sugar?'

'No. And black, please.'

When he returns, she has taken his place at the window. She accepts the coffee. 'Thanks. Beautiful, isn't it?'

'Move back a little, will you?'

'You think someone is out there?'

'Probably not,' he says. 'But you make a tempting target.'

'Good God.' She shifts further into the room. He can see a patch of deep indigo against the black in the east. A songthrush begins to sing just above the window, hesitantly at first, then finding full throat. Way across the valley on a hillside he sees a yellowish light flick on in a farmhouse building. They aren't the only ones up bright and early.

'Are you going to get into trouble?' Celeste asks.

'That depends.'

'On what?'

He smiles to himself in the half-light. 'Whether you really did smell smoke.'

'I did.'

'And whether the killing of Timmy was just a grotesque accident.'

She moves towards him. 'Thank you.'

'For what?'

'Coming down to the Alamo with your shotgun.'

'Roddy's shotgun.'

'How was he when you saw him?'

'Strange.' He drinks some coffee and cocks an ear. He hears an engine, but is pretty sure it is a tractor of some description. It sounds rough and agricultural.

'Yes, he has been acting strangely, even for him,' Celeste says thoughtfully.

'I saw him at the Turkish baths and he seemed, well . . . almost hysterical. Hyper, if you know what I mean.'

'I've only seen him looking hangdog. Maybe I should sell this place and let him have the money.' Celeste sits on the arm of the sofa. He can see the steam from the mug rising and wrapping itself around her face. For a second he imagines the tendrils are his fingers.

'But that would be a bad idea?' he asks.

'It would be a very bad idea. The trouble is, he doesn't really know what to do. He tries things, but . . . he has no calling.'

'Do you?'

'No, not really. That's why . . .' She lets it trail off, covering the missing part of the sentence with a gulp of her drink. He can fill in the blank anyway. 'How about you?'

'A calling? You're looking at it.'

'What, hanging out in the country, on the run, with guns, waiting for someone to find you?'

'No. Helping the good guys.'

'What if you get into real trouble this time?'

'I get fired.'

'Would they really do that?'

He looks up. There are footsteps across floorboards. Sasha must be awake and moving around. At least, he hopes it is her. He hears the toilet flush and relaxes. 'Yes,' he says, answering her question.

'Then what will you do? Become a private eye?'

He laughs at that. 'Yeah, there's a big demand for ex-FBI agents fired for incompetence. No, that's not what I would do.'

'Anything else in your portfolio?'

He looks out at a sky that is now streaked with pink across a deep turquoise background. The stars are going out from a huge portion of the heavens. 'Treasure hunter?'

'Really? Is that a job?'

'More a vocation, I guess. I want to find the lost treasure of the Seventh Cavalry.'

Hooper leans against the wall of the Underground station, keeping well in the shadows. As DeCesare suggested, this is Billing's thing. He can see the terror flickering over the guy's face, knows he has realised where he is and what is about to happen. Billing begins to pace the yellow line at the edge of the platform, keeping his eyes on the tethered man the whole time. The poor jerk begins to thrash, as if he could break free from the Quantico knots they have used on him.

After a while he slumps back, breathing hard. 'Is this about the diamond raid? 'Cos I didn't do that. I was offered the chance but I said no. For Christ's sake, it wasn't me.'

'It isn't about any diamonds.' Billing speaks slowly and deliberately, as if addressing a naughty boy. 'Now, son, let me explain what you might call the current situation. It is now . . . ooh . . . ' He looks at his watch ostentatiously. 'Four forty-five. The maintenance teams will be going home soon, getting off the tracks before the power kicks back in, in ten minutes. Now, first of all what happens is the lights on the platform, up here, come on. That's like your "on your marks" signal. Then the little lights over your heads, they come on. "Get Set." Then "Go." Two hundred thousand volts. You'll end up needing a lot of barbecue sauce to go with you. Know what I mean?' He pauses to let this sink in.

'What do you want?'

'An address.'

'Whose address?'

'Your sister's.'

'My sister's? Fuck off.'

'We want to know where she is at this precise moment.'

'Forget it.'

Billing checks his watch again. He reaches down and picks up a bottle of water. There is less than an inch left. He unzips himself, manages to work his dick into the opening and half-fills it with a stream of warm, pale liquid. He examines it, before upending the contents over Roddy, who thrashes once more, spitting and choking.

'You're dryin' out a touch there. Don't want to get a dodgy connection, do we? So give up the name, and we'll all nip down to Smithfield for an FEB.'

'I can't. Won't,' Roddy splutters.

'You know, back in the sixties, when I was a lot younger, I did a turn as a stunt man – did a couple of the James Bonds, and TV stuff – *The Saint, Danger Man, Man in a Suitcase*. You know, you wanted someone to jump out of the old Mark Two Jag just before it goes over the cliff and explodes, I was your man.'

'Before my time.'

'We filmed in a station like this once. A chase scene. Man jumps down off the platform, runs down the tunnel to try and avoid The Saint. Or was it The Baron? Anyway, turns out on the first rehearsal, they hadn't turned the power off. I did the whole scene not knowing that one touch and *woof!* I'd've been a gonner. Second take, they used another stand-in, for the shots of Roger Moore doing the chasing. He wasn't so, er, agile. I've learned to respect the juice down here ever since. Seen what it can do to a man. You tell us, we save you a grilling.'

'On one condition,' Roddy says, his eyes darting around desperately, as if help is on the way. Hooper knows there is no calvary hiding in the shadows.

'What?'

'You let me kill the man who is with her.'

'The American? Where is she?'

'You promise?'

'Why?' asks Hooper from the shadows, and Roddy is startled by the new voice.

'Because he killed my friend. Shot him. In the diamond raid.'

'That's a sod, isn't it?' said Billing. 'I read about that. They said there was blood in the chopper.'

'Lennie's blood. He was doing it for me.'

'You want to kill the Yank?'

'Yes.' He doesn't say he has already fluffed two chances. Once when Geoff told him how to get a handgun and he'd bushwacked him in the flat. He'd tried to kill him when he pressed the gun against his head, but he couldn't do it. He'd thought about leaving a note, telling him how lucky he was, how he had Celeste to thank for being alive, but in the end, he'd slunk off and got drunk, trying not to remember the look of disgust in Geoff's eyes at his lack of bottle. The second chance was when Piper had picked up the shotgun and he'd fantasised about blowing his head off with it. Maybe it would be third time lucky.

What was he thinking of? There would be no third time. He was stalling, that was all. Putting off the inevitable.

'You can have him,' says Billing with oily sincerity. 'The Yank. We don't want him. He's all yours.'

Roddy knows that tone. *Humour him. Give him what he wants for the time being.* He feels a warm sensation round his crotch, chilling rapidly. He is scared, but there is only one thing for it, one way forward. 'It's Squire Farm.'

'Squire Farm?'

'Near Harrogate. In a village called Ronton.' He once spent a weekend there with a schoolfriend. His parents owned it – might do still, in fact. He hopes he hasn't just got them killed, too.

'Is that right?' insists Billing. 'You're sure?'

'Yes. Honest to God,' says Roddy desperately.

Billing checks his watch. 'Because we ain't got much time.'

'Squire Farm, near Harrogate. Village called Ronton.'

Hooper writes it down and steps forward. 'Don't worry, Roddy, we'll take care of your friend for you. Right after your sister.'

'What? Fuck's sake, mate, get me off here. I told you—'

The ceiling lights flicker on and Roddy begins to scream, his voice echoing into the dark mouths on either side of the platform. There is a smell of ozone, and a low hum, and his body arches as the current comes back on, the power stopping his heart instantly, his flesh blackening and smoking where it touches the metal. His dead body goes rigid for a second, and then relaxes. A sickly charred odour fills the air.

'Jesus,' says Hooper to nobody in particular.

'My boys'll turn the juice off on this section and get rid of him,' Billing assures them, indicating over his shoulder. He has left two men guarding the escalator, just in case.

'Where are you going to put him?' asks Hooper, breathing through his mouth so as not to gag, wanting to run from this place. He stands his ground, though, conscious of appearances.

'Never you mind. Plenty of places down here.'

'Mr Billing,' says Kolski.

'Yes?'

'What's an FEB?'

'That? Full English breakfast – eggs, bacon, sausages, baked beans, black pudding, mushrooms, tomatoes and two fried slices. Mug of tea. Less than a fiver.'

Hooper doesn't like the sound of black pudding, isn't even hungry, but Kolski says: 'Sounds great. I'm starved.'

Twenty-one

'The Indians, as they were known back then, called the area where the Battle of Little Big Horn took place, Greasy Grass.' Piper drains his coffee. Outside it is light enough to be able to distinguish individual copses, fields and buildings, but the brittle dusting of frost has lent the landscape an odd luminescence, and it feels more like twilight than dawn. From the crumbling roof of a lonely ruined tower in the field opposite, noisy crows take flight. 'Because of all the blood spilled.'

'You've been there?'

'My dad took me, when I was small. He told me this story. I don't even know if it's true . . .'

'Go on.'

'The victorious Sioux hacked at the bodies of the Seventh Cavalry with stone knives. It was this mutilation that so incensed the US Army. You have to remember, though, the Native Americans were defending lands ceded to them by the US government. Unfortunately, at the time of the treaty, the Department of Indian Affairs didn't know there was gold in them thar hills. So settlers moved in, miners, building illegal villages . . .'

'Sounds familiar. Refill?' He shakes his head. Celeste moves to the kitchen and boils a fresh kettle of water.

Piper raises his voice slightly. 'Anyway, after the battle, Sitting Bull moves north, crosses the border into Canada, where he presents a gold medal showing that his grandfather had helped the British during the War of Independence and asking for sanctuary from you guys.'

'We gave it?'

'Kind of. He was allowed to stay on the border, moving between Saskatchewan and Alberta. A detachment of Royal Canadian Mountain Police kept an eye on him. We Americans, on the other hand, wanted him back.'

'I'll bet.'

'No, we were offering an amnesty. Of sorts.'

'Did he go back?'

A distant rooster starts its alarm call. Piper makes up his mind to take a morning walk as soon as it is fully light, scout the perimeter. He needs to blow some air through his head. 'Yes. Food was short. They were running out of goods to trade. Some lasted just three years. Sitting Bull threw in his hand in 1881, five years after the battle. But there was a problem.'

'Sure you don't want one?' She raises a cup.

He doesn't answer, just lets his gaze rest on her, the first dust-filled rays of the sun illuminating her face. Her hair is tousled, the eyes still sleepy, and for a moment he imagines he has woken up next to her.

'Vince?'

'Yeah?'

'Sure you don't want one?'

'I'm good.'

'What problem?'

'When they carved up the soldiers on the greasy grass, they had taken souvenirs. Guns, belts, hats, flags and, uh, more personal artifacts.'

'Scalps?'

'There was also a tradition of making little bags out of your enemies' scrotal sacs.'

'Ah.'

'So, knowing that such items might cause, uh, offence, Sitting Bull ordered all the booty from the Seventh Cavalry to be buried before he crossed back into the US.'

'That's the hidden treasure? A load of bollock bags?' asks Celeste, handing him a fresh mug. 'Here – I made you one anyway.'

'Well, the pouches aren't worth much, except to the odd freak. But very little Seventh Cavalry material has ever made it onto the collectors' market. There's guns, flags, uniforms, equipment and badges. They'd pay a fortune for it in Germany.'

'Why there?'

'For some reason all the big Native-American dealers are German.'

'And you are going to look for this?'

'My dad and I always used to say we'd do it one vacation. We figured we knew where he would have buried it. There is a hump in the prairies down there, a range of hills, some of them with caves.'

'You miss him, don't you?'

'The Wolf?' he says, using his father's old FBI nickname. 'Yeah.'

'Have you done any grieving yet?'

'Well—'

'Real grieving, I mean. Or have you just been the big tough, stoical FBI man?'

'I guess.'

'So, you'll be getting mood swings, irrational anger, feelings of hopelessness . . .'

'You qualified as a shrink while I was away?'

Celeste laughs. 'Not quite. Remember I told you I have a friend, Davina, who is a bereavement specialist. She does ceremonies . . .'

'I remember.' he says.

'She's a shaman.'

A bleary-looking Sasha drifts into the room, the strain still showing on her sleep-creased face. She grunts a hello, makes a quick, noisy cup of coffee and slouches back upstairs.

'Sash never was at her best in the mornings,' Celeste says loudly.

'Can someone shoot that fucking rooster,' comes Sasha's voice from the stairwell. 'Or I will. Tell the farmer we've got a shotgun and we're going to use it.'

'Isn't shaman next to charlatan in the dictionary?'

'An American dictionary maybe.'

'The best kind. OK, tell me something shamanistic.'

'I didn't say *I* was a shaman.'

'But you're tempted, right?'

'Well, I don't think it is quite the rubbish that sensible types, like yourself, might say it is.'

'Give me an example,' he yawns.

'Very well. If you want to cure a stomach-ache, use toasted onions.'

'Yup, the very thought'd cure you.'

'Steeped in urine.'

Piper pulls a face. 'Whose urine?'

'Preferably a young girl's. More lifeforce, you see.'

'Great. Is there much of a market for young girls'

urine? And how do you get it without being put in the slammer for ten years?'

'Strangely enough, a lot of it comes from Germany.'

'You can buy this stuff? How do you know it's genuine? I mean, you can pass an eighty-year-old's pee off as a fourteen-year-old's. And are there, like, production lines of young girls squatting over—'

'Enough,' says Celeste with a wave of her hand. 'You aren't taking it seriously.'

'On the contrary, I'm just thinking it through. What's it taste like?'

'Who knows? You use it as a poultice.'

'Oh. Good job you told me that. Next time I thought I'd skip the Pepto-Bismol, there could have been big trouble.'

The sun has cleared the horizon, the sky is a deep unblemished azure and the world beyond the window is sparkling and sharp. Judging from the completely still trees, there is no wind, just crisp clean country air to breathe. He doesn't really want to think of young girls' urine any longer. 'Wanna take a walk?' he asks. 'Then I'll do some breakfast for you and Sleeping Beauty up there.'

'It's a deal! Just give me a minute to change.'

Piper and Celeste stride up the footpath, walking south from the house, the ground rising steadily. Sheep eye them suspiciously, moving away on their stubby little legs as the two humans enter their personal space. The ground is hard underfoot, the mud frozen into uncomfortable ridges. Piper wishes he had some more suitable footwear. His Church's are pretty heavy-duty, with Commando soles, but there is no ankle support.

As they reach a stile, Celeste turns back and indicates the valley below. She is wearing a Barbour jacket and what she calls Brasher boots, with cream jodhpurs and a heavy Ralph Lauren sweater. All she needs is a staff, he thinks, and she could frighten the sheep into a pen.

'OK,' she says, her breath clouding around her face. 'That's our place,' she points down to the stable block, where their three cars are parked outside. 'Opposite, across that road, see the tower?'

He nods. 'Where the crows live.'

'Can you see those lines in the field leading from it? Ignore the sheep, look through them. Just slightly darker. It's easier in the summer – and when there isn't a frost.'

He squints, and he can just distinguish a rectilinear outline in the field, with the tower at one corner of it. 'I got it.'

'That was the Big House. The stables used to hold the horses and grooms for it. It was very grand, by all accounts.'

259

'What happened?'

'It burned down in the thirties, and only the tower remains now. There were all sorts of rumours about adultery and murder at the time, but I think it was an old-fashioned accident. They'd just installed electricity and central heating, you see. My father bought the stables sometime in the fifties. This was before this area became over-run with second homes and American tourists.'

'Hey, I'm workin',' he protests.

'Of course you are.' Celeste goes on, 'We don't own that field. The Landmark Trust want to convert the tower into a self-catering folly, but my guess is, it's too far gone.' She gestures past the ruin to a distant cluster of farm buildings. 'That's where the rooster's calling from,' she says. 'A lot of fruit-farming is done there now. See the wire frames?'

'Uh-huh.'

Her voice rises a tone, and there is a mixture of anger and passion underlying it. 'They are covered in ugly black plastic during the season. A real eyesore. People are trying to get that kind of farming banned, and I agree with them. In an area of outstanding—'

'Celeste.'

'Yes?'

'You don't seem like the other Celeste out here.'

'Which other Celeste?' She cocks her head coyly,

the mouth forming a pout, and he knows she is teasing him.

'That one,' he says.

She walks on up the field, following the thin ribbon of a path, the route quite steep now, and he is starting to sweat a little, his breathing showing the first signs of being laboured. He catches up with her, expecting to see annoyance on her face, but she flashes him a smile.

'I've been thinking about changing my life,' she says, puffing slightly.

'Changing it to what?'

'Shamanism sounds pretty good.'

'You could always come and look for Sitting Bull's treasure with me.'

She laughs. 'Vince, I've seen enough bollocks to last me a lifetime.' The smile disappears. 'Sorry, that sounded crude.'

'Don't worry. You'll cancel your contracts?'

'Don't rush me. It's just that with Timmy, and Natalie . . .'

'Later on today, we are going to sit down and write your life stories – at least, the professional part. Plus what you both know about Timmy and Natalie's.'

'You really think it has got something to do with that?'

'Yes,' he says with conviction. 'I just have no idea

what. But maybe some connections, a thread we can follow, will come out, and we'll know who is targeting you.'

'You know, Sasha was keeping a blog for Roddy. He tried to get us to write some sordid internet diary and we all said no, but Sasha confessed last night that she went ahead anyway. She wrote down on that most of what she has ever done and to whom.'

'A weblog? Why?'

'Titillation, mostly. Another one of my dear brother's get-rich-quick schemes.'

'She have copies?'

'It's on her laptop, but she didn't take it to the hospital with her.'

'I'll get it picked up.'

There is a buzzing from his pocket and he takes out the cell phone. Celeste looks puzzled. 'Pay as you go,' he explains. 'The office can't trace this one.'

'Who's got the number?'

'Only one person.' He presses the green button. 'Fletch. Hi.'

'Hi. Call Roth, Vince. You're not exactly in the clear, but you are getting there.'

'How come?'

'Natalie.'

'You found Natalie?' He can see hope flash in Celeste's eyes.

'There are bloodstains in her flat,' says Fletcher.

'What kind of bloodstains?' he asks, knowing there can be explanations other than violence.

'It's a Seeraj pattern.'

'I don't—'

'It's to do with the velocity and scatter of the droplets. This one's consistent with an arterial spray. Looks like she's dead, Vince.'

'Shit.' He shakes his head at Celeste.

'You OK?' Fletcher asks.

'Just out of breath. Hold on.' He reaches the top of the hill and sits on a boulder, its surface etched with the names or initials of others who have made the short climb. 'Go ahead.'

'There is one more thing. The British Transport Police stumbled across some activity early this morning. And I mean stumbled – it was a complete fluke. They found two men disposing of a body.'

'Which men?'

'They got away. The police were fired upon and couldn't get back-up in the tunnels quickly enough.'

He assumes the Transport Police aren't routinely armed and wonders when this country will ever learn that this is the twenty-first century. He asks the question he has put off. 'Is it Natalie?'

'It's Roddy Young.'

'Fuck.' He feels like a brick wall has fallen on him,

crushing his chest. He jumps and takes half a dozen fast jerky steps to move out of earshot. 'So, it looks like anyone who knows these girls is also at risk?'

'It could be, Vince.'

He doesn't reply, looking across at Celeste, who is kicking at a clump of iced grass with her toe. He will have to tell her, and he can already feel the pain that will swamp her. He's been there.

'How did it happen?' he asks.

'Electrocuted on the line.'

'No accident?'

'He'd been bound,' Fletch says quietly. 'I'm sorry, Vince.'

'Yeah.'

'Call Roth. Come home.'

'I will. And thanks – again.' He ends the call and dials Roth. 'Won't be a minute,' he shouts across to Celeste as it connects. 'Mary? Hi. Vince Piper.' He thinks he catches an intake of breath. 'Can you put me through?' He hears the connection being made.

'Vince?'

'Stanley.'

'You're not at Heathrow, are you?'

'No.'

Celeste has walked over the brow of the hill, where she can see most of the valley.

'You know about the Des Barres woman?' Roth asks.

'I do. And the other one.' He doesn't want to say the name, in case it catches her attention. He will have to play this very carefully, very gently, to pick his moment.

'Celeste's there with you now?'

'Yes.' He can't resist saying the next sentence. 'I'm right, aren't I?'

'You could be.'

'I am.'

'We'll see. We're bringing you in.'

'I can come in under my own steam.'

'No, you stay put. You're coming in under protection. I won't lose you too, or the other girls. Not on my watch. Now where are you?'

He gives him the address and directions. 'Who are you sending?'

'Brewster.'

'The Secret Service?' There is a sneer in his voice.

'Best bodyguards in the world, Vince.'

'OK. Brewster it is.'

'And his sidekick.'

'DeCesare?'

'Yes. DeCesare.'

Kolski has just cut into the thick, juicy sausage and watched the grease leak out onto his plate, when his mobile rings. They are in a café near Smithfield Market, the inside a rich stew of steam, fried bacon, and the first cigarettes of the morning. They are crammed into a corner, shunned by a crowd of surly, but well-muscled regulars, who bristled on hearing American accents, suspecting slumming tourists. Billing's loud navigation in his London accent through the menu chalked on a blackboard goes some way to placating them. Hooper no longer thinks they might have a fight on their hands.

Kolski takes the call, ignoring the scowls from other tables. 'Yeah.' He listens for a moment and snaps: 'We know that.'

Hooper can hear the upper register of the voice on the other end, but it is so distorted he cannot identify it.

'Near somewhere called Harrogate,' Kolski says.

Hooper watches his partner's facial muscles tighten. The veins stand out in his neck. The volume from the caller has increased. Whoever it is at the other end is shouting, and Kolski is having to take it. He grabs a napkin, and starts writing on it, cursing as the point of his pen snags or pierces the soft paper. He flips the phone down, the call over, his face clouded with anger.

'That little fuck.'

'What is it?' asks Hooper.

'We gotta go.' He stands, grabs a sausage and pushes it in his mouth.

'Get some of that put in a bap,' says Billing, pointing at the two plates of food. 'Shame to waste it.'

'You have it,' says Hooper. 'You earned it.'

Hooper only just catches Kolski's mutter through his chewing. 'Like fuck he has.'

Twenty-two

Jack Sandler welcomes his eleven o'clock appointment with a hearty handshake. This is one he has been looking forward to, an island of light relief in the usual concerns of the Ambassador, sandwiched between a trade delegation from Atlanta and a security review with the Secret Service.

'Roger, Roger, come on in. Tea? Coffee?'

'Some water, please.'

'Sparkling or still?'

'Tap is fine.'

'We don't do tap here,' replies Sandler. He pokes his head through the door and asks his PA for a large bottle of Evian, two glasses and plenty of ice.

Roger Marshall, still dazed by the security hoops he has been forced to jump through, and the number of times he has had to open his briefcase, examines the office. It is very masculine and quite daunting, the flags, photographs and mementoes seeming designed to intimidate mere mortals. However, amongst the photoplay of dignitaries and celebrities, he spots Sandler shaking hands with an old man across what looks to be a formless lump of metal.

He crosses the room and points at it. In his tweed jacket and sensible v-neck jumper, he looks like a geography teacher. 'Marsham?'

Sandler beams. 'Yes. That's Bill Prince, the man who pulled my dad out of his cockpit. The thing between them—'

'An Allison engine?'

'Yes. An Allison engine from my father's Lockheed Lightning. That was taken in 1984. He's dead now, of course, Bill – and my father. So what have you got for me?'

Roger Marshall, President of the East Anglia Aircraft Archaeology Society, clears his throat. 'There is no record of any downed plane in that area in *Franks* or *Chorley*.' These two books are the bibles on RAF losses in World War Two and crash-sites. 'So, if it is a US-made plane it was with the USAAF.' He extracts a map from his case. 'We've taken some more soundings . . .'

'Here,' says Sandler, clearing a space on the desk. He helps unfurl the large-scale map, and uses paperweights to keep it in position. One thing an Ambassador is never short of is memento paperweights. 'Right, so this is the shoreline, and these red dots . . . ?'

'That black line is the high-tide line. The red dots are positives on metal detectors. As you can see, the findings cover a large area.'

'There's certainly a hell of a lot of them. One plane?'

'Probably. But there is an outside possibility it's two. As you know, collisions were very common as the planes massed or when they returned. One US bomber group lost eight planes to collisions before it lost one to enemy action.'

'But?' asked Sandler.

'We know about the vast majority of collisions. Don't forget, one plane had thousands of parts – some of these could be ammunition from the guns. The thing is, these marshes are very active; they move things, bury them, then spit them out.' Marshall fishes another piece of paper from his case. 'The fragment that the birdwatcher found was stamped *Boeing*, which suggests a B-17. As I said, the chances are it was with the Eight Air Force. This is a list of all US B-17s from English bases that were unaccounted for.'

Sandler studies the typed list and flicks the pages over. 'So many?'

'Well, it's a small proportion of the thousands that served in the UK, sir.'

'Jack, please.'

'Twelve thousand B-17s were built. A goodly number of those came over here. All we need is one serial number. They were stamped on most parts, usually six or seven digits. With it we can trace its provenance, put a name to the plane and faces to the crew.'

Sandler nods. 'That would be a fine thing. It's not about the plane, it's about the people. So when do you envisage going out here?'

'As you know, we have a good low tide, just before Christmas.'

'The weekend of the twenty-first. I have it noted in my diary.'

'We have just received permission from the RSPB – you know what that is?'

'The Royal Society for the Protection of Birds, yes.'

'You see, most of this area is a bird sanctuary. They say we can explore this section here, where there is the greatest concentration of metal. We can run a path down here using flags – the flats are very, very tricky and the tides . . .' Marshall takes out a handkerchief and blows his nose noisily. 'Very quixotic. Still, we hope to be able to locate some-thing in the hours available to us. I will, of course, call you as soon as we know.'

The water arrives and Sandler pours two glasses.

He hands one across to Marshall. 'Call me? What do you mean call me, Roger?'

'As soon as we identify the plane.'

'Hell, you don't get off that easily. Call me my ass. I'm coming out there with you, Roger. Galoshes and all.'

Twenty-three

When he tells her, halfway down the path, she collapses against him, all the strength drained from her legs. He was going to wait until the house, but decided he had better do it while they are alone. Piper can feel the sobs shaking Celeste's body, and he pulls her in tighter, telling himself she is only holding him in grief. They are standing beneath a thick copper beech, magnificent even in its denuded winter state, a couple of the local crows eying them twitchily from its leafless branches.

He eases her away from his shoulder and kisses her forehead. 'I'm sorry.'

She looks up at him with empty, confused eyes. She is in shock of sorts, and he can imagine the collision of confused thoughts in her brain.

'How?'

'I don't know.'

Celeste punches him on the chest. 'Don't you dare lie to me! How did he die?'

'Electrocuted on the Tube.' Her expression changes and he says quickly, 'They don't think it was an accident.'

High clouds are beginning to obscure the sun, and a wind is blowing down the valley. Snow is forecast. It might even be a white Christmas. Not for them, though. It will be a very dark, black-hearted Christmas for them.

'I love you,' he says very softly, so quietly he thinks she can't have heard.

'I know,' she acknowledges. He starts to say something else, but she puts a finger to his chapped lips. 'But not now, Vince.'

'No. Not now.' He strokes her hair. Now he has to find out who did this, who killed Roddy, who is testing Celeste's sanity. Roth is right. He isn't the agent he once was. But that doesn't mean he can't be again.

'What's happening, Vince?' she asks in a voice thickened by tears. He finds a tissue in his pocket and gives it to her. She blows her nose. 'Poor Roddy. He never hurt anyone, not really. He was just a lost soul. He didn't deserve . . . Who is doing this to us?'

'I don't know.' He lifts her chin and speaks to her slowly, calmly. 'I need you to be strong. I need you to remember all the words you said to me when Martha went. I need you to put off mourning Roddy. There will be time, when we know what happened. I need Celeste, not the sister in black.'

'Why?'

'Because I don't know who is doing this. But Sasha does.'

Colonel Wallace lifts up the receiver on the second ring. He can tell from the quick, sharp wheezing that it is Pearl in Santa Barbara, and that he is agitated about something.

'Sir?'

'Wallace.'

'Yes?'

'I have called an emergency session of the, uh, investors.'

'You're in Washington?' The Colonel looks at the blowing snow outside, almost horizontal. He wouldn't have liked to have flown anywhere, in this weather.

'Never mind where we are. We have decided to put the London project into turnaround.'

Wallace tries to recall what that means in film-speak. He knows it isn't good. 'Can you be a bit more specific, sir?'

'We are pulling the plug. The tax incentives are not what we thought they might be. In fact, they are very disappointing.'

'You know principal photography is underway?'

'Yes,' barks the old man. 'And we know what it will cost us, but I repeat: wrap up this production at once.'

'Is that unanimous?'

There is a pause and Jerome comes on the telephone. 'Hello, Colonel. Yes, I just want to say you have done a good job, but we have considered this carefully. A document about the change of the tax incentives in the UK film industry was recently brought to our attention. It's on the internet and it makes depressing reading. They pulled the rug from under us, Colonel. Now all we can do is wrap the cables up very neatly, pay off the crew, and go home.'

'You have a replacement production in mind?'

'Yes, one in Florida.'

'Florida?'

'Yes. Not the project you are thinking of. Smaller budget. Independent.' Not the Governor then, which is a relief. That one was never going to fly nationwide. 'Now, can you take care of the other thing for us?'

'Yes, sir.'

Even as he puts the phone down, Colonel Wallace knows it is too late. The cameras are already turning.

He walks through to his study, once his sanctuary, now looking sad and neglected, with dust on the panelling and on the glass of pictures on the wall, all showing Wallace with various dignitaries. It was understood that his wife never violated this sanctuary. It wasn't until she passed on that he realised that the clubby room wasn't self-cleaning after all.

He boots up the computer, selects a search engine and puts the project's name in. He finds it three down. A transcript of a speech made in London, recorded in the *Wall Street Journal*.

Jack Sandler, addressing a group of bankers, economists and politicians.

The first part is some blather about holidays, but the second section lays out a hypothetical tax and spend strategy for governments, including the US, the tax being heavy on arms and defence contractors, insurance companies and the banking industry, which he claims is out of control. Their man has shifted to the left. Way to the left.

That's why it's a wrap. Pearl, who believes any tax increase to be a crime against humanity – or at least the most important part of it – no longer wants Sandler fast-tracked to greatness. The man's derailed himself. So people really have lost their lives needlessly. And, thinks Wallace as he picks up the receiver, the killing isn't over yet.

Twenty-four

Thanks to the early hour, the direction of travel and a total disregard for speed limits and cameras, Hooper and Kolski make it to the Evenlode Valley in a shade over an hour. They pull the car into a passing space about half a mile down the road from The Stables, and check their weapons. Hooper's sniper rifle is in the trunk, but it doesn't look like it will see action again today. He inspects the magazine of his Colt auto, rams it home, and looks across at Kolski.

'We sure this is the place?'

'Yes.'

'Not Harrogate.'

'For the fiftieth time, Hoop, he lied.'

'Brave man.'

'Yeah,' sneers Kolski as he pulls the slide on his

own weapon to put a shell into the breech. 'Was it my imagination that he pissed himself?'

'No, he did do that. He was scared shitless and he still managed to throw us a curve ball. So even as the juice fried his ass, he was thinking of saving his sister.' Hooper steps out of the car. 'Like I said, Roddy Young was a brave man.'

Kolski also exits the car and together they walk down the lane. Above them, the clear sky of dawn has been invaded by grey intruders, which have almost blotted out the sun. Wisps of snow are falling, and the air feels heavy with more.

The pair walk purposefully, but slowly, alert to movement, possible situations. Hooper just wants to get this over with, to move along. Even while he scans the countryside, Kolski is thinking about getting home for the holidays, getting wrecked and getting laid. The killings to come occupy just a dark corner of his brain, one he can easily ignore.

Hooper takes out his cell phone. The signal is weak. He dials anyway and gets through, although the connection is poor. He keeps his voice low, which doesn't help. 'It's me. Where are you? Yeah, we just got here. Slow it down. I said slow— I've lost you. Can you hear me? I said slow down. Give us thirty minutes. Right.' He turns to Kolski. 'Still on the M40.'

They cover the rest of the ground to the perimeter of the stable-block's grounds. 'The gang's all here,' says Kolski as they peer over the boundary wall. Three cars are parked out front. Smoke rises from the chimney, suggesting a roaring fire within. They duck out of sight behind the stone wall. Hooper loosens the weapon in his waistband. 'I'll go round the back, you take the front door,' begins Kolski.

But Hooper looks back over the wall once more, his face troubled. 'Hold on.'

He squints against the glare from the snow, peering over to the building's main entrance, where a white cat is padding in circles. He moves along to the gap in the stone fence occupied by a five-barred gate, which he vaults in one easy movement, and runs, crouched, towards the stable block's front door. When he returns, he has a large piece of paper in his hand, the ink on the note beginning to run as the flakes of snow hit it. *'Brewster. We've gone for walk. Back 30 minutes. Piper,'* he reads out loud.

'Gone for walk?' whispers Kolski incredulously, brushing the snow from his eyes. 'In this shit?'

'It's what folk do in the country.'

'Not where I come from,' he smirks. 'We gets us a warm body—'

'Shut the fuck up,' says Hooper, irritated by his partner's clowning. He stands and examines the surface of the ground. The snow is too recent to tell which direction they have taken. Nor can he and Kolski be sure how long it is since they departed. They could be back any minute. He scans the surrounding hills, but can see no figures picked out against the thickening white cover.

The cat is on the wall. It issues a piercing miaow, far louder than it needs to be, and Hooper makes to knock it down.

'Hey.' Kolski reaches up and sets the animal gently down in the snow. It pads off without a backward glance.

A murder of crows takes to the air from a tower in the next field and Hooper shades his eyes to examine it. There are windows on each side, on all three floors, giving a view over the whole area. If there are still stairs in there, or some way of climbing to the upper level, it will be perfect.

Now he does get a little buzz, an echo of former pleasures. Kolski sees the beginnings of a smile playing across his face and asks: 'What?'

'I'm going to get my gear from the car. I'll take the tower – you go and wait inside. I don't think you'll have to do much. I'll drop them before they reach you.' He mimes looking through the scope and squeezing the trigger on his sniper rifle.

'Call me on the cell when you see them coming,' says Kolski.

'Signal is shit.'

'Bound to be a hotspot up there.'

'Yeah.'

Hooper retraces his steps back towards the car, a little skip in them this time.

Piper watches the two men from his place in the tiny space behind the clock, in the tower above the stable block. He has wedged himself into here, just in case. They could be good guys, but on the other hand . . .

Now he knows – or thinks he knows – the reason for all this mayhem, he trusts absolutely nobody, nominally good or bad. When Sasha had heard about Roddy's death, Piper had cruelly taken advantage of her shock to get beyond her defences to the suspicions she hardly dared voice, even to herself.

What she told him is scarcely credible. It is unbelievable that anyone in this day and age could be quite so sanguine about their ability to influence the affairs of men. Look where it got them in Iraq. *We'll go in, they'll love us for it. We know what is best for them.* As if.

What they are trying to do is something similar, imposing their will on a whole nation of people. In this case, though, the nation is the USA. So what if some little people die along the way? Whores like Natalie, hustlers like Roddy – who cares?

Well, he does, for one.

He puts an eye to the latticework again and watches as one of the men points to the derelict tower and moves back towards the lane and disappears. Oh shit, thinks Piper. I called that one wrong. The other one lights a cigarette, takes a couple of drags and then, as if remembering himself, throws it down into the snow. He zips up his jacket and heads towards the stables.

She smelled smoke.

Piper hears him enter softly, only the rusty hinge on the front door betraying him. A minute later, the pipes in the roof spaces start to bang and groan. He's making himself something to drink. This one is cool. But what is his pal up to?

One thing is for sure, whoever they are, they aren't DeCesare and Brewster, their escort back to safety. Now he can see the other guy again, and he's carrying a case. His gaze seems fixed not on the building where Piper is hiding, but the remnants of the Big House.

This is confirmed when he drops the case over the fence, and clambers over the gate, and heads off towards the ruined tower. Piper grabs his cell phone and checks it. Zero signal. He can't warn them over there that this isn't Brewster and DeCesarè but . . . who? Black hats, that's all his gut tells him.

He is wondering what to do, when the decision is made for him. He hears a board creak. He has been in the house long enough to know that sound: the smoker is coming up the stairs.

Stanley Roth looks down the Christmas shopping list before him, then at his watch. He has two more meetings before he can get away. He still has to get some DVDs for his eldest, and something for Janet, his wife. Something sparkly or shiny, she has asked for. He doubted she meant firecrackers. So, he would have to trot across to Bond Street and pay through the nose for a trinket. He should go to Hatton Garden, he supposes, but because he knows less than zilch about diamonds, apart from the 4Cs – Colour, Clarity, Cut and Carats – he suspects he would be taken for a ride there, too.

Roth looks through the paperwork, wondering how much trouble the whole Piper affair will bring down on his head. He clicks the intercom. 'Mary, any word from Brewster yet?'

'No, sir.'

'What about the cops on the Young character, the brother?'

'Hold on. You have a call asking if the body can be released to a relative for burial. Post mortem completed.'

'That was done with indecent haste.'

'You want something done fast, schedule it just before the last weekend of the holiday.'

There is something in her voice that seems to be admonishing him. Ah yes, Christmas shopping. 'Mary, why don't you take off early today,' he says. 'I'm sure you've got errands to run.'

'I have, but . . . well, if you are sure.' She says it very fast, with no room for him to renege on it.

'Of course.'

'Thank you.'

'One thing before you go.'

'Yes?'

'Ask that Roddy Young's body be held until the New Year pending our own investigations.'

'Sir?'

'Tell them to keep him on ice. And I want a copy of that post mortem. Then you can go.'

'Thank you.'

Outside, a pneumatic drill coughs into sporadic life. Newer, higher barriers are being constructed around the Embassy. Soon they will be so tall they'll cut his light, and he's on the second floor. He wonders where Roddy Young fits into this whole cock-eyed turn of events. It could just be a coincidence. One thing is for sure, it isn't FBI business – or at least, it shouldn't be.

Except Piper has a way of busting through carefully constructed boundaries, physical and mental, and that makes him dangerous. OK, so maybe he was right about the girls, and Roth will push for the British cops to put together a team to try to come up with causal links. Whatever occurs, Piper won't be involved, though. He'll have to be shipped back to the US. Otherwise they'll all go to hell in a basket.

There is something nagging him about the case, but no matter how much he turns it over in his mind, it always comes back to this: why is the killing of English prostitutes a matter for the Federal Bureau of Investigation? It isn't. And for him to have to send a close protection detail from the Secret Service to pull one of his own agents in is pretty embarrassing. Maybe he should have gone with a detachment from Thames Valley Armed Response himself. No, best keep it in the whole dysfunctional family of the US Embassy.

He finds his credit-card bill in the in-tray and studies it. The total is too large, the transaction list containing too many items which cannot be put through on company expenses. The family has had a new plasma TV, a new recordable DVD and various bikes and skateboards in the last few months. His wife's diamond will have to wait. But he won't disappoint her. There is that cheaper stuff in Tiffany, up the stairs. After all, Sterling Silver is still pretty shiny.

By the time DeCesare and Brewster reach The Stables, the snow has been falling for close to an hour, in fat flakes that clog the eyes and mouth. They pull up next to Hooper and Kolski's car and turn the engine off. All is quiet, even the plaintive bleating of the sheep is muted. The landscape is wrapped in a thick layer of insulation.

'What do you reckon?' asks DeCesare, when the two men fail to appear.

'They'll want our congratulations,' says Brewster. 'Maybe a bonus.'

DeCesare laughs. 'A termination bonus, perhaps?'

'Yeah, something like that. Let's go see.'

Both men wrap up in scarves, but not gloves. Nor do they button their overcoats. They must suffer chilled fingers and cold chests for the freedom to get to their weapons easily.

They crunch through the snow, heads down but eyes staring straight ahead, looking for signs of life. They see signs of death first.

The blood must have been obscenely bright against the white background when it was fresh, but it is more a pinkish stain now. The body from which it leaked is sprawled out at the base of the tower, and the new fall of snow has half buried him. Brewster opens the gate to the field with some difficulty and slides through, signalling for DeCesare to wait. He doesn't have to be told twice. He has a Sig pistol in his hand, and he is no longer feeling the cold.

Brewster kneels down next to the body, looks up

at the tower and examines the fading pattern of foot-prints. He touches the small patch of skin that remains on the shattered face. The temperature will tell him nothing in these conditions about how long ago this happened. Not too long, is his instinct. He looks at the size of the indentations in the snow, guessing shoe size. A woman. A woman did this.

Brewster slithers his way back to DeCesare. 'Who is it?'

'Hooper,' he says flatly. 'I'd recognise that eyebrow anywhere.' DeCesare frowns. 'It's just about all that's left of his face. My guess is he opened that door and took two barrels in the upper body.'

'It kill him?'

'Well, he won't have to worry about shaving any more.'

DeCesare snarls: 'You know what I mean.'

'Yes, I know what you mean, you prick,' says Brewster. 'This has been one big fuck-up—'

DeCesare holds up his hands. 'We can do this later. First, we have to find Kolski.'

They locate him in the house, at the bottom of the stairs, a smashed coffee cup like a broken halo around his head, the contents splattered up the rough plas-tered walls. He has two holes in his chest. In his hand is a Glock 9. Brewster bends down and touches the neck. No pulse.

This isn't the way it was meant to be. Sure, these two were meant to die, but after they got rid of the others. Brewster feels a constriction at his temples, and a black, irrational anger building.

He unwraps Kolski's stiff, pasty fingers from the gun and stands.

'Dead?' asks DeCesare.

'No.'

DeCesare frowns and steps forward. 'Jeez, you sure?'

The fury in Brewster becomes cold and lethal. 'He's not dead, because he is going to kill you.'

'What the fuck you talking about?'

Brewster raises the Glock and fires two shots in or around DeCesare's heart. The wounded man flies backward, into the whitewashed wall, sending pieces of pottery and glass from the windowsill shattering onto the floor. Brewster walks over and bends down, oblivious to the weak rattle of a last breath and the glazing eyes. He checks for a pulse in the neck and it is there for a second, and then flutters away as the body gives one last jerk. Brewster stands, returns and puts the weapon back into Kolski's hand. He takes DeCesare's gun and fires a shot into Kolski, who twitches.

As he walks out, he kicks DeCesare's body. 'That was a terrible job, partner.'

He hears an engine cough in the cold then catch, as a car starts in the lane. This is followed by the whine of over-revving and the spin of tyres trying to grip on ice. He bursts back out and runs. He pumps his arms, weapon in his right hand, careful not to catch himself in the face with it. He keeps light on his feet, making sure he doesn't fall on his ass.

The hire car brought by Kolski and Hooper has pulled out of its place and is facing towards him. There is a grinding of gears and it reverses with a whine, gathering speed. Brewster can't be sure, but it looks like a woman at the controls. He raises the weapon as he runs, ready to fire. Then hears a noise like a banshee, a rising squeal from his feet. Something wraps itself around his ankles, and he stumbles.

He lurches headlong, his soles slipping on the compacted snow, hitting the ground with a winding thump, and sliding into a drift. Brewster rolls, raises his gun and fires a single shot at the cat he has just fallen over, but the bullet whines away harmlessly as the shape blends into the background and is gone. Damn animals.

He stands and brushes himself clean and limps up the lane, trying to ignore the pain in one ankle. The car he shared with DeCesare is down on one side, the tyres either slashed or deflated. Brewster pulls out his cell phone and checks the display. No signal. Fucking typical, he thinks, of everything connected with this project. He wishes he'd never heard of it in the first place. And never agreed to help in the second.

Twenty-five

The train crawls its way towards Paddington station in London. It has been inadequately cleaned: crisp wrappers, polystyrene cups and discarded newspapers litter the aisles. The windows are streaked with dirt and sleet, the view so blurred they can hardly see the passing countryside.

The three of them have found a carriage that is empty, and where Celeste can stretch out her stiff leg in comfort. Piper realises how tired he is, now they have stopped, the adrenaline that pumped through his body for hours having drained his batteries. He feels like those opponents that always play the Duracell Bunny.

Sasha is chewing her lip, a look familiar to Piper fixed on her face. What the fuck is going to happen now? she is thinking. There has been murder and mayhem, and her life has been tossed in the air like a pack of cards. She has no idea where they will land.

Celeste's face is harder to read, until you look into her eyes. They are worrying. He has a feeling she enjoyed pulling the trigger on the shotgun and blowing most of that guy's face away. When he asked how she'd managed to do it, she muttered something about shooting pheasants. Or was it peasants?

Piper was sure they were right to kill them. After all, they weren't Brewster or DeCesare, the designated escort team. What if they'd been an advance guard? asks a doubting voice. What if you just killed two Feds?

With a sniper's rifle? He looks down at the case between his feet. Why would an escort team need a Sig pro job like that? Besides, he'd checked the bodies. No creds. No ID of any kind. Just a collection of credit cards on one of them, in three different names. No, they weren't on the team.

So why had he run from the real thing, from Brewster and DeCesare? Because he has become paranoid, he reckons. And because he didn't like the sound of those three gunshots from the stables one little bit. As far as he knew, that guy on the stairs was already dead. So what were they firing at?

'Why did you dump the car?' asks Sasha.

He sighs. 'Because there might be a call out on the

plates. Because the congestion charge cameras in London can be set to flag up a fugitive plate for the Met.'

'The police aren't after us,' says Celeste quietly. 'Are they?'

'We don't know. But we just killed two people back there.'

'And they killed Roddy.'

'You can't be sure of that.' He slides his hand across the sticky plastic table that separates them, but hers is snatched away.

'I can.'

'Is this a shaman thing?'

He regrets saying it immediately, and she doesn't answer, but her lips purse in irritation at his perceived flippancy. Things have changed between them; there is a tension. Is she blaming him for Roddy's death? Or is she loading it onto Sasha? The latter says: 'They sent men to threaten me, you know.'

'Who did?'

'Two different men. They came up to me when I was least expecting it, just to remind me not to tell.' She begins to sob softly. 'I'm so sorry. I just didn't think that it could be anything to do with this. I'm still not sure you're right. He's a good man.'

No such thing any more, thinks Piper. And says aloud: 'Were either of the men who warned you off those guys back there?'

She shakes her head. 'I'm not sure. The one that Celeste . . . that one, I couldn't tell.' Well, it is difficult to identify a man whose face has been stripped back to tendon and bone, Piper concedes. 'I didn't recognise the other one.'

Celeste puts a hand on Sasha's shoulder. 'Don't worry. Vince will sort all this out once we get to London.'

Will I? he thinks. He hopes it can be sorted out. It still might be easier for all concerned to wrap this up by killing the three of them. No loose ends at all, then.

Celeste looks at him. 'Why did the note work?'

'How do you mean?'

'Two professional killers. You leave a "Gone Fishing" note and they fall for it?'

The train pulls into a station, and two girls get on, giggling, but they take a seat at the far end of the carriage. Last-minute Christmas shoppers, Piper reckons, heading for Oxford Street or the Harrods/Harvey Nicks nexus. He looks again, at the cheap shoes and gaudy fashion coats. Oxford Street.

He continues talking, his voice lower. 'Being able to kill someone is a skill, a mental gift. It doesn't mean the rest of your brain matches up.'

'Would you have fallen for it?'

'Probably not. But I'm really paranoid now. And

they had no reason to think we weren't expecting the Seventh Cavalry.'

'Do you think I should have cut their balls off for a souvenir?' Celeste asks, with an all-too malicious grin. Sasha looks puzzled and alarmed. 'Private joke,' she explains.

'Also . . .' Piper goes on.

'Also what?'

'The shaman in me,' Piper says, 'thinks that the man without a head wanted to use his little toy. He'd dragged a rifle all the way to the countryside and was reluctant to go home without having fired it. So we hand him a chance to play *Enemy at the Gates*, he isn't going to look a gift horse in the mouth. He'll believe we're going to come strolling along the road and he can pick us off. But that's just a guess. You OK?'

Her eyes have glazed over. He knows what she is thinking about.

'You know Roddy once tried to deal in drugs?' she says. 'Cocaine?'

'No.'

She can hear the disapproval in his voice. What did she expect from a cop? 'This is back when, well, it seemed a lot more innocent then.'

'It was never innocent.'

Celeste nods. In the mid-1990s a lot of her friends

had worn their nasal septums away using the corrosive powder, and many had ended up in rehab. Like almost everyone on the party scene, she'd tried it. It was the memory the next morning of the absolute crap she had talked – and been proud of – that made her move on.

Piper's objection is more practical. As case analyst for the FBI, he had traced a gram of street cocaine back through the supply chain. Even as a theoretical exercise, it wasn't hard to feel sickened by the number of lives ruined – or lost – by the lucrative trade. He was no moralist, he drank, he used to smoke, but as far as he knew, neither of those things were quite so blood-soaked as coke.

'Anyway, he bought a large quantity of the stuff, and it turned out to be fake. Rebaked or something?'

'Probably lidocaine roasted with baking soda and lighter fluid. Some movie prop guys do it. Crooks, too.'

'So you know what he did?'

'He took it back,' Piper guesses.

'Yes, he took it back.'

'Whereas, as we know, the drug world is the prime example of *caveat emptor*. And?'

'They gave him his money back. I think they were so surprised that he'd come in as if he was taking a faulty CD back to the shop.'

'He was damned lucky,' grunts Piper.

'He had charm and charisma.'

Yeah, and it ran out when he was strapped across the live rail of a subway station, he thinks, but doesn't voice.

Celeste's mobile rings and she pulls it from her pocket. She doesn't recognise the number. She holds it to her ear and says, 'Yes,' a few times.

'Who was that?' Piper demands.

'The funeral directors. They want to talk about . . . I'm Roddy's next-of-kin, you see. There's our mother, but I have Power of Attorney.'

'Right.'

'Can we?' she asks.

'What?'

'Go and see them. I'd like to find out what is going on. To see Roddy one more time.'

'Maybe,' he says. 'I have to think it through. See whether it exposes us.'

She flicks her head defiantly. 'I'll go anyway.'

His voice hardens. 'You'll go if I say it's OK.'

'Vince—'

'Celeste. You'll go if I say it is OK. I need a heads-up on how much danger we are in.'

'Who can get you that?'

'A friend.'

'You have some left?'

'One or two. Believe it or not.'

Celeste nods, but her mouth is set in a thin, pale line. He'll have to watch her. Grief makes people stubborn and foolhardy, and she has a head start in that department. Besides, they'd been reckless enough. He'd done nothing by the book, and it had worked. You don't get that lucky too often.

'Next stop, Paddington,' says Sasha.

'Thank Christ for that,' says Celeste, shifting position and banging her thigh. 'My leg is killing me.'

Twenty-six

Jacqueline Fletcher lives at the wrong end of Crouch End in North London, where it blends into Hornsey. The wrong end, that is, if you are one of the musos or journos and their ilk who gravitate to the Broadway. You can see them having breakfast – some with their spoiled DKNY-clad kids – at Banners most Sundays, and they drink in the Pumphouse or the refurbished Queen's, and have made the houses in the core streets unaffordable for the likes of Fletch.

So, she has a rather grand Edwardian house in what is considered by estate agents to be the wrong road, although it is fine by her – there are good all-night grocery stores and a police station within a few hundred metres. Her husband always wanted them to move up the road to family-friendly Muswell Hill, to cripple themselves with a quarter-of-a-million pound mortgage, that would rely on his salary. She is so glad she resisted.

The house seems empty without the kids. She will see them at Christmas, and is still undecided what to do about decorations. She always thought dragging a tree into a house and dressing it up was ridiculously pagan. 'Just stop and look at what you are doing,' she always wanted to yell. 'Next you'll be sacrificing sheep on the living-room carpet.' But voicing opinions like that only got her labelled a Scrooge, so she stopped.

Maybe she'll go for some holly, a sprig of mistletoe, the odd piece of silver tinsel just to cheer the place up. Keep it minimal.

She watches the black cab pull up in the street and the trio get out. Do they realise what they look like, she wonders. Tired, scruffy, they shuffle along more like tinkers than the metropolitan sophisticates they would like to believe. One of the women has trouble getting out of the cab, her leg stiff and clearly painful. Piper hinted at some trouble on the phone. 'Some trouble' with him is likely to be equivalent to a thermonuclear strike. She, too, is secretly glad he will go home soon, partly because seeing him reminds her of her embarrassing pass the other night. And partly because she has come to accept that where Piper goes, trouble follows, like a pale rider. Something else, though, tells her she ought to help. Because no matter what crap he has created, she senses he is on the side of the angels. He'd do the same for her, she is sure.

She opens the door as they come up the path and the taxi rattles away. It has stopped snowing, the pavements have turned to grey slush, and the air is damp and depressing. There will be a white Christmas in the country, the forecasters are saying, but forget it for London and the South-East. Sleet, at best.

'Thanks for this, Fletch.'

'Yes. I'd say you're welcome but I'm not sure yet.' She sees the look in the women's eyes and says, 'I'm joking. Come in. Make yourselves comfortable through there and excuse the mess. Tea, coffee?'

'Coffee,' says Piper. 'And do you have anything to eat? There was no food on the train.'

'I can do ham sandwiches,' she suggests.

Celeste smiles. 'Ham sandwiches would be fantastic.' She holds out her hand. 'I'm Celeste Young.'

'I know,' Fletcher says, taking it. 'I remember you from the Winfield House affair. I watched you get blown up on tape. Quite the stunt. Is your leg OK? Do you need anything?'

Celeste unzips her fly and loosens her belt. She grunts and groans as she extracts the over-under shotgun from her trouser leg.

'Jesus,' says Fletch.

'Phew – that's better.' Celeste throws it on the sofa.

Fletch can see that the stock has been cruelly hacked down to reduce the length, giving it a dangerous, mongrel air. This is no longer a sporting gun.

'You,' Fletch says to Piper. 'Help me with the sandwiches.'

They walk down the passage to a light, airy kitchen at the rear, with a recent extension that has added a glass roof, and steel and black fittings. Fletch spins to face him. 'What the fuck are you doing?'

'I know you are taking a chance.'

'A chance? Goodbye career, pension, everything. Sawn-off shotguns tend to change everything.'

'It's going to be OK.'

She points back towards the other room. 'Am I right in guessing you don't have a licence for that thing?'

'What – Celeste?'

'Don't be funny with me, Vince. Jesus Christ, I offered you a place to sort yourselves out. Not for you to start—'

'Whoa. Let me tell you everything. From the top.'

Fletch grabs a loaf of bread and begins buttering the slices, while Piper pulls ham and cheese from the fridge. He interrupts his tale only once to ask where the mustard is kept. By the time he has finished, there is a plate of sandwiches, a pot each of tea and coffee and biscuits all loaded onto a wooden tray. He goes to lift it and Fletch puts a hand on his arm. 'You fooled them with a note?'

'It was a very convincing note. Sincere.'

She shakes her head. 'If what you say is true . . .'

'It goes right to the top.'

'Jesus. How can you be sure of anyone?'

'I've got an idea.'

'Oh dear,' says Fletch to herself as he takes the tray out, heading back to the lounge. 'Oh dearie fuckin' dear.'

The sandwiches are consumed within minutes, and his two charges are allowed to go upstairs to freshen up. There are two bathrooms, one for the kids and one en-suite off Fletch's bedroom. Sasha selects the latter.

Fletch sips her tea and finishes the last of her sandwich, eyes fixed firmly on Piper.

'What is it?' he asks at last.

'She's very beautiful. In the flesh. I'd only seen the pictures.'

'Who?'

'Well, guess. I can see why I wasn't much of an offer.'

'Fletch, please. You're—'

'No. Don't start with the false flattery. She's gorgeous. That's why she can do what she does.'

Piper puts both hands over his face and breathes deeply. He wants to get into a hot bath, too, to soak away all this. 'Yes, she is. But it isn't a competition.'

Fletch laughs. 'Oh, yes it is. Every day it's a competition.'

Celeste puts her head round the door. 'Can we borrow some make-up? And maybe the odd bit of clothing?'

'The make-up'll be Boots Number Seven, not the sort of thing you're used to.'

Celeste shakes her head as if this is nonsense. 'Boots is fine.'

'And promise you won't look at the labels in the clothes. If they are something you've heard of, they'll be from TK Maxx.'

'Don't be silly. And Chief—'

'Fletch will do.'

'Fletch. Thanks – for everything. I know you are taking a risk for us.'

Fletch nods. 'I do too. But that's OK.' She glares at Piper. 'Polite as well as pretty. Are you sure you two are entirely suited?'

Celeste frowns. 'See you in a while.' She disappears and they hear her on the stairs.

'What did I say?'

'We're not really an item.'

'Oh, rubbish.'

'It's true. We've never . . .' He lets it tail off and feels himself redden. 'That's not why I'm doing all this.'

Fletch laughs softly. She stands and gathers up the plates. 'Come on,' she says. 'Help me load the dishwasher and I'll tell you how it is.'

* * *

Celeste comes down in a borrowed blouse, her face revitalised with a smattering of make-up, hair blow-dried. Piper and Fletch are back in the living room. He is going over the few options he has. It is getting dark now, the night taking over from a brief twilight. There are fireworks being let off from a party nearby, the bangs and whooshes making Piper jumpy.

'Water's hot again if you want a bath, Vince,' says Celeste. He nods. 'Sasha has fallen asleep on your bed,' she says to Fletch. 'Sorry.'

'That's OK.'

'You should get some rest too,' says Piper.

'We're staying here?'

'For tonight,' says Fletch. 'You are very welcome.'

'Vince, we can't.'

'I need to check some things out, Cel. Make sure we aren't still targeted.'

'How will you do that?'

'I have an idea.'

'Oh dear,' says Celeste.

Fletch nods her head: 'That's what I said.'

Celeste stifles a yawn. 'I'll leave you to it.' Her eyes fall on the shotgun, propped up against the wall.

'Take it,' says Fletch, 'if it'll make you feel better. You've got shells for it?'

'Upstairs.'

'Well, don't load it if you are going to cuddle it.'

Celeste grabs the shotgun and retreats back upstairs to one of the bedrooms.

'Did you see that?' Fletch sighs.

'What?'

'Did you see how great she looked in that twenty-quid blouse? Makes you sick. I don't look like that in it – and I bought it.'

Piper crosses the room and puts his hands on Fletch's head. He kisses her gently on the forehead. 'Stop it. It really isn't a competition.'

'Well, if it was, I know who'd win,' she says, pushing him off. 'You going to have a wash and brush-up before you go?'

He shakes his head. 'No. No point. Your husband . . .'

'What about him?'

'He leave any black or dark clothes behind?'

'Might have, I suppose.'

'Can you see for me?'

Fletcher is about to ask why, but thinks better of it. The less she knows, the less trouble she will eventually be in, she reckons. When she goes upstairs, Piper unfastens the case he took from Hooper, opens it, and checks he still knows how to put a sniper rifle together.

Twenty-seven

'Angel or star?'

'What?'

'Angel or star?' repeats Roth, a little louder.

His wife enters the living room, rubbing her hands on a cloth, her face red from standing over the oven. She is baking, the house is filled with the odour of mincemeat and pastry. She stares up at him atop the small steps, and he waves one of the decorations in each hand. 'Which do you want on top?'

'I don't know,' says Janet. 'What do you think?'

Roth laughs. He is a good Jewish boy, humouring his WASP wife, whom he married for love, swearing religion would never divide them. It doesn't. But its holiday conventions do, sometimes. 'You know, I've always been worried by the thought of this sweet little angel with a tree branch up her ass.'

Janet looks shocked. 'It isn't up her ass.'

'The alternative isn't much better.'

She smiles at that. 'The star then.'

He wires the star into place, then steps down. He glances out of the window towards Hampstead Heath when an owl hoots. He checks his watch. 'When are the boys due back?'

'Ben is bowling, he'll be back by ten. Max is sleeping over at Michael's.'

'OK. So we've got most of the evening alone?'

She appears in the doorway. 'Just us and two hundred mince pies I have to bake for the Selways' drinks party.'

'Ah. You have to do that tonight?'

She nods. 'I don't have to do it sober, though. Wine?'

'I'll get us a glass in a minute. How about some tinsel up here?'

'Why not? Let's go mad.'

As she leaves, he says: 'You know, when I was growing up I always used to envy you people Christmas. By the time I get to do it, I've missed the best bit.'

'What's that?' comes her voice.

'Being a kid. Looking at decorations and eating mince pies without having to put them up or cook the damn things. What I should have done is been a gentile up until I was twenty-five, then switched.' The phone rings and he shouts: 'I'll get it.'

'Stanley?'

Roth automatically lowers his voice. 'Vince?'

'Yeah.'

'I thought maybe the earth had swallowed you.'

'Thought or hoped?'

'A little of both, to be honest.'

'Be honest, Stanley. I need you to be honest.'

'Where are you, Vince?'

'What did Brewster say happened?'

Roth clears his throat. 'That someone got there ahead of them. You left one alive, Vince. He dropped DeCesare. Careless.'

'Bullshit.' Roth hears anger flooding down the line. 'The guy had two in the chest. He couldn't have dropped anyone.'

'Why did you run?'

'I heard three shots.'

'Your man taking down DeCesare.'

'I had no idea what it was. Someone told them where we were, Stanley – the goons who came to kill us. I told you where I was—'

Roth knows where this is going, and doesn't like the implication one bit. 'Hey, now wait a minute!'

The volume goes up. 'I told you, and the next thing, two guys are walking down the road with pistols and rifles and our names on a shopping list. How should I figure that?'

'I dunno, Vince. How are you figuring it?' There is a silence at the other end, except for the ragged sound of Piper's breathing. 'That I'm against you? Is that it?'

'I don't know, Stan.'

'Well, you should, Vince.'

'Who knew where we were?'

'Me. Brewster.' Who else? 'Your friend Fletcher, I guess.'

The thought hits Piper hard. Fletch? No way. 'I gave her a number, not the address.'

'You know that's not watertight, Vince.'

Another silence, punctuated by the rasp of his breathing. Roth can imagine the man's mind whirring.

'Who else your end?' Piper goes on. 'Brewster and . . .'

'The Ambassador. He wanted to be kept informed.'

'Did he now. How usual is that?'

'Not usual. Vince, you've got to come in. This is getting crazy.'

'I know how it feels. There's something bad happening here, Stan.'

'Not from me, Vince.'

'Am I posted, Stan?'

'Why should you be?'

'AM I FUCKIN' POSTED?'

Roth takes a deep breath. This is like hostage negotiation. You have to stay calm, not rile the other

311

person. What is Piper's state of mind? Verging on the psychotic, possibly. He might even have crossed that Rubicon into the full-blown genuine article.

'No,' says Roth emphatically. 'You aren't posted. There is an assist order out for you, that's all. We want to bring you in. Alive. Safe.'

'Can I trust you, Stan?'

'Yes. Where are you?'

'Turn around. Face the window.'

Roth does so.

'Look at your chest.' He looks down, knowing already what he will see. The little red spot from a long-range laser sighting device, a painter, dancing over his chest like an agitated firefly. He remembers it well from his Quantico marksmanship days, even though he always thought it was cheating to use one.

His throat tightens, but he swallows hard. No time to panic. It is a hostage negotiation, after all. And he is the hostage now.

'This baby has some nasty rounds in it. Copper Kiss. You know that round?'

'Yeah. Should be outlawed.'

'It was meant for me and Celeste and Sasha.'

'This is stupid, Vince. You are not posted. Nobody is after your ass this end. There will be an enquiry, that's all.'

'I haven't got all the pieces yet.'

'You won't have any if you kill me. Look, if there was a leak, we can figure it.'

'Did you tell them, Stan? The man with the Copper Kiss and his friend?'

'No. But how can I prove it?' He peers out into the road, but can see nothing but the glow of street lamps and the dark outline of the Heath and its trees beyond them.

'Come out and meet me.'

'Where are you exactly?'

'You know where. Come to the Heath. I'll find you.'

Stanley looks down, hardly daring to breathe now, and the little red spot clicks off.

The two men look startled as Roth pushes his way through the whip-like branches of the bushes that fringe the common, cursing as one slaps his face. The pair scamper deeper into the darkness.

'Oi,' one of them shouts back at him in disgust. 'Find your own place.'

'Sorry,' says Roth. 'Just looking for someone.'

'Aren't we all, mate,' comes the reply, and they giggle.

Roth steps over the perimeter ditch, with its frozen crust of dirty ice in the bottom. 'Vince?' he says, but the word is flat and dead and refuses to carry. He pulls his overcoat tighter around himself. The air is still and face-stingingly cold; the coating of snow is crisp underfoot, and he can feel the damp penetrating his shoes.

Roth looks back at his house. Through the branches, he can see his wife pulling the drapes as he told her. He tries to work out the sightlines, to figure out where Piper would have been. He is fighting hard to stay calm. His instinct will be to punch the guy on the nose. How dare he bring this to his house?

'Vince.' Some of that fury has seeped into his voice and he snaps it out once more: 'Vincent, for Christ's sake.'

'Stanley.'

He spins round and sees Piper crouched, his back against a tree, a case at his feet. He is tossing an infra-red sight from hand to hand. He switches it on and points the malevolent dot at Roth. 'You didn't think I'd aim a loaded weapon at my old pal, did you, Stan?'

Roth takes a step forward, his fist clenched, but stops himself. So he's been suckered. There are worse things than someone not pointing a gun at you. 'How did it get to this, Vince?'

Piper stands, stiffly. 'You know, my old man drove me down to the great Smoky Mountains when I was a kid – just to show me the view, and that blue mist above the trees. It seemed like you could see for miles. And you could – seventy or eighty. I read recently that these days you can see fifteen, at most. And that's not a blue mist obscuring the mountains these days, it's smog. The whole park is dying, Stanley. We just haven't realised it yet.'

'Your point being?'

'The world is getting worse, Stan. It's a fucked-up place.'

'Yeah. I hear guys are even playing sniper with their old pals now. That'd fuck with your head.'

'Sorry. I had to get your attention.'

'You have it. And can we move it along? I'm freezing my ass off here.'

Piper slips the scope into his inside pocket before he speaks. He stamps his feet and says: 'About eighteen months ago, Jack Sandler had a short affair with a girl named Sasha Zee. Not her real name.'

He hears a sharp intake of breath. Roth shakes his head. 'I don't believe it. How? How'd he get away with it?'

'If you want something bad enough . . .'

'Jack Sandler? You've seen his wife. Does he need to go over the garden fence? This is a man more turned on by old bombers than young bazoomas.'

Piper chortles at this. 'Oh, Stan. You're a little long in the tooth to believe that anything like logic applies here. She was brought to an Embassy function by someone, they got talking, he liked what he saw.'

'You are telling me that Jack Sandler . . .'

'I'm telling you that someone thought they were killing Sasha when Timmy was murdered. That the same people then decided to take out the right girl, and her circle of friends.'

'Vince, listen to yourself. This is such bullshit.'

'You ID'd the two guys at the stables?'

Roth hesitates before he confirms they have. 'They were two ex-specialists, if you know what I mean.'

'Our specialists?'

'Yes.'

'How many intersections?' Piper asks. Meaning how many times did their respective CVs overlap.

'Can we do this inside?'

'How many?'

'Dozens. We are still sorting them out.'

Roth begins to flap his arms and slap his body, trying to generate heat. Above his head, the owl he heard earlier gives voice once more. The ringing of deep laughter sounds from along the road, near the car park. 'I got some very fine Maker's Mark bourbon inside. And, Vince, if two guys stand around on the Heath for too long after dark, people get the wrong idea. You know what I'm sayin'?'

Piper picks up the rifle case and indicates that Roth should lead on. As they push through the undergrowth, he speaks to the rear of Roth's head, noticing a dime-sized bald spot for the first time. 'The pair have connections to here?'

'London? None so far.'

'When did they enter the country?'

'It's not clear. Nothing was marked.'

Piper touches his shoulder and Roth stops. 'You mean there is no immigration tag on them?'

'No.'

'Which means—'

'They could have come into the country any way.'

'Including the US back door,' says Piper grimly. 'Using the Air Force or a CIA Gulfstream.'

'Including that. It'll be checked.'

They continue walking, pushing their way through the undergrowth. 'Where's Brewster?'

'Leave. He made a full report, then went home for the holidays. Got a flight first thing.'

'Convenient.'

'Or predictable. You think Brewster is part of this now? People do go home for the holidays. Especially when they have just seen their partner shot.'

'By a dead man.'

'Says you.'

'Why are you stonewalling me, Stanley?'

They reach the road and its lights, and it is Roth's turn to stop to emphasise his point. 'Because I can accept that the view from the Smoky Mountains isn't what it was. I'm just having trouble believing that Jack Sandler is orchestrating a murder campaign against prostitutes. And why would he? Man slips from grace once—'

'Four times.'

'Yes, he'd be pilloried perhaps, but hey, he isn't the only one with a thing for ladies who rent by the hour. Is he, Vince?'

'I'm not the US Ambassador.'

'You are, or were, a Federal Agent, though. It's not quite up there, but the same rules apply. I ask again: why would he do it? To save face? Pah. I don't think Jack gives a rat's ass about face.'

Piper has been asking himself that very same question. He thinks he has an answer, but if he shares it, he will lose Roth altogether. It is, Piper has to admit, scarcely believable. 'I want to check some things out. You were straight with me when you said I wasn't posted?'

'I was. There is an AMNA flag on you, that's all. For now.'

An Agents May Need Assistance marker is no bad thing. 'I want a couple of days to stand this up. Or knock it down.'

Roth takes his arm and guides him across the road to the entrance of his house. He stops at the gate. 'You want me to forget about tonight? Is that what you're saying?'

'I am.'

Roth ponders this. Yet again, Piper has put him in a difficult position. Last time, when a bomb detonated at the Residence, they both survived, just. But the stakes on this one are so high, the fall-out will be enormous, whichever way it goes. Piper's theory beggars belief. But then, the choices made by politicians often do, as Roth knows only too well.

'You going to do anything really dumb?' he asks.

'Like?'

'Just tell me you aren't going to do anything really dumb. Like revenge.'

'I'm just going to do some digging, that's all. Not assassination. I'm a good agent, Stanley. Not *was*. It's why I'm still alive.'

Roth's anguish shows on his face. He rubs his chin, as if checking whether he had shaved that morning. 'On one condition.'

'What?'

'You give me that.' He nods down at the sniper rifle.

'I wasn't going to do anything with it.'

'I know,' Roth says, although he isn't sure he knows anything for certain right now. 'But it's a dangerous toy. I just wonder how you'd feel if you got the Ambassador in the crosshairs? Thinking you know what you know. Which, incidentally, I still think is bullshit.'

'That's all?'

Roth nods. 'That's all I need, Vince.'

Piper hands over the case and steps back. 'I'll take a raincheck on the drink, Stanley.'

'The sight, too.'

Piper tosses the black cylinder over.

Roth moves forward and puts a hand on Piper's shoulder. 'You thought about what your old man would make of all this?'

'My dad? I check in with him every hour, Stan.'

'What's he say?'

'He tells me to watch my back.'

'It's good advice. You know I like you, Vince, even when you do talk garbage. I liked your father, too. Come in, let us watch your back for you.'

'Sorry. Not yet. Remember my dad jumping off the freeway into a giant hopper that time? When they'd knocked an armoured car into it?'

Roth smiles. It is a famous incident in the annals of the FBI. 'You still teach that in case studies?'

Piper shakes his head. 'No. Because it wasn't by the book. Shouldn't tell them the rules can be broken till you tell 'em what the rules are. This is my moment of jumping off the freeway, not knowing where I am going to land.'

'You mess up and . . .' He lets it fade away.

'Stanley?'

'What?'

'Thanks.'

Roth doesn't reply; he just stands and watches Piper hurry off, head down, re-crossing the street, back towards the car park where he has doubtless left a vehicle. He feels sick to his stomach. He has to make a tough decision: should he honour his word to Piper, or press the red button and bring the whole US security apparatus down on him? The man is deluded at best, deranged at worst.

He heads back inside. Maybe a drink will help him decide.

Roth finally makes his mind up on the second tumbler. He is in his study, at the rear of the house, a pale imitation of his subterranean den back home, but it performs the same function, acting as a sanctuary from women and children. It is dark, and Frank Sinatra is playing on the Bose sound system, crooning to him about London. For the first time in years, he is feeling homesick. He wants to be home for the holidays like Brewster, enjoying a full-on US Christmas, not the strangely grudging, joyless affair they put on here, a mere interlude before they can get back to the real business of shopping in the New Year sales.

He drains the glass and splashes another half-inch of bourbon into the bottom. He is mildly tipsy, something he hasn't allowed himself to be for some time. It feels good, even if what he is about to do doesn't. He shifts in his seat and his foot bangs the case he took from Piper. He has looked inside. It is a neat, deadly piece of kit, more modern than the rifles he used back in the day, but familiar enough. He knows what the Copper Kiss round can do and he still burns inside from the thought of the man playing dumb-ass tricks on him, out there in the dark.

Vincent Piper, he thinks, you are a liability to all around you, friend or foe.

Roth takes one more sip of the bourbon, as if fortifying himself for the task ahead, then slowly reaches for the telephone.

Twenty-eight

Baker & Sons, the Funeral Directors, is across the river in Battersea. Piper has borrowed Fletch's black Saab 900, so he can drive Celeste to the appointment. Fletch let it go reluctantly; she knows Celeste's track record with automobiles, and has made him promise she won't get behind the wheel. Piper has convinced Fletch it is OK for him to do this. Celeste needs to make arrangements for when they release the body, and Piper is not posted, nobody is out to get him. Just to confirm Roth's assurances, Fletch has checked in with Scotland Yard; again, no mention of him on any apprehend or warning lists.

'So you can go back in any time you want?' she had asked.

'Yes.'

'Are you?'

'One more thing to do.'

'The Funeral Directors?'

'After that,' he had replied.

'Oh. You want to tell me what?'

'No. It's best you don't know.'

She had paused, biting her lip, and he told her that he appreciated her friendship, and the trust she put in him. She said: 'You aren't going to do anything stupid?'

Why does everyone ask him that? In the end, all he has offered was: 'No.'

The edifice of the funeral parlour is set back from the road, giving room for the hearses and limos to pull up, and is faced in the traditional sombre black marble, with gold lettering. Piper thinks of the brightly coloured, low building on the outskirts of town where his father was laid out, the fixtures and fittings all blond wood and soft pastels, as if death were no longer a dark, depressing affair, but just another day at IKEA. In retrospect, and for once, he prefers the British way.

They sit in Fletch's Saab for a moment and Piper turns off the engine. 'Want me to come in with you?'

She shakes her head. 'No. Do you mind?'

'Not at all.' She blames him for Roddy's death, he reckons.

She turns and looks at him. 'I don't blame you, you know.'

Spooked by this piece of telepathy, all he says is:
'Good.'

'Just in case you thought . . . I don't really know
what happened. I'd like to.'

He squeezes her arm. 'I'll find out. Promise.'

'I'm sure this won't take long.'

She gets out and hurries across the road, a wind
whipping at her skirt. He checks his pockets for
change, gets out of the car and feeds the pay and
display machine, putting thirty minutes on the ticket.

As he opens the passenger side to stick the printed
ticket onto the windscreen, he sees the door of the
funeral parlour open. Celeste is there, with someone
standing behind her. She mouths a few words, then
the door slams. Piper straightens up, just as he feels
the weight of the body behind him.

'Mr Piper. Don't turn around. It's a gun in your
back. Feel it?'

He nods as something hard prods him in the spine.
The accent is English, not American. This throws him.
He thought the bad guys were his fellow countrymen.
Maybe they're hiring locally.

'See the Jaguar?'

Piper looks along the road to where a deep maroon
XJ12 is pulled into the kerb, engine still running.
'Yes.'

'That's where we are going to go. First I need your

gun. And don't insult me by saying you haven't got one.'

This isn't a main shopping street, so there are few pedestrians around, but those that are, aren't taking much notice of him. They all have their heads down, trying to keep the east wind out of their faces.

'OK. I'm going to take it out,' he assures the figure crowding him. Piper removes the Sig from his belt holster and hands it over, keeping it between two fingers.

'When we get in the car I am going to frisk you. Tell me I am not going to find anything else.'

'You're not going to find anything else.'

'OK, let's go, Mr Piper.'

They cover the distance to the Jag in seconds; the rear door is opened and Piper has to climb in. He is made to kneel on the floor, head on the seat, while his body and limbs are patted down. A spare mag for the Sig is extracted and handed to the other passenger in the back, along with the gun itself.

'Sit up, Piper,' says the man next to him. 'Right – get us out of here, Geoff.'

Piper climbs off the floor and slumps back into the sculptured leather, which squeaks under him. Geoff, the frisker, is a big man, smartly dressed in a grey suit, the ensemble let down by white trainers and greasy hair. His face is expressionless as he leans across

Piper and clips in his seat belt. Piper recoils from his breath, which smells of old meat.

'Hands,' he instructs, and a black plastic retaining strap is cinched tightly around his wrists. 'Keep them where the Boss can see them.'

Geoff then gets in behind the wheel and the Jaguar purrs smoothly away. It isn't new, but it has been immaculately kept. The walnut trim gleams, and the smell of fine Connelly hide and polish is strong in Piper's nostrils.

'Where are we going?' he asks.

'Not far,' says the Boss, weighing the Sig in his hands. Even seated, Piper can tell he is not a tall man, around five-seven, with fine-boned features and delicate hands. He is dressed in a smart cashmere camel coat over a chalk-striped suit. His skin is dark enough to suggest foreign blood, but the ethnicity is vague. His eyebrows are thick and dark, the brown eyes beneath them are hard, and the skin around them starred with fine fissures. Piper suspects they aren't laughter lines. He knows that he won't be able to appeal for mercy, because there won't be any.

'Why?' he asks.

The man shrugs. Geoff makes a left turn into traffic, honks his horn, and forces his way through. They are heading further south.

'You could at least tell me why.'

'You have to answer for Lennie. And Roddy.'

'What?' Piper twists in his seat, and the gun jerks up to cover him, but he simply wants to make a point. The man slides back in his seat, putting distance between them, just in case. Unlike Piper, he doesn't have a seat belt on, or his hands tied, so can move more freely. 'I had nothing to do with . . .' The realisation of what he said dawns. 'Lennie is *dead*? Lennie as well?'

'You should know. You shot him.'

'I didn't.' He tries to remember the faces at the stables. The man without one was certainly not the Lennie he recalled, and neither was the one on the stairs with two holes in his chest. 'When?'

'He was in the helicopter.'

It takes a second for him to process that statement. Those wild shots into the chopper, the blood in the cabin. Lennie. Lennie was part of the diamond heist. 'So you are . . .'

'One of the investors in the project. Lennie, we'd have let go. Hazard of the job. Even Geoff here said so.'

Geoff turns round with a scowl that chills Piper's blood. He can tell the man is going to enjoy putting a bullet through the back of his head.

'Brothers, y'see. Geoff and Lennie. But Roddy . . .'

'Why would I kill Roddy?'

'To get information about us.'

Piper shakes his head frantically at the ridiculousness of the situation. They really do have the wrong guy. 'I'm not working on this. The Serious Crime Squad are probably on your tails. Not me.'

'We heard you are a bit of a renegade, Piper. Like the odd bit of unorthodox persuasion.'

'That's bullshit.'

'Learn it in Iraq, did you? We heard about the burn-marks on the body. Very nasty.' Piper opens his mouth but the Boss shakes his head. 'That's all you're getting. Now shut up, and be quiet.'

They are into the drabber parts of South London now, made grimmer by the blackened ice pushed into ridges in the gutters and along the pavements. They pass rows and rows of anonymous Victorian houses, some of them festooned with more lights than an airport runway. There are garish Santas, flashing Rudolphs, and whole choirs of angels. Somehow, it fails to lift the mood of the place, just suggests people with tacky taste and too much time on their hands.

So Lennie was in on the robbery. Perhaps Roddy, too. The call to Celeste from the funeral parlour was clearly a hoax, an easy way to get her – and Piper – to where they wanted him. A thought suddenly strikes him, something that never added up before. 'Who did my apartment that night when I got slugged?'

'Geoff got him in. He knocked you down. Left Roddy to do the rest. He bottled it.'

'Roddy?'

'Yeah. Think of that night as a reprieve. You've been living on borrowed time. Now, you've got to give it back.'

Christ, Roddy had tried to kill him. When his nerve failed, he had trashed the place. No wonder he was acting so weird in the Turkish baths. 'I didn't kill him,' he protests. 'I killed the men who did. Ask Celeste.'

The Boss raises an unbelieving eyebrow. Problem is, they both know people will say anything at a time like this. And others will gladly provide alibis for people they care about.

'It was Celeste who stopped him pulling the trigger,' the Boss says.

'Celeste was there?' Piper gasps.

'In a manner of speaking. He said the thought of Celeste being upset stopped him pulling the trigger.'

'We don't have such worries,' says Geoff with the softest of chuckles.

There are open green spaces outside now, a common or park of some description. A couple of sad snowmen built on the green are bent over, a limb or eye short of a full complement, features melted to mush. Piper doesn't know South London, apart from Greenwich and Blackheath, so he has no idea where they are.

'You are making a big mistake,' he says flatly.

'I think,' says the Boss, 'you made the mistake when you stuck your nose in. What's a few rich man's diamonds to you?'

What indeed? Why should he worry about obscenely wealthy Russians, who made their money carpetbagging their own country, then used it to play out their high-rolling fantasies across Europe, much like the Arabs during the oil boom. And just like them, the Russkies have become a magnet for every hanger-on, shyster and crook in the civilised world. So why did he care? Because it is his job. Because there are better ways to redistribute wealth than using RPGs and stolen choppers. And because he took an oath:

I do solemnly swear to support, uphold and defend the Constitution of the United States of America against all enemies, foreign and domestic, to obey the lawful orders and directives of those appointed before and above me, and that I enter into this office without any mental reservation whatsoever, so help me God.'

OK, so it didn't say anything about flying robbers, or acting on foreign soil in there, but he guessed you had to go with the spirit of the thing, or not at all.

His hands are beginning to tingle. The circulation is going. He could ask them to loosen the ties, but he guesses they will explain that his circulation problems are about to be solved for ever. He is surprised he is so calm. Not unafraid – there is a quiver of apprehension running through him – but it's controllable, cut by adrenaline, by a brain furiously working the odds. Even when there aren't any. *Die in a way that would make your father proud,* he tells himself. He glances down at the seat-belt release, but there is no way his bound hands can press it surreptitiously.

'Left here,' instructs the Boss. 'We'll do it at the garages. Then we'll go back to Bakers.'

Well, there was a certain expediency in arranging a snatch at a Funeral Directors, he supposes. 'I'm sorry about Lennie. I liked him. He helped me once,' Piper says quietly. Geoff twists his head, as if trying to shake off a worrying mosquito, but doesn't reply. 'But Roddy wasn't my call.'

'Boss,' says Geoff.

'He's lying.'

'Boss, get down!' Geoff yells.

The last word is lost in a thunderclap, an explosion of glass and metal, and the heat of discharged gases blowing through the car. It is immediately followed by the screech of metal as two cars collide, and Piper has a flashing image of a black vehicle at their side before the XJ begins to veer. The Boss is scrabbling for a handhold, a thin sliver of blood creeping down his cheek. Geoff is half slumped, yelling in agony as strips of flesh flap around where his ear had been. There is the protest of metal again, and Piper sees the lamp-post filling the windscreen. He is flung forward, his chest crushed by the belt as the tensioner kicks in, but not enough to stop him catching the headrest in front and, for a second, he blacks out.

The hands that grab him wrestle with the seat belt and the ties, and then pull him out onto icy grass. He rolls onto his back, his eyes hurt by the glare from the sky, feeling the damp penetrate his clothes. 'Fuck,' is all he manages.

'You'll live,' says Celeste. She hoists the shotgun up and leans inside the car. She pokes at the Boss, who is wedged between the two front seats, but he doesn't stir. He flew forward and seems to have head-butted Geoff, who is also out cold, face pressed against the steering wheel, his mouth ringed with blood.

'Who the hell is this?'

'I don't know. The driver is Geoff, Lennie's brother.'

Celeste ignores this. It is too much to take in. Explanations can wait. 'Can you stand? Let's get out of here.' There are clumps of onlookers forming, keeping a safe distance, but still too curious for her liking.

She yanks Piper to his feet and guides him around the wrecked Jaguar to where Fletch's Saab is leaking steam from its crumpled front end. He can smell hot metal. 'Some bastard grabbed me as soon as I got inside the parlour,' Celeste says tersely. 'I tried to walk out and he pulled me back in. I managed to stab him in the eye with the condolences pen. Thank God you left the keys in the car, Vince.'

'I didn't have much choice. Thank God I put the shotgun in there.'

'I only fired at where the roof and window meet. I don't think they're dead.'

He leans back against the car, the strength seeping from his legs. 'You think I care about that? This is nothing to do with . . . the other matter. This is us – you and me. They think I did Roddy.' His hands are still bound, so she opens the door for him and pushes him in. 'I didn't, you know. I didn't kill him.'

'I know you didn't, you idiot. I was with you at the time.'

'Oh yeah.' He feels himself swaying where he sits, and there is acid in his throat. As she gets behind the wheel, he turns and vomits noisily into the rear of the car. He must have hit his head harder than he thought.

'Oh, for heaven's sake!' yells Celeste as she powers away as best she can, the engine making a nasty grinding noise and the rev counter jerking wildly. 'Your friend Fletch is going to love this. Another car wrecked – then puked in.' She spins the wheel, and they are away from the Common, into back streets of tidy, expensive-looking houses that blur by. 'Where to?'

'Your place. It'll be safe now.'

A red warning light blinks on the dash and Celeste makes a small whimpering noise. 'Fletch is going to kill me. We promised to bring her car back in one piece.'

'You got a phone?' Piper manages to say as his stomach dry heaves. He holds up his hands to show that his ability to use one is impaired. 'Call her. All will be forgiven when you tell her who is in the Jag and what she can nail them for. She can have this one on us.'

Twenty-nine

Piper dreams of his father again that night. In it, his old man is in his late thirties. He is in the yard, in a short-sleeved shirt that reveals forearms covered in a tangle of curly hair, almost masking the mysterious, faded tattoos he would never talk about. He is flipping homemade burgers on the grill, and pulling on a bottle of Schlitz. He has a stogey in the ashtray, but rarely sucks on it. Piper notes that, in the dream at least, it is a Romeo y Julieta Havana and, therefore, technically illegal in the United States.

His dad is eyeing him up, shaking his head. He takes a hit of the beer and says: 'What you doin', son?'

'My job.' Piper is surprised that, although he has the body of a man, his voice is that of a little boy.

'That right? Seems to me you're tryin' to do ten people's jobs and a few besides. Focus, boy.'

'I am focused.'

A quick puff of the cigar adds to the billowing smoke from the barbecue. His mother lurks in the background; she is wearing a flamboyant sleeveless summer dress, and serving tall drinks to their friends and neighbours with a smile that could sear the steaks all by itself. She looks beautiful.

'Focused on what?' asks the old man.

'I'm doin' OK.'

'You know at one time, German almost became the official language of the United States. It was a close-run thing. The Yanks hated the English, and there were a lot of Germans, and Slavs who spoke German, on the East Coast. Imagine what would have happened if it had gone through. Where would the US have been on the subject of two world wars? Would they have gone against Hitler?'

'Would we still be called Pfeiffer?' Piper's grandfather had anglicised the name.

His dad laughs. 'Most likely, son. Most likely. Want a word of advice from The Wolfman?'

'Sure. Can I have a beer?'

His dad shakes his head. 'When you're twenty-one, boy.'

'I am twenty-one, Dad,' he insists in his squeaky voice.

'When you start to act it. Listen, you need a partner, someone you can rely on. Back-up.'

Piper's voice deepens and slows as he says: 'I have a partner.'

'Her? What's she ever done for you?'

He points across the garden to where Celeste is surrounded by The Wolf's fellow FBI officers. She is dressed in a scoop-necked top that displays the curve of her breasts, and she has a coquettish grin on her face as she listens to each of the men in turn, giggling appreciatively at their jokes and compliments.

'She's a good girl,' booms Piper.

'Yeah? She looks like she's a good-time girl to me, son.'

Piper reaches for the Sig. It's gone. He left it in the car when he was rescued. But the shotgun is there, propped against the fence. He surges past his father, pushing him aside, spilling a stack of burger buns, and picks up the shotgun, which has had its stock renewed. He pumps the action and heads over to the group surrounding Celeste, shoulders the weapon and—

He wakes.

A soft, fuzzy dawn is leaking through the windows, a lighter shade of grey than London has seen for a while. Perhaps it will be a bright day, for once. Piper rolls off the bed in Celeste's spare room and rubs his eyes. Where did that dream come from? There is a streak of jealousy running through it, he recognises, but there is also possibly a subtext of resentment. It just might be he doesn't like having his ass hauled out of the fire by an unqualified woman. Again.

Unqualified for what, though? She drove like a demon, and fired a shotgun with one hand, and she hit just right: at the roofline, showering Geoff with debris, but not killing him. Quantico would have approved.

Fletch had sent him a tame police doctor the night before, who checked him out. He has maybe a slight concussion, and chafed wrists, but nothing permanent. Not physically, at least, but it is yet more baggage; the memory of another time when he nearly died, another snap from the image bank to wake him up at nights in a cold sweat.

He finds a towelling gown on the back of the door, puts it on and pads downstairs in bare feet. It must be six at the latest, he figures. There is noise from the kitchen, though, and when he enters he finds Celeste chopping vegetables with one of the Global kitchen knives from the steel block on the marble worktop. She looks up as he enters, careful not to add a fingertip to her diced carrot. 'Sorry. Did I wake you?'

'No. I had a dream.'

'I think someone beat you to that line,' she says. 'You OK?'

'Yeah. What you doin'?'

'Juice. Want one?'

'Coffee?'

'Junkie.' She nevertheless sets up the machine for espresso and continues her chopping. 'What was the dream about?'

He explains the gist of it, leaving out the finale.

'Me and your father? Hang on, I think we need my Harley Street therapist on this. Is it true that you are German?'

'Of German descent. The Pfeiffers changed their name as an act of patriotism during the last war – and so they wouldn't get bricks through their window. It's also true that German nearly became the official language of the US, although I'm not sure what my dad's point was.'

She finishes chopping and whizzes the machine. 'It was just a dream, Vince.'

'I did leave the Sig behind.' Fletch had told him the pistol was recovered in the Jag, but protocol dictates it will remain with the cops until it can be officially released back to the FBI. Which could be a couple of weeks.

'It wasn't exactly a healthy kind of place to be hanging around in, trying to find your gun. Besides,' she nods down at her feet. The shotgun is there. 'We're not completely defenceless.'

She crosses to the table with her juice and sits. 'Vince, did you see something when we got into the Saab?'

'Not much. Why?'

She shrugs and sips. 'Nothing.'

'What was it?'

'A cat,' she says quickly. 'A white cat. With blue eyes. Looking at us from across the road.'

'Lots of cats in London.'

'Not like that.'

'You think it came from the Cotswolds?'

She is aware of how silly that sounds, so she simply shrugs once more.

'It could at least have brought your Mini back with it,' he jokes.

'I knew I shouldn't have said anything.' Celeste goes back to drinking from her glass, staring straight ahead, and he studies her for a few moments, enjoying the comforting familiarity that has returned.

'Celeste.'

'Yes?'

'I appreciate what you did. So does Fletch. It took balls.'

Her features drop as she relives those moments. She looks worn and older, the events of the last few weeks etched in lines on her face. 'I still don't understand what happened with Roddy,' she says in a low voice.

Piper collects his coffee from the machine and sits down opposite her. 'I reckon that Lennie tried to persuade him to solve his financial problems with a robbery.'

Celeste shakes her head violently. 'Roddy wasn't a criminal.'

'Didn't he deal drugs once?'

'Hardly. And he thought that was a victimless crime.'

'He was wrong.'

'I know. But a robber?'

Piper reaches across and takes her wrist. He can feel her heart thumping under his thumb. 'These days, you invest in robbery. The overheads are enormous. Take that one. Training a pilot, hijacking a chopper, getting an RPG. Weapons. So just like angels in the theatre, you can buy a share of a heist.'

'Are you serious?'

'Absolutely. Remember how incredulous people were when they discovered you could buy a slice of a racehorse? That seemed bizarre, but this is no different. A thoroughbred team comes along and says, "Here's the deal. You want ten, fifteen, twenty per cent? Well, here's what it'll cost you".'

Celeste shivers at the thought. As if to comfort her, somewhere in the house he hears the whoosh of the central-heating boiler. 'Not Roddy,' she whispers.

'No, maybe not. But Lennie was there. I shot Lennie, apparently. Roddy wanted to kill me in return, but couldn't. Because he loved you. Because he couldn't bear to hurt you.'

'That's meant to make me feel better?'

'It's all you've got,' says Piper slowly. 'Trust me, I know. He loved you. I liked Roddy, no matter what he got himself into. I don't bear him a grudge.'

'But the people who took you?'

'They thought I was after them, because someone had snatched Roddy and . . .' He stops, not liking where this is going. 'Look, they didn't want to cap me first time round, because it was just business, me hitting Lennie. With Roddy, it was personal, so they set me up for him. But once they thought it was me using Roddy to trace them . . .' He clears his throat. 'Whereas in fact, someone else had snatched Roddy and . . .'

'Go on. I can take it.'

'And,' he has trouble saying the word, 'tortured him for information – about where you were, I would guess.'

'Did he give them us?' she asks glumly.

'If he did, I wouldn't blame him, but we'll probably

never know. I think they got to us through Roth. Not directly, but I think Roth told too many people, which makes it my fault. I think Roddy did his part.'

'Thank you,' she says, her eyes filling.

'For what?'

She just shakes her head, unable to answer. After a while she sniffs and says: 'What now?'

'I need a haircut. I look like Crusty the Clown.'

'That's not what I meant. But I can do the haircut.'

He waves a hand at the thought of it. 'No, that's OK.'

'Oh, don't be silly. I've cut all my girlfriends' hair at one time or another.' Celeste stops, aware of the fact that she now has two fewer girlfriends than she once had. 'Sit here. I'll get a towel.'

Piper does as he is told. She wraps a towel around his shoulders and pulls at his hair in the disdainful manner of a professional. 'I'll dry-cut it.'

She begins to work quickly, and he enjoys the sensation, the intimacy of her fingers in his hair, on his neck, gently pushing him this way and that. 'It's going to be hard,' he says. 'Roddy.'

'It is already. I keep catching myself thinking: I'll ask Roddy. Or: Roddy'll know what to do. Then it hits me.'

'I was the same with Martha.'

'Does it go away?'

No, he should say. It happens less often, but when it does the realisation still punches you in the gut, just as hard as always. 'A little,' he says. 'And slowly.'

She stops cutting. 'I'm not sure I want it to go away. At least I am remembering him when it happens. Do you know what I mean?'

'Yes.'

'I wish I believed in an afterlife.'

'Me, too.'

He feels her arms around his neck and her cheek on top of his head. He reaches up and strokes her arm, letting the sobs shake him as well. It lasts perhaps two minutes before she straightens up and resumes cutting. 'Sorry.'

She walks to the window and lets the blind up. A crisp light fills the kitchen, the new sun having found a break in the clouds.

'Don't be sorry. It's what friends are for.' He picks up a clump of hair from his lap. There is more grey than he imagined in there. He lets it float to the floor. By the time this is over, there will be plenty more where that came from.

'What are you going to do now, Vince? Is it back to the Embassy, tie up loose ends?'

'No. I haven't got all the ends to tie up yet.'

'What then?'

'I go and ask questions of the one man who has the answers.'

Celeste places a hand on his shoulder. She knows who he is referring to. 'And how do you get to him?'

Piper reaches up and squeezes her fingers once more, and reluctantly lets go. 'I get to him at low tide.'

Thirty

'You've missed the Skuas, you know.'

'I beg your pardon?' asks Piper.

The publican swipes his credit card and points to the binocular case Piper has over his shoulder. 'Here for the birds? We had all four Skuas up until last month. Sabine's Gulls, too. They've moved on by now, though, in all likelihood. I think you might be lucky with the Little Auk, though.'

He has driven here to the North Norfolk coast in Fletch's Saab, which she hasn't seen yet. A local mechanic knocked a couple of panels out and fixed a split hose to make it roadworthy, but there wasn't much he could do about the cosmetics. Or the smell of vomit, which means it is best to drive with the windows open, no matter what the weather. Celeste is right. Fletcher will tear their heads off and beat them with the bloody ends.

She is pleased enough about the collaring in the Jag, even though there isn't a decent case against the two men yet, and Piper doesn't want to press charges for abduction. As Fletcher said, he's given them the dots, now they have to join them up. Celeste's escapade with the shotgun is being explained away as inter-gang warfare.

The pub he has chosen to stay at is, as he expects, dark, twisted and crepuscular, its ceilings browned by smoke, its wood panels scuffed by the years. The reception desk where they stand is in a wide corridor between the public and saloon bars, a distinction most pubs have lost long ago. The rooms are behind the desk up a staircase that looks as if it would challenge a sober man and, he has been informed three times in a tone that expects a challenge, breakfast finishes at nine. Still, the village is close to the bird reserve, which is where his business lies.

'We've had a good year,' the publican continues. 'Look in the species book in the public bar. Just in October, Ferruginous Duck we had, as well as Radde's Warbler, Siberian Stonechat and the Marsh Warbler, and that's not counting the Great Grey Shrike, Arctic Warbler, Greenish Warbler, the Dotterel, Short-toed Lark—'

'I'm not really—'

'—Grey Phalarope, Night Heron, Aquatic Warbler, Booted Warbler, and let me see now . . . the Lesser Grey Shrike, Rosy Starling, Rustic Bunting, Great White Egret, Western Bonelli's Warbler and mustn't forget the Tawny Pipit, Red-throated Pipit, Olive-backed Pipit . . .' He paused to catch his breath.

'Not really here for the birds,' Piper manages to say.

The landlord stops and eyes him suspiciously, as if this was anti-social behaviour of the highest order. 'Oh. I thought with the binoculars . . .'

'I'm just going to take a look at the plane they're excavating out there.'

The landlord reaches under the desk and produces a key that could double as a sea anchor. 'There's no plane out there,' he scoffs. 'Bits of metal maybe, but not a whole plane. Not after all these years. Waste of time, layin' out all those flags. And if one of them steps off the path . . .' He makes a sucking noise. 'Got to know your way around out there. Shouldn't be lettin' amateurs crawl all over it, just for a few bits of metal.'

'I heard it's a Flying Fortress.'

The man places the key on the desk. 'Here you are, Room Fourteen, second floor. No lift, I'm afraid. Could be one of those. I remember seein' them as a lad, coming over. Them and, what was the other one? Liberators. Hundreds of them sometimes. They found one of those Liberators in the reed bed at Bulham, twenty year ago. Hardly anything left of it. What hope have they got out there?'

'I think they just want to identify it.' Piper picks up his bag when it becomes clear he will be carrying his own luggage up those lethal stairs.

'You're American.'

'Yes.'

'You got a connection with this plane then?'

'Just curious,' he says. 'Just a curious American.'

'Right. Did I mention breakfast service is only till—'

'Nine o'clock,' Piper finishes. That's OK. He'll be long gone by then.

Celeste finally tracks down Father Gavin in Chiswick. He has moved three times since he officiated at the funeral of her father. They were never a particularly religious family, but her father requested a priest – albeit a high C of E one – in his final few days, and the young Father Gavin rose to the occasion. Not only did he manage an eloquent and moving speech about a man he had known for less than a week, he also kept in constant contact for the tricky six months afterwards.

His vicarage, not far from Gunnersbury Tube

station, is a darkly Gothic late-Victorian building that suggests dour sermons and joylessness from the outside. When he opens the door, however, she can see how the stained glass floods the interior with light. If it dazzles under a winter sky, she thinks, it must be glorious in summer.

He is blinking sleep from his eyes and brandishing a chequebook. It takes a moment for him to focus. 'Oh. I thought you were the milkman.' A second later, recognition hits him. 'Celeste? Celeste Young?'

'Hello, Father.'

He remembers himself and steps aside. 'Come in. Sorry, it's just such a surprise. My goodness, you are up early.'

'I wanted to catch you. I know it's a busy time of year.'

'Yes. I mean, no. I can always make time for you.' He is a little thinner on top, a little more careworn, but there still shines from Father Gavin the aura of a good man.

He takes her through to a dated country-style kitchen, where he fetches cups from a stripped pine dresser and they drink a pot of tea at a similarly honey-coloured table, piled high with Minutes and notes, Bibles, and Christmas decorations. He manages to get most of it onto one of the other chairs, before he sits and asks: 'What can I do for you?'

'Roddy is dead.'

His features collapse into a mask of sadness the way they must have done a million times, but nevertheless he manages to look sincere when he reaches across and touches her hand and says, 'I am sorry, Celeste. How?'

'Oh, that doesn't matter. He got in with some bad people.'

He shakes his head, pain etched across his face. 'Oh dear. I always felt Roddy was a good soul, a little lost.'

'That's why I'm here.'

He cocks his head to one side. 'You think he's somewhere, suffering? A hell of some description?'

'No, Father.' Celeste took in a deep breath, knowing how this was going to sound. 'I think he's become a cat.'

Thirty-one

The car park for the bird reserve is situated between two spits of land that jut out into the North Sea, perhaps two miles apart. In front of this tarmac-ed area, now full of vehicles, stand four elevated wooden hides, spaced out on their stilts at 200-yard intervals. They look a little like watchtowers at a prisoner-of-war camp, except that they are pleasingly ramshackle. The thick crust of salt and lichen that covers the boards means that, from seaward at least, they blend into the background. Which is, of course, the idea.

No bird lovers are in them today, however. Most of the twitchers are in the car park, haranguing anyone who will listen about the hordes of outsiders who have come with their metal detectors and cameras and sample nets, about the man from the War Graves Commission – his status proclaimed by a stencilled sign – who sits next to the hot drinks vendor, sipping tasteless tea, about the RSPB and the Imperial War Museum and Duxford, and anyone else who may have ruined their day's birding.

Piper parks the Saab behind a Chrysler Grand Voyager with blacked-out windows and diplomatic plates. Not too difficult to guess who that has transported up here. He steps out, his boots crunching through a film of ice formed in the ruts, and fetches his binoculars from the passenger seat. He threads through the knots of people towards the line of hides, and the gateway that gives access to the dunes and the tidal marshes. He puts the binoculars to his eyes and scans the scene out on the mudflats.

There must be thirty people out there, all scrupulously keeping to a complex network of search areas linked by pathways, the limits of each marked by red and green flags. Many are digging into the mud, others sweeping the area with metal detectors, their eyes fixed firmly on the sludge at their feet. A contingent of Royal Engineers is on hand, in case dangerous ordnance is uncovered. They are all ignoring the swirling clouds of displaced birds above their heads, their alarmed cries distinct even on shore.

The sea is a distant fuzzy line, but Piper can see it is hardly moving, just a few flecks of white showing where the waves are breaking. Although the air temperature is low, and his breath clouds in front of his face, mercifully there is next to no wind.

He walks over to the concession van and risks a coffee, nodding to the War Graves man who is sitting in a canvas chair, wrapped in a waxed jacket, woollen hat and scarf. 'Busy,' Piper says, indicating the activity.

'Too bloody busy,' comes a voice from behind. 'Bloody idiots have scared half the birds away. What the hell do they think they're playing at!'

'Soon be gone,' says Mr War Graves, in a slightly plummy voice. Piper guesses he is just past thirty – young, thinks Piper, to be raking over such old traces. This is an old man's game. 'You'll have it all back by lunchtime.'

'We'd better or the tide'll have 'em.'

'Quite.'

Piper points at the sign which is propped next to him. 'You here in case there are bodies?'

He nods, but says: 'There won't be, not after all this time. Sometimes there are. We recovered a Mosquito in The Wash in 2004 which had two bodies in it. But that was intact. This one . . .' He spreads his arm to indicate the scattering of wreckage. 'But yes, Home Office rules insist one of us is here, and we identify ourselves prominently. You another American?'

'Another?'

He gestures over at the flats. 'Quite a few of you

out there. Mind you, it's one of yours, I suppose.' His mobile rings and he answers. After listening, he consults a bound buff-coloured folder balanced on his knee. 'No, I think you'll find that's an oxygen cylinder. The number is the model type. Not an aircraft ident, I am afraid.' He flips the phone lid closed and answers Piper's unasked question. 'This contains the numbers and squadrons of all unaccounted planes believed to be in South-East England.'

'You do this for a US plane? I mean, if there were bodies, they'd not be British citizens.'

'*In loco governmentis.* You do the same for us. There is the odd British pilot who disappeared on training missions over there. It was safer to train our boys in the US in forty-two and three, you see. Besides, I have been doing this for five years now. Time has taught me that you never know who was on a plane – Brits, Yanks, Czechs, Kiwis, South Africans, Poles. It was a world war, after all.' He raises his voice. 'How much longer, Roger?'

Piper turns to see a ruddy-faced middle-aged man dressed in waders, carrying detection equipment over his shoulder. 'Less than two hours,' he says, looking at his watch. 'The RSPB guys are getting twitchy even now.'

'Twitchy. Very good,' laughs the War Graves man, before he realises it wasn't a joke. 'Royal Society for the Protection of Birds,' he explains to Piper. 'This is their back yard, really.' The phone rings again and Piper slips away with a wave of the hand.

He ditches most of the coffee in a wire trash bin, and moves towards the gate which gives access to the reserve and shoreline. It is festooned with signs, full of dos and don'ts and birdwatching etiquette. Next to it is a Secret Service agent whom Piper vaguely recognises. It is clear this is mutual, because the man tenses when he sees him. Piper gets out his creds, just in case the guy needs his memory properly refreshed.

'Agent,' the guy says with a nod. 'What can I do for you?'

'Hi. I'd like a word with the Ambassador.'

'I am afraid no firearms are allowed out in the reserve.'

'I wasn't planning on wildfowling.' The square face doesn't register anything. Piper raises his arms and is frisked.

'You are not carrying a weapon?' the man asks, surprised.

'No,' says Piper. 'The Met are using it as part of criminal proceedings.' Because the Sig was still in the Boss's hand when the police got there, it has given them something to charge and hold him with while they tie him to the chopper heist. It means that the few weeks until Piper sees his gun again have become an indefinite period.

'Mr Ambassador is over there. On the left. Do not deviate from the area laid out by the red and green flags.'

Piper puts the binoculars to his eyes, and scans the scavengers out on the flats. He finds Sandler way over to the left, next to a ragged wall formed by foot-wide wooden poles that run off the gravelly headland. Even from this distance, he can make out that the wood of the groyne is soft and rotten and covered in molluscs. Sandler is patrolling the base of it, away from the others, a solitary figure lost in his own thoughts of what happened to that plane.

'OK. Thanks.'

He walks across the marram-grassed dunes towards the mud, past one of the towers, the canvas covers of the hide itself rustling slightly in the breeze that has sprung up. At the high-tide mark, a grouchy-looking official with a clipboard asks: 'Name?'

'Vincent Piper.'

'With?'

'US Embassy.'

From his pocket the man fishes a plastic disc the size of a gambling chip and hands it over. 'Number forty-six. Return that when you come back. You been out there before?' Piper shakes his head. 'Make sure you—'

'Stay between the flags. I know.'

Within a dozen paces Piper realises that his hiking boots aren't up to this job. The substratum is a gooey mess, traced with tiny rivulets of water, that means the top three inches are just sludge that sucks at your feet. Here and there are rounded hillocks, which must poke above the water even at high tide, capped with spiky dark-green plants. As he strides on, labouring hard, these outcrops diminish in number until he is on the flats proper.

A strange smell rises with each footstep – the tang of saltwater cut with a musky organic smell and ripe with the tinge of decay. It isn't gaggingly unpleasant, but it suggests fish flesh, just on the turn, or, he thinks, the gradual decomposition of human bodies, as micro-organisms and bottom feeders all take their turn at the flesh. He shakes the image from his mind. As the man said, if there were crew out here, they have long been fed back into the planet's great carbon cycle.

Now he is away from the shore, Piper can hear the voices of the searchers, calling across the flats to each other, and pick out the small wide-tyred pull-along trucks into which any finds are being placed, after being bagged and tagged. Above him, the birds still screech, the sound piercing and disturbing, a cry of real anger at the intrusion.

The groyne where Sandler is working is further away than it seems. The path to the large oval he occupies is delineated by flags, and averages three metres wide. Beyond this safe passage, the ground looks pretty much like what he is walking on, apart from the odd pool, whose depth is difficult to judge. He bends, picks up a white stone, so honeycombed with holes it could be the remnants of something once living, and tosses it into one of the circles of seawater. It plops in and disappears. He is still none the wiser.

A group of crabs scuttle away before him, and slide into one of the foot-wide channels of water that form a reticulate pattern all over the flats. A gull the size of his head alights on one of the flagpoles and eyes him with disdain.

Sandler has straightened up and is examining something in his hand. From his belt he takes a water spray and atomises a mist over the chunk of metal, turning it in his hand. Something tells him he is being watched and he looks up. 'Vince,' he calls. 'You made it.'

'I said I would.'

'And I said you were lying.' He holds out his hand, and Piper has to speed up, sliding through the mud in order to take it without an embarrassing period elapsing. 'Look.' The Ambassador displays a piece of oxidised aluminium eight inches across, a few flecks of paint clinging to the line of rivets that cross it.

'What is it?'

'Beats the shit out of me.' Sandler bends down and drops it into a rubber bag. 'What's on your mind, Vince?'

'B-17s?'

Sandler grins and shakes his head. 'I don't think old planes would get you out of bed, Vince, let alone up here. Drink?' From his rucksack he takes a chrome flask and pours Piper a half-cup of coffee. Piper takes it and sips. It is still hot.

'Thanks.'

'So?'

The wind finally remembers it is meant to blow on this exposed coast, and it whips at them, droning softly around the exposed, spongy uprights of the groyne. The sea has become more agitated, and it looks to be closer. 'Mr Ambassador . . .'

'Jack.'

'Jack. What are you going to do once this gig is up?'

'The dig?'

'Gig. The Ambassadorship. What ambitions do you have?'

'I have a ranch that needs some money spent on it. I'd like to get back to flying, I'm a little rusty. Why?'

'I think you are an ambitious man, Jack. Under all that good old boy bonhomie, you have designs. Political designs.'

Sandler laughs so loud the seagull vacates its perch on the flag, and the other searchers stop and stare in their direction. Piper doesn't crack a smile. 'You're serious?'

'Tell me about Sasha Zee.'

'Whoa, whoa, son. That's a change of tack. Sasha who?'

'Sasha Zee. She claims you had an affair with her.' The Ambassador makes a snorting sound. 'Well,' agrees Piper, 'affair might be too grand a term.'

Sandler's features harden. His fists clench so hard, his knuckles shine white. 'Damn right. How dare you come here and—'

'I dare come here because people have died.' Piper throws the anger back in his face, and Sandler steps away as if he has been scorched. 'Other people have nearly died. Including me, including Celeste Young. And I think it is because of you.'

Sandler stares him down for the best part of thirty seconds, his jaw working, but no words coming. Two blasts on a whistle drift across the flats and he relaxes. 'Tides turning. We don't have long. Thing creeps round, cuts you off. Because of me, you say?'

'Yes. Because of you.'

There is something about the flat, emotionless answer that unnerves him. 'You come to kill me, Vince?'

'No. I've come to listen.'

Sandler walks across and places the bag against the slimy timbers of the groyne. The seagull from the flag-pole alights on the top of the structure and peers down at them. 'To me?'

Piper nods, takes a gulp of the coffee, throws the dregs away and says: 'Tell me about Sasha.'

Sandler considers for a moment. He looks up at the fat seagull, which squawks noisily at him, the yellow beak agape, head thrusting back and forth. 'Someone else who doesn't trust me. OK, let me tell you about Sasha.'

Thirty-two

Father Gavin tries to keep his features impassive as Celeste talks what he considers to be, at best, claptrap. 'Do you remember my friend Davina? She was at Daddy's funeral – blonde, pretty, had quite a loud laugh. Well, she is a shaman. I know, I know, you are suspicious of such things.'

Father Gavin tops up their cups of tea and says softly, 'I think the devil works hard to dazzle us in many ways.'

'The *devil*?' Celeste blurts out.

'Yes, the devil. I don't mean Old Nick, with horns and a tail. I suppose I mean devil*ment*, rather than an actual being. I think something conspires to blind and seduce us when we are vulnerable. As you are now, Celeste.'

She stands up and paces the slate-tiled floor, her

heels clicking out a staccato rhythm. 'I am. But Davina once told me that she believes that when we die, we split into three parts. The body, obviously, which is just a shell.'

'I would have to agree with her there,' nods Father Gavin.

'The spirit and the soul. She believes the spirit is like a universal force. Perhaps like the Holy Spirit? That goes to some kind of big powerhouse. And then there is the soul. Each one of those is unique, imprinted in some way with us. Our being.'

'Go on.'

'But she thinks the soul can move into other vessels, into animals, so that they can communicate with us. She swears her father visits her as a robin.'

'Really?' Now he lets the disbelief creep into his voice. 'Celeste, I have no dispute with the various theories of how our soul and spirit are transmuted when we die. That is a legitimate part of the theological debate. But my religion does not countenance souls moving into animals, nor animals popping along for a quick chat.'

Celeste runs her fingers through her hair. 'But you don't know, do you?'

'I don't believe—'

'But you don't *know* if any of this is true. God, the devil, the Holy Spirit – it's all guesswork, isn't it? Like all that guff about angels on pinheads. Mere conjecture.'

'Celeste, sit down. Please. You're wearing me out – and my floor.'

She smiles at him and takes her place at the table once more. One knee, though, refuses to keep still, and pumps up and down nervously.

He checks his watch. 'I have to take a service in forty minutes.'

'I'm sorry, I shouldn't have come.'

She reaches for her bag, but he slides it out of her reach. 'No, not at all. I am glad you did. Look, I feel that I am getting snapshots, very blurred and grainy snapshots, of what has gone on. Do you think you could tell me everything from the beginning?'

Celeste laughs. 'I'm not sure you are ready for everything, Father.'

'Oh, you'd be surprised. Now look, I'm going to grab a razor and toothpaste and I'll get ready next door.' He indicates the downstairs lavatory with wash basin, off the hallway. 'You just carry on talking. I'll be able to hear everything you say.'

'Like a confession box?'

'But with hot and cold running water.'

She finishes thirty minutes later, and within that time Father Gavin has transformed himself into someone approximating a Man of God, ready for the first services of the day. His face, though, looks troubled, as if he has taken the weight from Celeste and let it drop onto his own shoulders. He places a hand on hers. 'I take back what I said. If you think Roddy is trying to communicate, to help in some way, I can't believe it is a sin.'

'You don't think he is, though?'

'I think it might be wishful thinking.' His voice drops to a whisper. 'But, if truth be known, who knows how much of this job is just that, eh?'

'Father, you'll burn in hell for that.'

He wags a finger at her. 'Perhaps. Now tell me, this American . . .'

'Vincent.'

'Is he a good man?'

She hesitates before answering, though she isn't sure why. 'Yes.'

'Do you love him?'

A bark of embarrassed laughter. 'Father, I just told you what I do for a living!'

The house phone rings three times and stops. Father Gavin glances at his watch once more. 'That's my you're-on-in-five-minutes warning. Come, walk with me to the church.' He holds out a crooked elbow and she slides her right arm through, slinging her bag over the other shoulder. 'So. I know what you do for a living. I also know how you talked about this Vincent.'

She makes a contorted face of distaste at him. 'OK, act like a schoolgirl. But you haven't answered my question.'

'No. I haven't.'

'Are you going to?'

'Yes,' Celeste says as they step out into a cold light that hurts her eyes, and blinks a sudden film of moisture away. Father Gavin unhooks himself from her to mortice-lock his front door. 'But give me a minute.'

'She was a nice girl. I . . . it's indefensible, isn't it? Here I am, happily married, kids, good job. Hell,' says Sandler with feeling. 'Great job in some ways. But it's never enough, is it?'

'I'm not judging you,' says Piper. 'That isn't what this about.'

'You see it in the terrible tabloids they have here. Soccer players and managers, TV stars, businessmen. People who have it all, caught with their pants down.'

'You weren't.'

Sandler shrugs. He helps himself to more coffee from the flask, leaning back against the seaweed-slippery wood of the groyne, not worrying about marking his ski-jacket. 'It didn't last long. It wasn't particularly sordid. There is a theory, you know, that what we men need is variety, constant stimulation. It is the chase, the change we want. The sex, when it happens, is only like signing off on the adventure.'

Piper isn't sure how most women would feel about being described as a dotting of Is and crossing of Ts, but he can see what the other man means. 'It's a depressing thought. But you could be right.'

'So. That's my dark, dirty secret. Not very dark or dirty. Not in the grand scheme of things.'

'Not unless you're running for public office. Then it's a stain on your soul – and a deal breaker.'

'So we are back to that. What public office?'

The wind has strengthened; they are being buffeted now. Piper can feel his face stinging as salt is flicked at it, and the breaking surf is within earshot. The searchers are beginning to move back towards the shore. Out at sea a bulk carrier is making slow progress, heading for one of the ports, its hull low in the water. 'The biggest there is. President of the United States.'

Sandler holds his arms out as if he is about to be crucified against the rotting wall behind him. 'Do I look like I am campaigning for the Presidency? You think this is a vote winner?'

'I think you are being groomed, Mr Ambassador. The only question is: was it with or without your permission? Did you know about the killings done in your name?'

It takes a moment for Piper to identify the squelching sound as that of large feet being pulled free from the tight grip of the glutinous mud. He turns to his right, and sees Brewster rounding the head of the groyne, steadying himself with one hand. In the other is a pistol held pressed to his thigh, the stubby cylinder of a suppressor prominent on the end. 'I told you, sir,' he says. 'The man is crazed.'

'Yes, you did tell me.' Sandler shakes his head as if he is very disappointed with Piper. 'You think that a person or persons unknown are bowdlerising my life. Making it more palatable to the voting public. Rubbing out that little stain you mentioned. Is that correct?'

'Your life. Maybe some other lives too. I doubt if they'd put all their eggs in one basket.'

'Who are *they*?' the Ambassador demands.

Piper lets his voice drop. It barely carries as the wind funnels between them. 'I don't know.'

'Oh, you can do better than that, Vincent. The Illuminati? The Masons? No, no wait. The Knights Templar?'

'*They* are people who can get two trained killers into this country through the back door. *They* are people who can find me in the countryside. *They* are the people who tortured my friend to death.'

'You carrying, Piper?' asks Brewster.

'No. Your boy did me at the gate.'

Brewster eyes him suspiciously. 'Put your arms above your head. Just for a second.'

Piper does as he is told, and Brewster looks for the tell-tale tug of the weight of a weapon. 'OK. Mr Ambassador, you can leave us now. Vincent and I are just going around this wall here.' He points at the groyne.

'No,' Piper says. 'I'm not.'

The gun swings up in an arc, still close to Brewster's body, so it will be invisible to any observer, but pointed at Piper's stomach. Sandler has not moved a muscle. 'Mr Ambassador, will you leave us now, please. This is my job. This man is a danger to you and your office. A clear and present danger with serious delusions. Will you leave now?'

Sandler, confused, bends down and picks up his bag with exaggerated slowness. 'Brewster, if you are going to do what—'

'Leave now. It's best you don't know.'

'Best you don't know,' Piper repeats, trying to keep an edge of hysteria from his voice. 'See? He's one of them. Best you don't know.'

'Listen to yourself, Piper,' Brewster sneers. 'Mr Ambassador?'

Sandler nods and turns, his back to Piper. As soon

as he does so, the pistol is pointed at his chest, the suppressor indicating he should walk. Walk or be dragged, he is sure it is all the same to Brewster.

The three shrill blasts on the whistle stab across the flats. There is a pause, then they are repeated, with even more urgency, then a third time. There seems to be panic in the car park. People are shouting with hands cupped over their mouths, but little of it carries; others are waving arms frantically.

'What's that?' asks Piper.

'The Royal Engineers' emergency evacuate signal,' says Sandler as he turns back to them. 'It probably—'

But his explanation is drowned out by the roar of an explosion that ripples the semi-fluid ground beneath their feet, then throws up a vast dark wall of mud and saltwater, blotting out the sun, and hurls all three of them against the timber with a slap of soft flesh on hard wood.

Celeste arrives home from her meeting with Father Gavin feeling even more unsettled than usual. She sits in her kitchen with Radio 4 a soft burble in the background, tearing the *Independent* newspaper into smaller and smaller strips, until she has a substantial pile in front of her.

She then tears each strip into tiny irregular shapes, until it begins to resemble inky confetti. Confetti?

Hardly suitable for a funeral. That will be the next thing to get through. Perhaps she ought to face up to that. This unlocks a floodgate of questions. She still has to break the news to their mother: will the latter be well enough to attend? Will she be certain what is going on? Should it be a secular or religious service? Religious, probably. Then what hymns, what music? Should there be a choir? What about drinks afterwards? Who should she invite?

The world seems to go crimson for a second as she sweeps the torn newspaper onto the floor with a yell of: 'Fuck it!'

She isn't strong enough for this. She, the woman whose whole world was all about control, of men, of money, of desire – all that seems like just a conceit now. She is as vulnerable to the eddies of life as anyone else. It was sheer vanity to think otherwise.

There is a noise at the window, and she turns, but there is nothing. A cat again, perhaps? Roddy?

Something else is making her jittery, something out of place, not quite right. She stands and scans the kitchen, checking off each section, ensuring all is as it should be. Finally her eyes alight on the silver knife block. There is one of the Globals missing, the one that she uses to chop the fruit and vegetables. Which is odd, because she distinctly remembers washing it and putting it back, because you have to handle the razor-edges so carefully. So if she hasn't taken it, where is it?

Celeste feels her stomach contract, as if she is about to throw up.

Piper spits out a mouthful of mud, levers himself off the groyne, and wipes his eyes clear. Ahead of him, a thick coil of smoke is twisting across the flats at ground level, and within it dazed ghostly figures are moving. Fine particles of sand and silt float through the air, turning the whole scene sepia.

There is a loud groan to his left, and he recalls exactly what was about to happen before the blast.

The Ambassador is still dazed, shaking his head. He is lying against Brewster, who roughly pushes him away. The Secret Service man hasn't lost the gun, Piper notices with regret. Piper lets the Global knife slide from his sleeve into his hand, feels the edge cut into his skin, but he can't worry about that.

He steps forward, his fingers tightening around the knurled metal handle, picking out the impact point. Into the neck, sever the carotid artery. Brewster will last less than twenty seconds. He'll doubtless use that time to kill Piper, but every plan has its flaw.

He is within three feet of Brewster, raising the knife when he sees the other man's eyes clear, and the pistol flick up and steady, and he braces himself for the impact of the slug. If he can just keep the forward momentum, stop being blown off his feet by the impact of the slug, he might still take him out.

'*Nooo.*' The body barrels past him and into the Secret Service man. Together Sandler and Brewster slither through the mud, feet working for a grip, but eventually Brewster manages to untangle himself, using his spare hand to shove the Ambassador away.

Piper stands facing him, his knife in his hand, but now there is so much distance between them, it might as well be his dick.

'Now,' puffs Sandler, his chest heaving with the exertion.

Both Brewster and Piper hesitate, wondering what the hell that means. Brewster assumes he is meant to kill Piper, and reacts accordingly.

'NOW.'

Piper is aware of a crack in the air, the punch to the eardrum as something whistles by. It impacts Brewster in the left shoulder and he spins around, his feet once more slithering, and he reels back further out into the flats past the red-flagged pole. His face is a mask of shock and surprise, his body too damaged for him to do much more than sway, panting through a curtain of pain, an agony that makes both his hands clench.

The finger tightens and the pistol fires, and Piper feels a burn in his upper thigh, and the leg goes numb.

A second shot punches into Brewster's chest, and his head flies back, a mist of blood flicking from his mouth high into the air. There is no need for a third. He is going now, the one good arm windmilling, his body haemorrhaging internally from a thousand burst capillaries, cruelly sliced by the little copper discs which have ricocheted within him.

He falls back into one of the pools with a soft slap. He floats for a second, then there is a greedy slurping sound and the water and mud roll over him. His face is the last to go under, his unseeing eyes filled in by the sludge, until there is just the merest indentation in the mud to show where he has fallen.

Sandler and Piper both let long-held breaths out. The Ambassador's phone rings from within the rubberised bag, and he fishes it out. When he takes the call, his voice is thin and reedy. 'Yeah. It was what? Jesus. Yeah, He's OK.'

He looks at Piper who nods in confirmation.

'Me, too. Son of a bitch. No, we're coming in.'

Piper glances down at his leg, but the wound is little more than a gouge and, for the moment, he feels no pain. His hand, however, is stinging from the thin paper-like cut across the palm.

There are more whistles being blown. Piper realises they are just about the last ones left out here, and that he is standing in several inches of water, which is rippled and wrinkled like old skin.

'Tide's running like a bastard. Come on.' Sandler picks up his gear and offers Piper a shoulder to lean on. Just then, the cross-shore wave hits them, pushing Piper, who staggers but remains upright, but side-swiping the legs from under Sandler. He falls onto his knees, his eyes wide with surprise.

Piper splashes forward, and is reaching for the raised hand when there is a sound like an enormous sink emptying. Within a second the water is over Sandler's waist, the suction clamping his legs unbelievably. An eddy encircles him, accelerating like a whirlpool, and his eyes bulge. 'Vince!'

The seabed beneath him seems to open as it changes from mud to a treacherously insubstantial mixture of salt particles and seawater. His fingers brush Vince's, but the ocean seems to reach up and grab Sandler, pulling him under, spinning him over as it does. He takes a mouthful of water, his throat burning, the world beneath his feet refusing to give any purchase.

He collides with a flagpole, and he knows he is being drawn out to sea, to join Brewster. He manages to grab hold of the metal, but the post starts to move, dragging under his weight. His head breaks the surface, and he spews the water from his throat and lungs and takes a gasp, before the shifting, feckless sands have him once more.

The pain in his head is intense, a sharp agony that makes him want to scream. It is only as he feels fingers grab his ears that he realises someone or something is pulling at his scalp. He breaks into air once more and sees Piper, one hand on the pole, the other with a fistful of hair.

'Kick, there's still some solid patches,' Piper yells, a tremor of fear in his voice. 'Jack, for fuck's sake, *kick*.'

Sandler moves his legs in bicycling motion, and finds something to lever on. He pushes himself up, manages to stand, surprised to find the water is only just over his knees.

'Come on, Jack,' urges Piper. 'Again.'

He staggers forward, the mud beneath his feet reluctant to let him go, but each step feels firmer. Piper gets an arm under his elbow and heaves him, and they half run a few yards, until their knees are free of the water.

'Jesus,' gasps Sandler.

'Keep going,' warns Piper. 'It isn't going to give up that easily.'

With the sea still sucking at them hungrily, they head between the flags, fleeing on treacherous ground which, for the moment, takes their weight. Sandler reaches across to take the dangerous Global still sticking out of Piper's pocket and is about to toss it away when Piper stops him.

'I've got to take that back. It's Celeste's.'

'Yeah. I can see how you might have to do that. You and me, eh? Two peas in a pod.'

'Yeah, but I'm not going to be President.'

Sandler gives a rueful smile. 'Trust me, neither am I. And not just because of my fall from grace.'

Piper can taste the salty particles of carbon and explosive material in the air as they walk through the thin haze of smoke. 'What the hell happened out there?'

'That call I just had, before I went under? It explains a lot.'

'About what?'

'About the fireworks. The plane we've been looking for was an Aphrodite.'

'I don't understand. That explosion was nothing to do with you?' A thought occurs to him and he reaches over and unzips Sandler's sodden jacket. He can see the fine filament of a microphone across his chest. 'Because I have the feeling you knew exactly what I was doing out there, even before I got here.'

Sandler grins and ups the pace. The water is swirling around their knees again, tugging them back once more. 'Son, you got that right. I know you might think you are a bit of a maverick, but you do have some friends left. You should be thankful you have people down here who like you. As for Aphrodite, well, you need another history lesson.'

'Hello, Susan.'

'Hello, Mummy.'

The old lady looks up at Celeste and smiles. Only her mother recalls the few years at school when she was embarrassed by her name and wanted something normal, and had hit upon Susan. Mrs Young is still incredibly beautiful, her face soft and marked by only the most delicate of lines. Her heavily veined hands, tinged with blue, give the game away, but no frowns or cares criss-cross the visage these days, because she has none. Her world is shrinking, week by week.

They are in the lounge of the care home in Roehampton where she now resides. It was once a very grand vicarage; now it houses just a dozen privileged clients, who pay, or whose children pay, well over the odds for a place that is clean, brightly lit and devoid of the smells that normally characterise such establishments.

There is a Christmas tree in one corner, with plenty of presents stacked underneath, and streamers billow from the ceiling. There is not a surface that doesn't hold gold or silver tinsel or a piece of holly, it seems.

'Happy Christmas,' Celeste says, and hands over the box. 'But don't open it till the twenty-fifth, will you?'

'Of course not.'

'I'll be in for lunch. I've asked Claire.' Claire is the owner, very sweet, but also very businesslike. She will, of course, charge Celeste extra for her roast turkey and all the trimmings.

'Will you?'

'Yes.'

That slightly vacant smile again. 'That will be lovely.'

'Mummy, I have something to tell you.'

'You're getting married?'

'No.' But she sees a twinkle in the eye, for once, and pinches her mother playfully. 'As if.' She swallows, braces herself. 'It's about Roddy.'

'Oh, what's he done now? He was in this morning, you know.'

'Was he?' she asks. Her father visits sometimes, too.

'Yes. He hasn't been gambling with other children's dinner-money again, has he?'

'No, Mummy.' She feels herself welling up, and chokes back the tears. 'He's . . .'

'Not running an unofficial tuckshop? I said that was just youthful entrepreneurism.'

'No, not that. He's . . .'

'Yes?'

She can't tell her. Those clear eyes seem to drill right into her, daring her to shatter the innocence, to drive a shard of misery into her heart.

'Just that he's going away for Christmas. He can't be here for lunch.'

'Oh.' She looks confused. 'He didn't mention that this morning.'

'Last-minute change of plan.'

'Oh, well. Perhaps you could come?'

'Yes,' she says. 'I think I will.'

'Good. You must mention it to . . .' For once her brow furrows in concentration as she scans her depleted memory banks for a name.

'Claire.'

'Yes.'

'I will. I've got to dash. I've got a cab waiting.' She leans over and kisses her mother on the forehead. 'See you on Christmas Day.'

As she leaves she stops by the office. Claire, a stout lady in her early forties given to tent-like floral dresses, is supervising Iva, one of the young foreign girls who make up much of the staff, who is mopping the black and white tiles of the hallways.

'Sorry, Miss Young.' Claire sprays a large aerosol can of scent in the air.

'Someone had an accident?'

382

'No. Some dratted cat crept inside.' She wrinkles her nose. 'Must be a tom. I hope you didn't smell it when you came in.'

'I came in through the conservatory. Didn't smell a thing. I just wanted to re-confirm lunch on Christmas Day.'

'Of course. You can have a table just for you two, if you wish.'

'That would be lovely. Thanks.'

As she reaches the heavy front door, with its stained glass showing a scene from the Sermon on the Mount, Celeste hesitates. 'Claire?'

'Yes?'

'Did you see the cat?'

'No.' She shakes her head, making her chin wobble. 'Just smelled him.'

'I did,' says Iva. 'Big cat. I chased it, but too late – *pssssst*. All over my floor.'

'What colour was it?'

'Oh, white.'

'With blue eyes?'

'Yes,' she says, puzzled. 'You are right, miss. Blue eyes. You know him?'

Celeste smiles and begins chuckling to herself. She is still laughing by the time she gets into the cab and it pulls away from the kerb, heading back to Chelsea.

Thirty-three

As he does every morning, Charles Pearl wheels himself over the tracks that criss-cross Three Pines until the odometer attached to the wheelchair shows twenty kilometres. Then he coasts down the gentle slope to the belvedere, letting the breeze dry the sweat from his face and body. There, waiting as always, is Carlos, with cold towels and a pitcher of orange juice.

It is a slightly overcast start to the day, and there is rain in the air, but Pearl is of a mind to breakfast out of doors. He orders toast, two poached eggs, some hash browns and two pieces of crisped Canadian bacon. The boy leaves with his order, and Pearl watches the flames flickering on the horizon.

London was a pity, he thinks. Jack Sandler would have been an easy sell. Only one indiscretion to launder from his call sheet, and then they had a man with everything – charisma, youth, principles, right-of-centre policies, the works. And then he goes all liberal on him with that tax-hike bullshit. Just goes to show, people are unpredictable.

He wonders whether they shouldn't just shut the whole exercise down. Go back to leaving it to luck and the will of the people. Except that has led them to disaster, to the body bags in Iraq, to a free-falling dollar, to the devaluing of the Office. All he is trying to do is pre-select, to ensure that people he thinks will serve and serve well have a decent shot at it. A little bit of social engineering, a tweak to the carburettor, no more.

A news helicopter judders overhead and sweeps left to pick up the coastal highway. He can see a thin plume of smoke, more a soft haze, in the far distance, more or less in the direction it is heading. It is possibly a small forest fire, although it is the wrong season. Perhaps an early-morning commuter smash, although no, it is the weekend. But there is a lot of holiday traffic out there, the final flurry of repositioning prior to the celebrations. All it takes is one driver to have been getting into the bottle a little early, and *boom*. Carnage. Dying just before Christmas – what a terrible thing to inflict on friends and relatives.

The first pain has an epicentre just below his left armpit, radiating across his ribcage. He grabs the cramped muscle in his upper arm and frantically kneads it. The second punches him in the solar plexus, driving the breath from his body in an extended wheeze.

Might have overdone it today, he thinks. But he had a check-up only weeks ago. His father lived until he was ninety-five.

The steel band whips around his chest and contracts, hard. He feels the air forced from the depths of his lungs and his throat constricts. The world darkens on the left side, the vision shutting down, like an old television set, until all that is left is a small, white dot.

He leans forward to reach the intercom, but he is too far away and pitches forward, out of the chair. His forehead thuds into the wooden floor of the belvedere, drawing blood, but that is the least of his problems. He lies there, struggling with limbs and senses that are rapidly fading, for a few more minutes, but he is dead by the time Carlos arrives with his breakfast.

'Aphrodite was a response to the V-1 programme,' says Sandler as they trudge through shallower water towards shore. Both are shivering, from shock and cold, but the Ambassador's voice has regained its firmness. 'However, it was a Model-T compared to a Ferrari. Or maybe that should be a Mercedes. They took old, clapped-out Flying Fortresses and loaded them with explosives. They were called Babies. Up above, a Mothership used radio control and would guide them to the targets – mostly V-1 and V-2 launching sites.'

Piper stops for a minute, taking all this in, his teeth chattering. 'They could take fully loaded planes off by remote control back then?'

'No,' says Sandler. 'That was the devil of it. A volunteer aircrew had to fly it up to operational height, point it in the right direction and bale out.'

'Bale out?' he repeats. Parachute jumping with primitive silk canopies from a bomber wasn't quite like modern skydiving.

'Yup. Which is why one Aphrodite mission counted as five regular sorties. Of course, not all of them made it to jumping height.'

'How come?'

'These were old planes. True, the engines were recons, but the airframes had been through hell. Plus they had twenty thousand pounds of explosive on board, sometimes an early version of napalm. You know that is how Joe Kennedy died? Joe Junior?'

Piper shakes his head.

'He was flying a PB4Y-1, the Navy version of the B-24 Liberator, packed with three hundred and seventy-four boxes of high explosives. The idea was, he would arm the detonator by pulling a pin, hand over control to the B-17 mothership, and then bale out. The target was the bunkers at Mimoyecques, France. Kennedy and his co-pilot Bud Willy took off at 5:55 p.m. on twelve August, 1944. The weather monitors were two Mosquito bombers, one of which, bizarrely, was flown by Elliot Roosevelt, the son of the President of the United States. Kennedy and Willy were meant to bale out near Dover after ensuring the plane was ready to be controlled by the mothership. Kennedy removed the safety pin at 6.19 p.m., and signalled all was as he expected with the agreed code phrase "Stay Flush". The four-engined plane exploded at 6:20 p.m. Joseph was twenty-nine years old. It was kept secret for years. You know it was Joe Junior the old man was grooming for President? It was then he had to switch to Jack. Might've been a different world without Aphrodite.'

'Jesus. Was it worth it?'

'No. In fact, none of the planes ever hit the intended targets. Most were thought to have been destroyed, although there were reports of a few rogue ones that had to be shot down by shore batteries.'

'You knew it was an Aphrodite out there?'

'Hell, no. What do you think we are – crazy? We got some questions to ask about how come nobody knew what was out there. We're lucky half of Norfolk hasn't gone up.'

People are splashing towards them now, several of them holding blankets.

'I owe you another one, Vince.'

'I'll call this one in now.'

'Name it.'

'Did you know about the killing, Jack?' Piper asked softly. 'About getting rid of Sasha?'

The reply is equally soft, and very heartfelt. 'No, Vincent. No, I didn't.'

The two men emerge from the breaking waves onto the shore, and hands reach out to grab them.

'Are you OK?' shouts a voice.

'What happened out there?'

Piper's attention is caught by the man clambering out of one of the hides, the bird observation towers. It is Stanley Roth. And in his hand is the case containing the Sig sniper rifle.

Sandler and Piper, their outer clothes stripped off, swathed in both woollen and foil blankets, are fed hot tea from the catering van. The car park is full of bodies, curious, alarmed and hyperactive in turn. Piper hasn't had a chance to speak to Roth, but he says to Sandler, 'I think we need to get some dry clothes.' He shakes a naked leg.

'We ought to get that wound dressed first.'

'It's not much,' says Piper.

'Didn't think an Aphrodite had survived,' comes a voice from behind. Piper turns. It is the War Graves man from the Home Office, looking unfazed and addressing Sandler. 'Nobody has been badly hurt as far as we can tell. Everyone on the list is accounted for.'

Piper looks at Sandler, who winks. Brewster hadn't signed in on the roster; he must have approached the groyne from the other, the westerly side.

'Thing is, they found part of the AFCE panel,' says Mr War Graves. 'The Automatic Flight Control Equipment was the crude autopilot. As soon as I saw it, I knew that it was a Baby. But, my God, I didn't think there would be live ordnance. Just as I blew my whistle to warn the Engineers, one of them out there clunked something and it began making a strange whirring noise. Thank goodness they got away in time. Minor injuries only.'

'I think we had a lucky break,' says Sandler. 'You reckon we might be able to trace its history?'

'From the serial number on the panel, certainly.'

A police car appears, its blue light sweeping the car park. The Home Office man looks worried and says: 'I'd better go and reassure them that World War Three isn't imminent.'

Roth walks through the crowd towards them. Piper holds out his hand and it is taken and pumped. 'You set this up, didn't you?'

'I did,' says Roth. 'With a little help from the Ambassador here. I called Doc Turner after I spoke to you. He took a peek and confirmed that Kolski was shot *after* he was dead. Then we started looking at where Kolski, Hooper, DeCesare and Brewster might interface. We found a link in a training school in the US. All had been trained by a Colonel Wallace.'

'Who killed DeCesare?'

'Brewster, I would guess.'

'Why?'

'Because, thanks to you and your half-assed ways of doing things, it was all going tits-up.'

'So you stopped Brewster going back home?'

'Didn't have to. He decided to stay and kick over the traces. Which meant taking you out. So the Ambassador here told him that he thought you were stalking him. Reckoned you'd confront him up here with some crazy-sounding conspiracy theory. Brewster volunteered to stay close, undercover. We needed to draw Brewster out. See what he was capable of. Sorry about the leg. I couldn't get a clear bead on him before that, and in the old days the first shot would have been enough. I'm a tad rusty.'

'It's not much,' Piper repeats, although the wound is starting to throb. 'You two cooked this up off your own bat?'

'We did,' says Sandler with a hint of pride.

'I wasn't always a desk jockey and family man,' says Roth, indicating the rifle case at his feet.

'Remember? And Jack here, well Jack liked the sound of going off-piste for once.'

'You can have a life that's too safe, you know,' says Sandler.

Piper shakes his head in disbelief. Chance would be a fine thing. 'But . . . it sounds like the kind of half-assed crazy thing I'd do.'

Roth grins. He points to the ambulance that is crawling along the lane, and takes Piper by the arm, leading him towards it. He lowers his voice. 'Yeah, it does, doesn't it? But keep that quiet, eh? I want to hang on to my job.'

The next day, a story appears on the much-visited website www.whattheywonttellyou.com, claiming that British aviation archaeologists had inadvertently uncovered the scattered remains of a flying saucer which was brought down by RAF Meteors in 1953 off the North Norfolk coast. It details several strange phenomena, and noises that occurred during the dig – the discovery of panels made from an advanced carbon-fibre-like material, the convenient explosion which cleared the beach, and the instant vaporisation of one man when he unearthed one of the saucer's death rays.

Furthermore, it continues, the US government, anxious to add to its Roswell crash-site knowledge, has sealed the site while it packages up the debris for transport back to New Mexico.

The story is picked up by the more credulous press worldwide.

The idea that a sixty-year-old USAAF bomb was accidentally detonated, that the reserve is closed while Royal Engineer teams search for any more unexploded ordnance seems tame in comparison. From now on, twitchers will report strange lights in the sky, spooky happenings on the shore. Britain has its very own Area 51, powered by half-truths, lies and wishful thinking. Which is how the FBI wants it.

Those people who swear they heard shots on the beach, the flat crack of a high-powered rifle, perhaps, are told it was the sympathetic detonation of unstable .50 ammo from the Flying Fortress's waist and turret guns. Enthusiasts who know the Aphrodite ships had no need of such ammo, are told that the Imperial War Museum has ascertained it was not a remote 'Baby' drone, but a regular bomber, returning from Germany, with at least one bomb still jammed in the rack.

And those who claim that day that they saw a man fall, flailing into the mud, and disappear? There is no evidence of a missing person at all.

While the reserve is closed, Brewster's body is eventually located by a team from the US State Department and quietly removed for cremation. He has no immediate family. The cause of death is put as heart failure.

Back in London, Jack Sandler stores away his B-17

model before catching a flight with his family to the USA. He will never build it. Nor will he ever be seriously tempted either to be unfaithful, or stand for high office, again. He should never have listened to Charles Pearl, even when the old man convinced him that nobody, not even those doing his dirty laundry, would realise that the Ambassador had an inkling of what was going on.

He would be ring-fenced, untouchable. Only Pearl would know they had even spoken about it. He didn't have to do anything, just watch his step in future, and follow the pathway laid out for him over the next ten years, a route that should lead him to the White House. A road paved with greed, vanity, hubris. Sandler had only realised when the killing actually started, just how monstrous the whole scheme was. By then it was too late.

Which was why he had made the liberal, left-wing speech, of course, to let Pearl know, indirectly, that the deal was off. He was no longer a contender. There would be no more deaths, that was the idea. Sadly, it didn't work: once the first domino is pushed, the run goes on until there are none left standing. Even as he boards his 747, Sandler has a feeling that the run isn't finished just yet.

Thirty-four

Colonel Henry Logan Wallace Junior finishes his third reading of the obituary of Charles Pearl and lays it on his desk next to the other newspapers. He removes his glasses and rubs his eyes. The light is fading as the sun goes down. The room is illuminated only by the afterglow bouncing off the snow outside, and reading has become difficult.

Pearl, businessman, visionary, film-maker, right-wing activist, patriot – all the touchstones are in the obits. Missing are killer, assassin, master manipulator.

All day the Colonel has been fielding calls from other members of the Committee, all scared for their hides or their wallets, all wondering what will happen now. Well, with the money dried up, and the prime motivator gone, it seems very likely that Operation Palimpsest will wither on the vine. Wallace can't say he's sad.

On paper, it sounded so simple and straightforward.
A little discreet airbrushing, that was all. The problem
was, they were going to do it with real human beings,
not static photographs of them. Its demise means that,
yes, the best possible people may not make it to the
White House. There is a good argument to suggest that
they never have, for one reason or another.

As Pearl had always said, it wasn't the intended
Kennedy who got to the White House. So, just to make
certain the family enjoyed its manifest destiny,
Kennedy Senior steered JFK, his next-in-line, to the
Oval Office, with a mixture of bribes, bullying and
media manipulation. And the Mafia, of course.

Pearl saw no reason why he couldn't do the same,
minus the Mob. But times had changed. The Kennedys
had plenty of skeletons, but back then none of them
mattered a damn. Now, every last bone in the closet
is brought out for general inspection. So you have to
launder the past, wipe it clean and over-write it with
a rosier version, a *palimpsest* of the guy's personal
history.

Now, the immediate past is about to catch up with
Colonel Wallace.

A National Security Agency employee called
Spencer had called him two hours previously to say
they would like to ask him a few questions. About
what? he had enquired. Spencer declined to discuss

it over the phone – said they would be down later that day. On Christmas Eve? he'd protested. The NSA doesn't recognise holidays, had been the priggish reply.

What will he tell Dwight, his son? That is what worries him most. How will he be able to explain about how easy it is to cross the line, without realising what you are doing. Because there is no line, not really. You only find out where it is when you're on the other side, looking back.

The phone rings and he reluctantly picks it up. 'Wallace.'

'You know who this is?' The voice is calm and quiet.

'I think so.'

'Remember Irwin Rommel.'

'I beg your pardon?'

'You know about Rommel?'

'I know who he was.'

'The guy was implicated in the July twentieth plot to kill Hitler by one of the men under torture. There was no real evidence against him, but that didn't matter. The problem was, they couldn't kill a much-loved Nazi war hero by hanging him from a meat hook with piano wire, could they?'

'No, I guess not.'

'So he did the honourable thing. He committed suicide, and word was put out that he had died a noble death. Military funeral, the works. Family allowed to hold their head up.'

'I heard about that.'

'Do we understand each other?'

'Family not told the truth?'

'Correct.'

'Then we understand each other.'

'Good,' says Jack Sandler at the other end, and the line goes dead.

Wallace hears the crunch of tyres on his driveway, the throb of an SUV's engine, quickly silenced as the key is turned off in the ignition. A doors slams. Then a second. The NSA, no doubt.

He can hear carols bleeding through the wall from next door. Bing Crosby. The doorbell rings. Spencer and his friend. Wallace reaches into his desk and brings out his pistol, oiled and cleaned.

Can he trust them to bury what he has done? To forget the aberration of the last two years? To concentrate on his achievements, the highs rather than this terrible low?

The bell rings again, two impatient stabs.

Yes, he can. Because it is in their own interest to inter Palimpsest so deep, it never sees the light of day again.

Apart from wanting to protect his son, he has no regrets about what he is about to do. He is ready. He hopes Margaret is waiting for him, but he isn't entirely sure he believes that is possible. Either way, it is with a sense of peace that he places the barrel of the Colt in his mouth and squeezes a trigger one last time.

Thirty-five

'Roderick Marshall Young was one of the most remarkable people I have ever met. It would be fair to say that his was not a conventional life, but it is that which makes him all the more memorable. I recall the first time I actually met Roddy . . .'

Father Gavin settles into his stride, delivering the eulogy at Roddy's cremation. Celeste has already read the poem 'Do Not Weep', in a shaky voice, and there have been other tributes. A gospel choir has sung 'Let the River Flow'; a musician friend of the family echoed it with a slow, mournful version of 'Take Me to the River'.

Piper is at the back of the bland, joyless chapel, waiting for the inevitable Punch and Judy moment when the curtains are drawn and the coffin grinds away on its track. Piper doesn't necessarily believe in

God, but he does believe churches are more dignified for this kind of thing. That, or a totally secular service. Not this halfway house.

The congregation is sparse. It is between Christmas and New Year, and many of Roddy's social circle, his original one anyway, before Lennie took him East, are away skiing or sunning themselves in Barbados.

Father Gavin finishes and commits the body to the Lord, and the curtains close. A piece of classical music, all swelling strings, starts up, and Piper is fairly sure this is Celeste's, rather than Roddy's, choice. Roddy probably would have gone for 'It's Getting Hot in Here' or 'Burn, Baby, Burn'.

Keeping ahead of the pack, he gets up and limps on a still-stiff leg outside, to where the flowers have been laid on the grass verge for inspection. The snow has gone; it is another bleak London winter day, a spiteful wind spitting rain in your face. He pulls his overcoat around him.

Father Gavin has stationed himself at the door and is shaking hands with each mourner. Celeste, as she emerges, sees Piper and nods. Behind her is Sasha, wan and pale.

Celeste strides across the gravel, stops before him, then stands on tip-toe and kisses his cheek. 'Thanks for coming.'

'Don't mention it. Least I could do. You OK?'

'Yes. Not much of a turn-out.'

'It's fine. He wouldn't have wanted a fuss,' says Piper.

Celeste smiles and her reddened eyes widen. 'Yes, he would. He'd have wanted a big party. Instead, there are sandwiches at Cobden Working Man's Club.' She sees the look of surprise on his face. 'No, it's ironic. It isn't for workers or men. You coming?'

'No. I . . . No. I was hoping I'd see you afterwards, in private. I hope you don't mind.'

Sasha has reached them, and she, too, kisses Piper. 'Don't mind what?'

'Vince has to go. More hush-hush business.'

He laughs. He'll be lucky to have a job once this is over. 'What about you two? What now?'

Sasha digs into her bag and produces a folder. 'Two-round the-world tickets.'

His heart sinks. 'For?'

'Sash and me,' says Celeste. 'We both need time to sort ourselves out.'

'So it's . . .'

'It's over. We're out of it. I might even go back to being Susan.'

'Susan?'

'It's a long story. But round the world, we'll be stopping off lots and we're going west to east. So America's our first stop. You're going back to the States, aren't you?'

'Yes. Contract here terminated. Future uncertain.'

'E-mail me your address and contact details over there,' says Celeste. 'I'll be on Hotmail.'

'When do you leave? Maybe we can get together before then.'

'Tomorrow,' Sasha blurts out excitedly. 'First thing.'

'It was all a bit last minute and spur of the moment,' explains Celeste softly. Her voice drops, and she touches his arm. 'Sorry. Really.'

Others start to crowd round her, offering their condolences, and he slowly pulls away, fading to the edge of the throng, until he spins on his good heel and leaves, hands in pockets, head down. He exits from the crematorium and turns right, heading for the nearest underground station.

'Vince.'

He looks up and sees Roth, standing next to a Cadillac parked across the road. With him is a character he doesn't recognise, shivering in what looks to be unfamiliar cold, judging by his tan. Piper crosses over.

'Vince, this is Special Agent Michael Johnson.'

They shake hands and Piper says: 'Of?'

'I am a Liaison to the Office of the Secretary of State,' the man drawls.

'Riiigghhht,' Piper says, stretching out the word while looking quizzically at Roth.

'What it means, Vince, is that Special Agent Johnson is empowered to do pretty much what the fuck he likes.'

'Or what the Secretary of State likes,' adds Piper.

'You wanna get in the car?' Johnson asks. 'It's just that the last thing the Secretary of State asked me to do involved four weeks in Florida.'

They climb inside, all three squashing in the rear, and the driver starts the car. 'Whoa,' says Piper, thinking of the last time he got in the back of an unfamiliar car. 'What's going on?'

'Relax. Tell him, Michael.'

'I have been empowered to prepare a report on the events of the past few weeks which you have been privy to, prior to action by either the State Department, the NSA or the Office of the Attorney General. Now, Stanley here saw the list of people to be interviewed and told me I was missing a trick.'

'What's that?' asks Piper.

'Getting you on board,' says Roth with a wink.

'As what?'

'Federal Bureau of Investigation, right?' says Johnson. 'Stanley says you still know how to do the investigation part. I can get you on the team. Maybe we can make sense of this can of worms.'

'Because,' says Roth, 'we've thrown up some pretty interesting intersections. Vince?'

He has spun round and is looking through the rear window of the Cadillac and can see Celeste at the crematorium gateway, her eyes scanning the road, searching for someone. Someone she wanted to have a word with.

'Vince?'

He spins back. 'Yeah. Right. Sounds good.' He knows Stanley is helping him out once more, moving him from defence to attack. It's clever. Especially as Stanley knows that if the enquiry ever starts to question Roth's role in all this – in particular the part with the sniper rifle on the beach – he at least has one ally inside. He is padding the jury.

'Where will it be based? Washington?' In which case, he thinks, Celeste can make that her first stopover.

'No,' says Johnson. 'Right here.' He slaps his knee. 'You're staying in London, Vince.'

Vince curses under his breath. He hasn't grown any fonder of the place, and one of the few reasons he has for staying is about to jump ship. There are a couple of pluses. He can visit Martha's grave once more. Maybe even risk a meeting with Judy.

Then another thought occurs to him.

'You know, Agent Johnson, we may have a problem.'

'What's that?'

He takes one last hurried look at the shrinking

figure of Celeste, before the Cadillac makes the turn and she is gone. 'I think two of our prime witnesses are about to go on a long vacation.'

Roth shakes his head. 'Who?'

Piper explains.

Roth laughs, sensing, perhaps, the hidden agenda here. 'No, Vince. Not on your watch, they're not. We'll pull the plug on that, pronto.'

Piper smiles to himself, leans back in the leather seat and relaxes. Maybe it'll work out OK after all.

Author's Note

The details of the USAAF Aphrodite missions using volunteer crews and remote-controlled planes, and the death of Joseph Kennedy Junior while piloting one, are substantially true. However, although there is an FBI Legat office in London, at the request of the Bureau all operational details have been altered in some way.

My thanks go to D'Arcy Paladeau of Calgary, Canada for the Sitting Bull story (we'll go looking one day, for sure) and to Davina Mackail for shaman advice of the highest order. I am also grateful to Dylan Jones and Bill Prince of GQ, to my agent David Miller and to my editor Martin Fletcher for his invaluable advice and input. And thanks to Johnny Bongo for the beats.

Steel Rain

Tom Neale

It comes like a sudden blast of fog, then the noise, a dull crump that he has heard on countless training videos . . .

Special agent Vincent Piper of the London FBI Field Office rushes to the scene of a terrorist bomb attack. His daughter is one of the victims. She dies in his arms.

Now he has only one focus. He knows who planted the lethal device: all he has to do is find him.

His search becomes entangled in the lives of two women, but who is friend and who is foe? As Piper digs deeper into the ever-darker world of crime and political subversion, will he take out his man before the steel rain falls once more on the innocent . . . ?

0 7553 2239 8

headline

Now you can buy any of these other bestselling
Headline books from your bookshop
or *direct from the publisher*.

FREE P&P AND UK DELIVERY
(Overseas and Ireland £3.50 per book)

Never Fear	Scott Frost	£6.99
The Last Sunrise	Robert Ryan	£6.99
The Four Courts Murder	Andrew Nugent	£6.99
Steel Rain	Tom Neale	£6.99
Smoked	Patrick Quinlan	£6.99
Cover Up	John Francome	£6.99
Dead and Buried	Quintin Jardine	£6.99
The Art of Dying	Vena Cork	£6.99
The Year of the Cobra	Paul Doherty	£6.99
Last Rights	Barbara Nadel	£6.99

TO ORDER SIMPLY CALL THIS NUMBER

01235 400 414

or visit our website: www.madaboutbooks.com

Prices and availability subject to change without notice.